Spicy as Puck

by

Debbie Charles

Texas Tornadoes
Book 3

Trade Paperback ISBN 979-8-89044-414-1
Digital ISBN 979-8-89044-415-8
Audio ISBN 979-8-89044-416-5
Cover by *Wicked Smart Designs*

Dedication

To Sreylak (the real life Saylet) with love

Spicy as Puck Playlist

Saylet

Single Ladies – Beyoncé
Girl on Fire – Alicia Keys
We Can't Stop – Miley Cyrus
Firework – Katy Perry
F**kin' Perfect – Pink
Hips Don't Lie – Shakira (featuring Wyclef Jean)
On The Floor – Jennifer Lopez, Pitbull
Unwritten – Natasha Bedingfield
This One's for the Girls – Martina McBride
Don't Be so Hard on Yourself – Jess Glynne
Breakaway – Kelly Clarkson
Glamorous – Fergie, Ludacris
Chandelier – Sia

Drew

Chandelier – Vitamin String Quartet
Radioactive – Imagine Dragons
Fireflies – Owl City
Apologize – Timbaland, OneRepublic
Root Beer Rag – Billy Joel
A Thousand Years – The Piano Guys
A Sky Full of Stars – Coldplay
Warm Weather – Pieces of a Dream
Bohemian Sunset – Jazzanova
Riptide – Duomo
I'd Really Love to See You Tonight – England Dan &
John Ford Coley
Just the Way You Are – The Piano Guys

Chapter One

Drew

It's Christina Donovan's birthday. Thankfully, her brother specified no gifts because what do you get your boss's boss's boss who is one of the owners of your NHL team, and a billionaire?

As we sing *Happy Birthday* around a ginormous multi-tiered cake that somehow manages to avoid looking like a wedding cake, Mattie—Mathieu du Près, left wing on first line to my center—catches my eye and nods at a swaying Kyle Scott, a defender in our top six. Dammit. Several of us have noticed his recent increased drinking, but to do it at the owner's place is downright stupid. And we have an early practice tomorrow.

Our captain, Gabriel St. John, isn't around. Which has also been happening more recently. So as alternate captain, it's up to me to deal with this. I sidle closer and drag the younger man back a few steps toward a doorway. Giving him a chin nod, I try for casual. "What's up, man?"

"Nothin'," he says in the surliest tone I've ever heard from the guy.

"Got something on your mind?" I ask quietly.

Kyle skids a furtive glance toward Coach Steele and shakes his head.

"I'll get you out of here. Don't worry about Coach

seeing you."

He grimaces, then shakes his head again.

I herd him through the doorway to the short hallway and into the grand entryway. "I'm concerned about you. You seem"—*frequently drunk*—"unhappy."

"Nah. Living the high life. Players and playas. Let's fucking go and all that." He waves a hand and nearly falls over.

"Yep. Not everyone could be hanging at a party like this one and making millions to play a game the next night. Speaking of, we have an early skate tomorrow, and I'm about to head out. Why don't I drop you home on my way?"

"No way, man. I have my car."

"I'm not sure it's a good idea for you to drive right now."

"I need my car to get to practice," he says with a set jaw and a wobbly arm fold. Great, he's going to be an ornery drunk.

I glance back at the party, afraid to leave him alone long enough to find someone to drive him and his car home with me following.

On cue, Saylet walks through from the kitchen. She takes us in at a glance. "What can I do?"

Anyone else offering to help would have been preferable. Okay, well maybe not Coach. But no. FML, it has to be Saylet Young.

The tiny, tight package of dark-haired sexiness otherwise known as our PR Director is my biggest weakness. She also runs circles around us players, like a corgi nipping at our ankles keeping us in line.

I sigh, giving in to fate. Peeking behind her to ensure no one else followed her, I summarize the situation.

"Kyle and I are heading out. He's not quite in driving shape, and he has to get to early practice tomorrow."

"I can drive his car, and you follow?" she asks.

With Kyle becoming belligerent, I'm forced to accept her offer. For sure I wasn't going to ask Mattie to leave his girlfriend stranded at the party when they only just became a couple.

Why Kyle, who we call Scottie, was drunk at an owner's birthday party, I have no idea. Saylet probably won't get that out of him, so I'll ask him when he's sober.

Right now, I have bigger things to worry about, like how to avoid popping wood when she climbs into my car with her unique scent. Whatever it is, shampoo, perfume, or other, it's a lovely mix of sweet and spicy, with a touch of floral. Not that I could name a flower smell other than a rose to save my life. Her, I could pick out of a room of a hundred people blindfolded. Dammit, I'm already at half mast thinking about it.

When we get to his house, I jump out to help him. He's gone from irate to weepy, and I do not have time for this. I have to get Saylet to her car then go rub one out. Possibly in my car with her fragrance lingering since today is the first and last time she'll be in it.

But first, as alternate captain, I have responsibilities. She heads to the kitchen for a glass of water, and I lean against the wall of his bedroom as he slumps on the edge of his bed to yank his shoes off. He tosses them in the general direction of the closet and drops his head in his hands.

"Sorry, Buzz," he mumbles to the floor.

"It's ok, buddy. I wish I knew what was wrong, so I could help."

"No you don't." His head shakes side to side once.

"Hey, that's not fair. I said I did, and I meant it. Try me."

"I can't. You don't. Trust me."

I sigh. "Ok. I'll be here when you're ready. Judgment-free zone."

Saylet is back and chimes in, "It better be. If it's not, they'll answer to me."

He flinches.

I sigh again. She means well, but her in-your-face brand defense of her players is not what he needs right now.

"Set your alarm, man. Then make sure you've eaten enough to absorb what you drank so you're not puking on the ice. No one wants that."

He nods and reaches for his phone.

I brace myself, hold my breath, and take Saylet's arm to gently guide her out of the room.

As we reach the living room, I inhale a deep breath as though relieved to have Kyle home. Instead, I'm wishing I could roll around in her sugar and spice.

She turns to me. "Perhaps I should stay with him."

I shake my head. "Would you want anyone beyond a very close friend to see you drunk? Worse, to babysit?"

She twists her lips. "I see your point."

"Now imagine being a 'macho'," I put the word in quotes with a half smile, "hockey player."

"Okay. He's a big boy. And I'm sure it's not the first or the last time he'll be in this state." She throws up her hands and walks toward the door.

I hustle around her to open it for her, then speed walk to beat her to the car to open the passenger door. Mostly so I can smell her again, but also, my grams raised me right.

Sliding into the driver's seat, I say, "Okay, back to the Donovans'."

"Actually, I rideshared there. Lucky for you, I live on the east side of town like you. Unless you were planning to return to the party for a while?"

"No, I don't know how much longer it went on after we left." But holy hell, now I'm imagining her inviting me in. I shift in my seat, my cock plumping and pressing against the seam of my shorts uncomfortably. I usually reserve puck bunny hookups for road games, preferring to keep the drama to a minimum and out of my home town, but I might have to bend that rule to release some of this tension. Because there's no way in hell I'm messing around with someone within the Tornadoes organization, particularly someone who has my public image in her hands. And I'm not risking my hockey career for one night of fun.

"Why was Kyle drunk, at Greg's house, no less?" Saylet asks.

The Donovans, along with their other sister Amy, are the team's owners. They're young, and Christina and Cameron "Prancer" Hill, our goalie, are in love, so we spend more time with them than most teams do with their owners. But no one other than Cam should forget that a business relationship exists.

I reply, "I was hoping you got that information during the drive to his house."

"Yeah, no. He went from annoyed muttering to weepy mumbling. But nothing coherent, and he wasn't answering questions." She twists in her seat to face me more. "At least it was a private event, and we got him out of there before any damage was done."

I'd have preferred to handle it without alerting her to

the situation, but I guess it's better she's prepared in case it blows up. Gabriel "Saint" St. John, and I will do what we can, as will the rest of the team, to ensure that doesn't happen, but we can't babysit him all the time.

"All right, I'll see what I can get out of him when he's sober. Right now, your guess is as good as mine."

"Maybe it's sexist, but if he was one of my girlfriends, I'd guess man troubles."

I tilt my head. "Could be. He's young. For the first half of the season, he was chasing skirts with Jack after every game, but now that I think about it, I haven't seen that as much recently." Jack Landry, star defenseman, is our team clown, party guy, and slut, all rolled into one, off the ice. Thankfully, he's a super focused, deadly serious player on it.

Saylet's tone holds a bitter note when she says, "Don't you mean letting the bunnies chase him? None of you have to work for it."

I scoff, and reply without thinking. "It's not like you do, either. You could have any man you want."

There's a deafening silence in the car. I'm pretty sure neither of us is breathing. When I slide a quick glance to her, she's staring at me with her mouth hanging open, and damn if that doesn't make me think about what I'd like to put in it.

I concentrate very hard on parking in a visitor spot for her apartment building.

When I glance back, she's looking forward again and says with a hair toss, "Yeah, well, maybe my standards are high."

With that, she's out of the car before I can open her door, racing into the building.

I watch her until she's out of sight, cursing my idiot

big mouth for making things awkward. Now I'd feel weird jerking off to thoughts of her, despite sniffing the last whiff of her fragrance.

* * * *

I slam into the locker room, pissed despite our win. We played Winnipeg, who has little to no chance of making the playoffs, and it was a tie game for the last two periods, forcing us into sudden death overtime. As if we need to elongate our play time at the end of a long season. We should be conserving our stamina for the playoffs, but not at the expense of a regulation win.

Coach's admonishing congratulatory talk is way milder than mine would be. I look at Saint to see if he's going to say anything as our captain, but he's staring at the floor, either in his own head or exhausted. He and I are among the few players on this team who have been through the playoffs before coming to the Tornadoes. I touch his shoulder and ask low, "Shall I say something?"

He nods once.

As Coach walks out, I stand. "We have to do better. Just because we clinched our spot, we still need every advantage we can get as a first-year team in the playoffs. We need home ice advantage, we need to be in their heads if we meet them again, we need it all. Tonight, we were sluggish and uncoordinated. And it cost us. It cost us energy that will be essential in the coming weeks. Less than half of us have been in the Stanley Cup playoffs before, but I can tell you, if you thought regular season was long, try tacking on a few seven-game series. We're not in the minors any more. No five games and done, with lag time between them because the arena is in use. This is the big leagues, boys, and we have to play like it."

"Maybe we were trying to conserve our energy." F-ing Milo "Quasi" Petrovsky always has an answer.

"And where did it get you? An extra four-plus minutes of play until your captain here put it away for us. And because Coach agrees with me, we'll likely have an extra hard practice tomorrow instead of him taking it easy on us. Now step. It. Up. All of you."

I stalk off to the showers, still half dressed.

At home, I'm still pissed. Not at my teammates. Regardless of my motivational slash chastising pep talk, we're all tired and trying our best on any game night. But there might have been something I could have done to get us to the win.

There are only a few things I've splurged on since I was first called up to the NHL and bigger money a few years ago. New cars for me and my grams, despite her protests. Two-bedroom condos in both cities I played for, and a decorator to help me make them warm and inviting for when Grams visits. And the NHL satellite package so I could see as many games as I want.

I recorded our game, so I grab a protein shake and rewind to the spot in the first period where I had an intercepted pass. I should have seen that defender coming, dammit.

I've tortured myself for twenty minutes when the phone rings.

"Hi, Grams. You're up late."

I've tried to get her to wait until the morning to call me after games, but as she's been mother, father, and grandparents to me most of my life, she's too invested in my happiness to wait that long. She also knows I'll obsess all night if I don't talk it out, but I'd never put my needs before hers. She's all I have.

"Don't start that with me again, Drew. You know I won't sleep until I check on how you're doing. You'd better not be rewatching what you call your 'mistakes.'"

Thank god I muted the TV before answering.

"Nah."

"Don't lie to me either, young man. You could not have seen that defender coming; he was directly behind you until he poke checked you."

I should have checked. "Yeah, okay. But what about—"

"You know that goalie gets paid millions to block shots, don't you? You did your job trying to score, he did his by stopping you. It's really that simple. It's happened before, and it'll happen again. It'll happen more if you don't get your rest, so turn the TV off and go to sleep, my boy."

"Yes, ma'am. I love you, Grams. Thank you for talking me off the ledge as always."

"I love you, too. They wouldn't have given you the "A" if they didn't think you were essential to the team's success." She makes sure to add on her customary farewell.

"Yeah, yeah. I'll talk to you in a few days. Miss you."

I still replay the other moments in the game I could have improved, but I see them with more rational eyes after my conversation with my biggest cheerleader. In the morning, I'm refreshed and ready to be a positive role model for my team again.

Chapter Two

Saylet

As usual, I swing by Kayla Morrison's office. The Operations Manager and I joke that we're mirrors. I manage the guys' public lives whereas she manages the behind-the-scenes stuff. She has a small team to help organize their travel arrangements, partner with me for public appearances, and assist with everything from hiring housekeepers to moving players here as they are traded. Not that that part has happened yet in our inaugural season.

We're a tight team, and while I have zero say in who stays and who goes, I really hope Greg and Stephen Link, our GM, keep most of the team together after this year. Us making the playoffs will help. I'd only make a few minor adjustments to support my passion—to gain diversity in this sport.

"How was your family reunion?" I ask when she joins me at the fancy espresso machine in the kitchen.

"Oh, you know. The usual drama, fun, drinking, and more drama," she answers with an eye roll. "How was the birthday party?"

"Fine, until Kyle Scott over-served himself."

"At an *owner's* party, of all things?"

"Right? Thankfully, for every young Kyle and Jack, there are two Cams, Gabes, and Drews."

"Buzz? Isn't he a ladies' man with Scottie and Landry?"

"He's single, sure, but he's...I dunno, more respectful about it?"

"Hey, at least you've never had to bail anyone out."

"Yet." My tone is flat. "And please don't put that out in the universe. Someone will take it as a dare."

"What happened with Kyle?"

"Drew and Mattie extracted him from the party, but he wanted to drive home. And Mattie came with Nicole."

"Such a cute couple," Kayla interjects.

I continue. "So I drove Kyle's car home then Drew drove me home. I missed cake, dammit, and I love cake."

"Maybe they'll bring leftovers." She wiggles her eyebrows. "That was nice of Drew. That boy may be young, but he's a leader. They were right picking him as alternate captain. When he's ready to settle down, he'll have the pick of the litter."

"Terrible analogy aside, yes he is and will. Those bright eyes, big shoulders, and neatly trimmed beard will make some young woman very happy, not to mention his gentlemanly nature."

"Said as though you're my age." Kayla's about a decade older than me. "He's in your league, girl. Go for it."

I do a double take. "Me? No way. I'm too old for him and nowhere near puck bunny hotness. And anyway, don't let Greg hear you say that. Chris and Cam aside, it's against company policy."

But damn if she didn't put ideas in my head, especially as Drew said almost the same thing. I swear he didn't mean to say it out loud, but what do I do with that? Maybe Kayla's right and I have a shot.

I press my lips together, annoyed at myself. We're coworkers, nothing more. He's not looking for a relationship, and I'm sure as fuck not looking to hookup with a player. Talk about unprofessional.

* * * *

Regular season is over, and the first round playoffs have been determined. We secured our spot a few weeks ago, and are second in our division, so are up against the Minnesota Wildcats. Despite them being third, they're a strong team and will be tough to get past, but I have faith in our guys. We also plan to hype the fact that Drew is a Duluth native, hoping to encourage some Tornadoes support when we play on their ice.

I'm in the practice facility's tunnel with LaRhonda, our Social Media Analyst, and Sara, our cameraperson/videographer, waiting for the guys to suit up for practice so we can ask them for a snippet about the playoffs.

When Coach signals me it's safe, I step into the locker room behind him. The guys all have their lower gear on, and most of them have their pads and sweaters, ready to run drills. I catch movement out of the corner of my eye, and look over. Drew's abs disappear as he pulls on his under layer then reaches for his pads.

Swallowing, I blink and refocus. I'm a pro; I've been in this room before and will again. There's no reason to act missish, even if those abs will be burned into my brain forever and will serve as fodder in my quality alone time for the foreseeable future.

The guys call greetings and that helps bring me back to the reason I'm here.

"Hi, y'all. I have LaRhonda and Sara in the tunnel.

We're going to have you come by one at a time. I'll prompt you onscreen again, but here's the gist: state whether this is your first time in the NHL playoffs, and what you're most looking forward to doing as a Tornado. And please try not to say 'kicking Wildcat butt.' Be original."

"Sure. 'Kicking *Wildpussy ass*,'" Milo sasses.

A few players snicker, but Drew gives him a sharp look.

The guys come through and most manage to come up with something personal. A couple mumble, "kicking Wildcat butt" despite my request, but that's okay. These are young guys, with barely any life experience, whose whole world is hockey. They're feeling the pressure.

I thank each of them, no matter how eloquent or reticent they are.

Then Drew is there. Almost a foot taller than me in bare feet, he towers over me in skates. Most of them do, but thanks to his and Kayla's recent comments, I am more conscious of all our differences now.

"Buzz," I start, using his nickname on the team, "you've been here before, although not as alternate captain. And now it's against your home town. What are you most looking forward to?"

"Austin is my town now. I'm psyched to help Saint lead the team through the playoffs and show the world what a young expansion team can do when handpicked by the Donovans, our GM, and Coach Steele. Look out Minnesota—and all the other teams in the playoffs. We mean business."

He flashes a smile, his bright eyes shining brighter, and nods as he heads to the ice.

Phew, it just got hot in here. I'm a little worried for

the ice. I've caught glimpses of a caretaker nature underneath his single hot hockey player shenanigans with Kyle and Jack. But him saying I could have any man I want turned up the heat, and Kayla's encouragement doesn't help. A mild attraction is quickly becoming a fixation—on one of the few men I can't have, no matter how hot I might be. I'd lose all credibility if I slept with a member of the team.

I spend the afternoon reviewing edits from the players' mini-interviews and scheduling a few publicity appearances for the next week, now that we have the team's schedule. Managing PR for an organization through playoffs, where you don't know the calendar more than a week out, is challenging.

* * * *

The day of our first playoff game, I work right through until the pre-game warmup, trying to keep ahead of things. Knowing there will be a decent assortment of food in the company luxury box allows me to skip lunch and maximize my worktime.

Greg Donovan built the back offices onto the suite level of the arena, so I literally could walk down the hall to the game. And I will watch from there, but I can't resist going down to the tunnel first to check on our boys before they head out to the ice.

I hang out near the end of the tunnel, separate from the training and equipment staff and whoever else comes out to send them off. Sara is always there, and I try to stay out of her way, but I like to be present for the guys in their element.

Too many times, I'm dragging them to some PR opportunity or charity gig, or giving them a tongue-lashing for getting caught in some less-than-flattering situation on social media, or worse, the news. Whether they notice me or not, I also want to show them that I'm here to support them in their area of expertise. Not because it pays my salary, but because PR is about championing the team. Mostly ensuring public support, but I prefer to live my truth. Call it method acting.

Mattie and Remi Boulanger come through first, followed by Saint, who always curls a glove to give me a gentle fist bump. Behind him is Drew, close cropped beard and dark eyes stark against his ivory skin under his helmet. His mouthpiece hangs from his teeth. He doesn't notice me, totally focused on the arena as though there is already a game playing in his head.

I lick my lips. That intensity is hot. He's pretty chill off the ice, but this reminds me that he's alternate captain for a reason. Even in his mid-twenties, he's a leader. And I can relate. I'm young for a PR Director, and I've been called intense a few too many times for my comfort. Not that I dislike being intense, I'd just prefer to have a thicker veneer.

He must feel my stare, because his gaze veers to me as my tongue swipes across my lips. Heat flares in his eyes.

I gulp. The testosterone must be flowing to hype him for the game. But fuck if it doesn't make him even more captivating.

He dips his head once in a short nod then is past me.

I wilt back against the concrete wall and give a small wave to other team members who notice me as they stomp by on skates. Jack makes his usual gesture as though he's going to mess up my hair with his disgusting hockey glove, and I give my usual glare to let him know he'll be assigned to all the smelliest animal-focused PR appearances for the rest of his natural life if he does it. But my heart's not in it after the thump Drew's look caused.

As they hump the ice, then circle and take shots on Cam's goal, I make my way back up to the suite level. I grab some crudités and hummus on a small plate while I assess who's joining us tonight. The morning of every game, the list is sent out to those of us who are coming to the owner's box. Whenever possible, management puts two seats into a lottery for back office folks to win. Tonight it's a member of the operations department and her significant other who haven't attended before, so I welcome them, ensure they're comfortable, and point out the restroom.

Then I scarf my snack down before I have to shmooze. I can multitask with the best of them, but talking, eating, *and* trying to follow the game is a bit much. Amy Donovan, who heads the Tornadoes Foundation, shmoozes as well, but hers is less about public image and more about securing donations to support her passion, providing long-term housing and a supportive community for men and women who are coming out of chronic homelessness.

Thankfully, most of tonight's invitees are interested in watching the game. The stadium seating at the front of the suite fills in, with only a few guests back in the bar area keeping an eye on the game via the television hung over the corner of the bar. I grab a seat in the front section.

A Tech Brad plops into the seat next to me, and I straighten a bit. Greg is finalizing sponsorships with companies whose names will go on the ice, and this guy is with one of them. I have no idea if he's a decision-maker, but he wouldn't be here if he wasn't at least an influencer.

For the first period, he points out players on both teams and spouts statistics, living down to my expectations. During the first intermission, I share with him more about Greg's vision for the team, including statistics of course, like the fact that this team's average age is about two years younger than the league average. Encouraging him to talk to Amy about our charitable efforts, I excuse myself to greet more people.

But when I return to my seat, he's back as well.

Drew gets the puck on a pass from Jack almost immediately, and he's sprinting up the ice. I lean forward, loving how fast he is. He manages to look hot even in bulky, sweaty hockey gear, and it makes me wonder how that stamina would play out in bed. The other team is also fast, though, and gets there in time that our guys have to set up an organized play rather than going for the quick shot.

Tech Brad (I know his name of course, but I can't resist thinking of him as this) shakes his head and tsks. "Not sure why they went for Busbee. He underperformed in Tampa."

"Maybe, but he hasn't here. He has more goals *and* assists this year than he did the past two, and his SHG is particularly impressive." I manage to keep my tone mild, but barely. Inside, I'm fuming that he'd pick on one of our leaders. "Is that a function of having a strong team around him? Sure. But SHG go to the fastest and most skilled. If you'll remember, he was voted into the All-Stars skills competition. Personally, I think we made the right choice."

TB slides me a side glance. He nods and scrunches his mouth as though he's thinking it over.

I confess to surprise. A lot of TBs don't hear an opinion that differs from theirs easily, and almost never when it's given in a woman's voice.

"Okay, okay," he says with a half-smile. "I'll reserve judgment. After all, the team did get to the playoffs."

"Exactly." I smile. "And it's always good business to associate with a winning team."

Chapter Three

Drew

The visitors' dressing room at the Wildcats' arena is nearly vibrating. Excitement and nerves have all of us bouncing. We need to get on the ice and let this energy loose.

We had home ice advantage for the first two games, and won them both, although not without effort. The number of Busbee Tornadoes jerseys scattered throughout the crowd was gratifying, and I make a mental note to thank Saylet for that particular PR campaign. We managed to eke out another W in Game 3, and I swear we were all a bit surprised, although no one owned up to that, including the coaches.

So here we are, with the possibility of taking the series in four straight games, securing an entire week break before the second round starts. Adrenaline ratchets the nerves and excitement in the locker room, and none of us can sit still except of course Cam. He's leaning forward, gaze on the floor, ear pods in. Our goalie is younger than me, but has the Zen of a seventy-year-old Buddhist monk.

I'm doing the thing I seem to always do when the pressure is on. Recalling that I was exposed by my old team in the expansion draft, questioning my abilities, and wondering if the others are doubting themselves, too. Or is it just me?

Saint has been quieter than normal. As captain, he's given encouragement to the junior players both one-on-one and in pep talks at practices and before games. But he's stopped hanging with us socially, not that his high maintenance wife, Jessica, let him much before now. Unfortunately, she hasn't won the hearts of the team, and while I'm pretty sure she doesn't care, I'm equally sure Saint does. Or maybe he's feeling his age or something's up healthwise. I dunno, but it's getting in my head.

Cam and Mattie have stepped up with me as leaders, coaxing and mentoring others no matter what their ages. Based on those two, I'd say romantic relationships are helpful to players, but Jessica Freakin' Rabbit is always at the edge of my conscience. No, thank you. I'd rather focus on hockey and not jeopardize my place on the team with any distractions. Hockey is my ticket to security, to never being poor again, and to taking care of my grams in the style she deserves, if she'll let me.

I heave a sigh of relief when I spy Saylet in the tunnel. She doesn't always fly with us. But as a first-year team in the playoffs, I suppose there are lots of PR possibilities and risks, so she's been with us on this road trip. Tonight she's wearing high-waisted wide-legged trousers in a dark purple with a thin pinstripe and a high-necked white blouse. In them, her petite frame manages to be arresting. I've always seen her there, looking hot as hell as she roots for us. But now, because I acknowledged her with a nod before the first game, I try to repeat everything I did that night to keep our luck going.

I nod. No wink, no smile, just a nod, before refocusing on the players we're up against, and how they've been playing in this series.

My skates hit the ice, and it's on.

Fifty-one minutes later, I'm panting and spraying water in the general direction of my mouth, back on the bench. Lack of oxygen or not, I'm ready to go back in the minute Coach gives the signal. The score is 2-1, and I can taste the four-game win. So can the crowd, based on how quiet they are.

Mattie leans in. "Look at number 12. He isn't as aggressive as he normally is, and I think he's favoring his right leg a little."

"Hmm, maybe," I say after watching him for a minute. "He took a hard hit from Quasi last game. You think that did it?"

"Could be. Plus, these have been close games all the way along. He's one of their best players, so he's had a ton of ice time, on top of travel."

"Okay, duly noted. He's on my side so I'll play accordingly." No one wants to worsen another player's injury, but each of us also have to own our decision to play. Most coaches, docs, and trainers will defer to the player unless there is a serious long-term risk if they play. He chose to play, as I probably would. If he didn't and they lost because of that, he'd regret it. It looks like they may end their season even with him in, though.

We flow back over the wall for another shift change. I mutter to Saint as we go over to get me the puck if he can. He nods.

Lukas Kucera, our second line defenseman, sends the puck to Saint to take it over the blue line. We all follow as he drops it back to Lukas, who sets up the play. Saint and I hover near the crease while Mattie jockeys with a Wildcat toward the corner. Lukas flicks it to Saint.

Dammit, number 12 snags it before Saint can get his stick on it. My heart starts pumping as I crouch and push off my blade; my entire focus is on catching him. He starts up the ice.

I close in fast and poke check. Our sticks clash, but I have the puck. He tries to get close to me. Nope. I pass the puck to Saint even though he's in the thick of the Wildcats defense. Saint is like an eel, slippery as fuck. He manages to untangle himself, gets the biscuit, and sends it sailing at the goalie with a snap shot.

Shit. It's deflected off the post, and they grab the rebound, bringing it to our end.

I hover near number 12. It's risky, but I don't crowd him. I'm confident I can get the puck away from him again, so I'd rather them send it to him than to someone faster.

Lukas frowns at me, but I ignore him. I've got this.

The black disk flies toward number 12. As it makes contact with his stick, he turns. All I need is the quick second that he spends checking his path to the goal and his teammates, and I'm on it. With a sweep check, I grab the puck and pass to Mattie then race a skate's length behind him across the blue line, blocking the Wildcats from interfering. My legs burn.

Saint is somehow also ahead of the pack, and it's three-on-one for their beleaguered goalie. Mattie dekes toward Saint then flicks a wrist shot, and I swear my heart stops for a beat. The goal lamp lights. 3-1. Hell yeah. We're so fucking close I can taste the Second Round.

As we switch out with the second line, Minnesota's goalie gets pulled for the last two minutes of their game as they try to catch up.

From the bench, I keep one eye on the clock and one on the game. Twenty seconds. Even with the extra player on ice, we hold our lead. Ten. I hold my breath.

The buzzer sounds. Oh my god. We, the first-year expansion team Texas Tornadoes, have swept the first round of the Stanley Cup playoffs. I don't care that we aren't with our home crowd. This way, we'll have more chances to play in front of them.

Tonight, we'll celebrate. As we come off the ice, Saylet is there again, tagging Saint and me to speak to the press. I lean in impulsively. "You're part of the team's success. Come out with us tonight. Change into flats, and come celebrate our win."

She blinks in surprise, I'm past her and in front of the bloodhounds before she can reply.

I nurse my beer and watch the hotel bar entrance all evening, but she doesn't walk through it. Most of the time, I sit back and nod at my teammates' antics while I argue with myself that she's being smart. It was stupid to invite trouble when I don't want any complications in my life, and a member of management is not a hookup candidate. I still go to bed disappointed despite our win.

* * * *

Back home, we enjoy the slightly longer break between the first and second rounds that winning in four afforded us. We eat massive quantities of healthy food so we're not run ragged in the games, sleep, and do light workouts and practices.

The trainers are getting more of a workout than we are, as everyone books time with them to ensure lingering injuries or soreness improve as much as possible before this next round.

We'll be playing the Chicago Icedogs, who have deep history as Stanley Cup contenders. They have outplayed us in the regular season, they outweigh us, and they out-stat us. The only thing we have going for us is they're also an older team. So while they've had more time to come together as a unit, the Icedogs are injury prone and tire easily—I hope.

The week goes by fast and we're in Round 2. In Chicago, I thump down the tunnel in my uniform to warmups. The whole team is tense but amped. I spy Saylet at the tunnel opening, smoking hot as always. It's a good thing she didn't take me up on my invitation in Minnesota. Not only would it have been hard to hide my crush all night with her in close proximity. Then I would have wanted her there after every win for superstition, and I doubt she'd go for that. I give her my usual solemn nod and refocus, all hotness pushed to the back of my brain for my personal celebration later.

The game is brutal. Their offense is dialed in from years of play together, and they out-maneuver us no matter what we try. By the second intermission, we are down 1-0. We come into the dressing room drenched in sweat, to ice and hydrate.

Coach tries to be encouraging. "This is a team that has been to the Stanley Cup twice in the last five years, and the playoffs seven out of the last ten. They know how to do it."

"We do, too. We just have to do it better, harder, faster," Saint chimes in.

"Right. And you may not do that every night. So I'm telling you—just get the fuck out there and do your best. Play your hearts out for another twenty minutes and then we'll break it down and prepare for the next game. Now, bring it in. Do. Your. Best."

Jack chimes in with, "Leash the Icemutts! Let's fucking gooo!"

I've been in the playoffs once with my last team, as have some of the guys. But somehow each year, I forget how much a full season then post-season play against the best teams of the league take out of a body. We may only spend a couple minutes at a go on the line, but we're moving at over twenty miles an hour on razor-sharp blades, banging into players, walls, and the ice.

Coach's pep talk keeps our energy high long enough for frustration to take over as fuel. The Icedogs' number 4 slams Petrovsky against the boards with a shove. Our irritable winger drops his gloves and it's on. Saint and I exchange eye rolls. Quasi is such a hothead. If he wasn't so fast on the front line he'd make a decent grinder. But this team doesn't need a grinder. We play clean, and on average we're faster than our counterparts. Saint and I had a private conversation about Quasi being traded, but as captain, Saint can't propose something like that. The players all have to see him as our support and representative to management, so he has to wait until it's asked or suggested before he weighs in.

Quasi's hair trigger temper gets him time in the sin bin, so now we're on a penalty kill. Fucking Quasi needs to play smarter. Saint, Jack, Kyle, and I all drop over the wall to help Cam protect our goal. The same player rams Saint into the boards. Now, I'm pissed. Saint is the cleanest player of us all.

I'm not risking another penalty, but it's time to get physical. Fighting for the puck in the corner, I dig my elbow under number 4's pads. When I send it down the ice and the ref's attention follows it, I shove off with an extra hard push of him into the boards. In another battle for the biscuit, my stick happens to tangle in his skates. He gets the message, growling at me, and I growl back.

Two line changes later, I'm back out, and Quasi is released from the penalty box. I blink and they've got the puck in our end with Jack and Scottie racing to catch up. Right as Jack throws himself forward, the winger hauls back. He's done this several times, faking a slapshot and passing it to a teammate. My shoulders drop in relief, only to have him send it right between Cam's knees as they come down to block it. As always, Cam maintains his equilibrium, standing and banging his stick on the ice three times to shake it off, but his eyes are frustrated.

We're down with a score of 2-0. Two and a half minutes left.

We pull Cam so we have a hundred and fifty seconds to score two goals with an advantage, and to ensure they don't get another one on us.

It doesn't happen. We head to the dressing room, trying to tune out the home crowd cheering for their team.

By the time I've showered and changed, I'm wiped. The game is already replaying in my head. It loops as I try to figure out what I did wrong that cost us the game. Grams and I will talk, and she'll attempt to make me feel better. Worse, I have to manage a call with her without swearing. Her hard and fast rule has always been that cussing is only allowed during hockey games, but all I want to do is yell "FUCK" at the top of my lungs.

Saylet is nowhere to be found, and I'm relieved. I have to get over this crush already. As Cam's younger sister likes to say, you don't shit where you eat. Cam being the exception, of course, having successfully navigated that minefield to be with Christina.

But as I have zero interest or capacity for a relationship, it would be a terrible idea to act on my desire to take Saylet's hot little body to bed and make a sex pretzel. Besides, my mood is so foul no one needs to see that.

Chapter Four

Saylet

Holy fuck, I almost—*almost*—hope we don't make it to the Finals. I've been running nonstop. We're a new team in a new town, and it's hard to sell next round tickets until we make it through the current round.

Player interactions have been limited to interviews to the fan favorites to give the guys as much space as possible to focus on their game, nutrition, and rest.

Today was an even longer day than the ones before, and it's close to midnight when I pull into my building's garage.

When I turn my car off, I'm plunged into darkness. I'm so tired I hadn't noticed that the garage security lights weren't working. Sighing, I grab my pepper spray, turn my phone to flashlight mode, and slide the strap of my laptop bag over my right shoulder. When I trudge to the elevator, I discover yellow tape across it. Fuck. If I was less exhausted, I might have been able to predict that the electricity for the whole building was out.

Sighing, I turn to the stairwell. There's a sign taped on it so I shine the flashlight up. I read aloud, "Building is closed until further notice due to an electrical emergency. Call the number below for access to your belongings. Financial arrangements will be communicated within the next three days." I stare at it, unable to process that I do not have a home for the foreseeable future.

Finally, I call the number. It takes two calls to get someone to answer, and when they do, they're groggy. The guy tells me it'll be half an hour before he can get here to walk me to my apartment. I debate trying to get him here early tomorrow, but I don't trust that he'll show up on time, and I am too freaking busy to deal with this all over again. Deciding to wait, I give him the number of my parking space.

Sitting in my car, I consider my options. I could go to a hotel, but that's expensive. My salary doesn't come close to what the hockey players make. It's also too late to call Kayla or anyone else. At this point, I might as well go back to the training facility, crash in the players' lounge, and then use the women's locker room off the gym to change clothes. Once I get the "financial arrangements" communication and an estimate of how long we'll be out, I can figure the rest out.

When the on-call security guy arrives, who I thankfully recognize, I climb out of my car. "What happened to the electricity?"

"Apparently, rodents got into the wiring in the basement and ate through some of it. There were several shorts. The electrician who came out to look at it said that the work needed is significant enough to classify as a renovation or upgrade, which means the building has to be brought up to current code."

"Um…" My brain is too sluggish to follow all this. "What does that mean for the tenants?"

"Y'all have to find somewhere else to live for a few weeks."

"A few *weeks*?" I recoil, stopping mid-stride to lean

against a wall. If only this could have happened in a month, after the Stanley Cup. The players' superstitions have rubbed off on me, so I can't think about them being out earlier than that.

"I can't afford a hotel for weeks. Do they have any short-term rental suggestions?" Even an Airbnb would be outside my financial comfort zone.

"I don't know, miss. Maybe they'll send some in the emails they're working on, or you can ask."

As immigrants, my meak and ba taught me to be prepared for anything. My siblings and I still call them by the Khmer titles for mom and dad. Heck, Meak still wears multiple bracelets on both arms because they hid their wealth and made it portable in Cambodia so they could escape the Khmer Rouge when the opportunity arose. Growing up in Colorado, I learned to not rely on friendships outside my siblings. Too many times, I ended up hurt or excluded because of my race.

Meak instilled in all of us that our careers are the equivalent of her bracelets, that we should preserve those as our fallbacks should things go wrong in our life.

I have friends here, but I'd never be comfortable asking them to put me up for a night, much less weeks. Plus, some of them are on tight budgets, sharing apartments with roommates to pay down student loans. Others are married with young children in the house, not able to flex to the hours I'm working right now. And if I was willing to ask her, which I'm not, I only have the vaguest concept of Kayla's living arrangements. She's pretty closed-mouthed about her personal life.

All in all, I don't know how I could have prepared for being homeless for weeks on end.

What had been an exhausting week pales compared

to what I'm facing. Overwhelmed, I pack whatever I think I might need in a large suitcase and an overnighter then follow the guard back to my car. So it's decided. I'll sneak into the players' lounge tonight and shower in the locker room, and hopefully I'll figure out a plan in the morning.

* * * *

The Tornadoes support staff are running ragged to make this first playoff season a success on all levels.

The teams split the first two games in Chicago and the two home games, unexpectedly.

Once I crashed in the players' lounge that first night, it was easy to make it a habit. I made sure I knew when the team had an early practice and was either up and out extra early or managed on the too-small couch in my office.

Eight days later, we are back in Illinois. A road trip never felt so good. The pleasure of sleeping in a real bed cannot be overstated, giving me a new reason for being invested in our guys winning the Cup. Sadly, we lose the away game, so we are coming home down 2-3 in the series. The next game is make or break for us—if we lose, we're eliminated.

Being home also means I'm back to sneaking around. I'm racing around trying to sell reserved tickets to Conference Finals, even though there is no guarantee we'll get there. Between that I'm juggling the kickstart of two summer programs I'll be spearheading—Greg's bid for sponsors for the team and arena, and the PR campaign on diversity that Stephen approved. We'll run several spots on local TV, radio, and social media about being the *diverse* new face of the NHL. While I love my work, it's challenging to keep my attitude upbeat on a few hours of sleep on a sectional that often holds sweaty player asses.

Along with a bed and a private bathroom, I miss cooking my preferred food. I don't have access to the kitchen at the practice facility and the one Cambodian restaurant in Austin has watered down the seasoning for American palates. I'd rather make my own, but that's not a possibility for who knows how long. Even spicy Tex-Mex, an adopted favorite, is better when I can enjoy the Zen of preparing it.

I wouldn't mind, but after the first emails assuring us they'd refund that month's rent and not charge us for as long as it took to restore power safely, the property manager has been radio silent. So I have no idea how long it will be until I get back to living like a grown-up.

I'm sure I could call my family for financial or emotional support, but I'm loathe to do so. My parents used what money and jewelry they had to get us to the U.S. Here, they got whatever jobs they could find until they re-credentialed. Now Ba is a doctor and Meak a nurse in Denver. If they did it without help, so can I.

I'm the youngest of four. Some of my favorite memories are my mother teaching us to cook after a full day of work. With almost a ten year gap between me and my oldest sister, I was too young for some of it. But I started with rice, using a stepstool to reach the counter. I loved every minute of it and look forward to teaching my daughters and sons. My father would sit in the living room and study after his workday. Then when he passed the boards, my mother went back to school, confident we could feed ourselves.

None of us played sports, joined clubs, or learned an

instrument. At first, there wasn't money for the extras. Later, as my siblings went to university and my parents restarted their careers, there was no one to pick me up if I didn't make the bus, whether it was for an extracurricular activity or tardiness.

So I became self-sufficient. Smiling, I realize that was probably the start of why my coworkers call me a control freak these days. And I continued to refine my cooking skills, trying to impress my parents with delicious Cambodian food when they got home from work. More often than not, they shoveled whatever I made into their mouths as they discussed their workday, then went to bed without commenting on the food.

Despite that, I still find cooking therapeutic. But being homeless means I don't have my usual path to relaxation. Between that and the lack of sleep, I've started falling behind at work. At first, it was a couple missed emails, forcing coworkers to follow up with me.

Kayla catches me the morning of the day before the game. "How the heck are you managing to work out with this schedule?"

"What?" I belatedly realize my hair is still wet from showering in the practice facility locker room. "Oh. I'm not sure how often this will happen, but I'm trying." Thankfully, I am at least eating healthy, even if it's not my preferred cuisine, as I sneak premade meals from the players' lounge when I can. I'm careful about quantities, as those are portioned for professional athletes, not 5'2" female desk jockeys.

"Did you see my email yesterday?"

Oh no, there's a third one I missed? "No, I'm sorry. What's up?"

"Hey, don't worry, I sent it late." She cocks her head.

"You look stressed. And you haven't been your usual high octane self. You okay?"

"Sure, I just want to be responsive."

"It was just something funny, no response required. Look at it when you have time or need a break," she says with a wave and a smile.

By three o'clock most afternoons, I'm yawning and sluggish. A knock on my door startles me out of a nod, and I jump in my chair. Stephen leans in, "Are you coming to the meeting?"

I glance down. It's 3:35. I've lost half an hour and am late to a meeting.

Grabbing my laptop, I apologize and hustle behind him.

That night, instead of sleeping, I lay awake and stare at the lit fire exit sign hanging from the ceiling in the lounge.

My siblings all have graduate degrees and are excelling in their chosen professions. I stopped with a Bachelor's degree and have bounced through a couple industries before hockey. I was PR Director for Austin's minor league team when the Tornadoes rehomed them. When they offered me the same role with them, citing my familiarity with Austin's hockey audience, I was euphoric.

Now I'm jeopardizing this dream job. Or I could ask my parents for a loan. Both those thoughts make me feel sick. If I can power through these next few weeks and get back in my apartment, all will be well. Especially if we win the Cup.

The more I worry about the job and my parents' expectations, the later it gets. Then every time I look at the clock, I worry more about my lack of sleep affecting my performance. I'm spiraling, but I can't seem to help it.

Our guys have to win tomorrow night's game. I need a road trip to catch up on sleep.

Chapter Five

Drew

Saylet is standing in the tunnel again as we head out for warmups, smiling and clapping to wish us luck. I nod, taking her in. She looks hot in a form-fitting black dress with a purple scarf and purple heels. Even her eyeshadow and fingernails are Tornadoes purple. Dammit, I have to stop noticing details like this and focus on our opponents, and how we can kick their asses in three blocks of twenty minutes.

But as I near the ice, I realize I don't usually notice her makeup. Those were smudges of exhaustion, and her eyes looked dull. She spends so much time taking care of all of us; I wonder who takes care of her. Making a mental note to check in on her later or tomorrow, I shut everything except hockey out. My skates scrape the ice, my world ends at the glass.

After warmups, the dressing room is tense. If we lose tonight, our season is over and our shot at the Cup lost. Not many people expected an expansion team to get this far this fast. Screw them. I want to go all the damned way. Every game that gets us closer gives us more of a taste of what that might look like, feel like.

Some players are focused on performance bonuses based on playoff rounds. Just about all of us know that the deeper into the Cup run we go, the more likely we are to get long-term contract renewal offers from the Tornadoes.

Separate from all that is the hunger every NHL player has for the Cup. There are only so many names that will get on that Cup, and having your name etched there makes history, even if you never play again after that.

The problem is, the other team wants it that bad, too, and they've been playing together for longer.

Coach and Saint try to raise our spirits. Their words sound the same as the last few games, but that might be my mindset. Or maybe it's because there are only so many ways to say "Go get 'em. Win!"

My leg is bouncing, along with half the team's. We explode onto the ice, everything other than the brightly lit rink blurs.

And finally, tonight, everything clicks. There's always someone on the other end of my passes. I'm in the crease when Saint looks for me. Mattie gets my rebounds, and I get his. Jack is fiercer than ever, crowding the Icedogs offense against the boards to fight for the puck, or stealing it away and racing up the ice to set up our play.

We go up 1-0. First intermission. We're all strung tighter than an overtuned piano. 2-0.

Second intermission. Cam is a lake, calm and smooth. He's in the zone, and he'll stay there. My front line is in a similar headspace, hearing Coach's feedback on the second period through a haze. He says something about minutes in zone, but I don't catch it. I'm eager to get this to a W, and on to the Conference Finals.

Then we're back out, racing up and down the ice. Chicago has tightened their defense, and I can barely see the goal, much less try for a shot. The second line comes over the boards, and I head to the bench. Even Petrovsky has been calmer tonight. But now I see the other team needling him. Unfortunately, Quasi is on the opposite side of the ice, out of earshot for Saint and I to encourage calmness from the bench as he skates past.

An Icedog slams him against the glass in a tangle of skates and sticks, competing for the puck. Quasi sneaks an elbow and gets enough breathing room to flick it backwards to Kucera.

I breathe a sigh of relief. The gloves stayed on, and the whistle didn't blow.

The game clock shows under three minutes remaining when Chicago pulls their goalie.

Cam hasn't had a lot of experience with six on five, with this being his first year goaltending in the NHL. But his stats are among the best in the league so I hold my breath and hope.

The puck is down our end for too long. Victor Gauthier, playing at center, gets it away and starts toward their goal, but their defense is ready and gets control back, pushing it into our zone.

I risk a glance at the clock. Two minutes. In the second I glance away, the crowd sighs collectively, and I turn back to see the goal lamp lit with Cam shaking his head.

Okay, it's still 2-1, with less time on the clock. Cam bangs his stick on the ice three times to shake it off as my line flows over the boards for the faceoff. Their goalie is back in place, but before they have time to pull him and replace him with another player, we win the faceoff.

Sure, we're going to try to score, but our gazes

connect and we nod at each other. We have to keep the play at this end of the ice and run the clock down, so score carefully. Jack and Kyle cycle the puck between us. Finally, some Icemutts start making jabs at each of us and it's getting too close. I get the puck and pass to Saint, who is close to the crease. He tries to slap it in, but the defense is on him, taking the puck to run it back up to our end.

He and I check their D-men while the rest of our guys race up the ice. There's no way we're going into overtime after starting this period up by two, dammit. The five of us are furious yet energized.

They get by us with a long pass, but Jack shoulder checks the guy with the puck. He swats it back to Saint, who is jammed against the wall by an Icedog defenseman. The mutt steals the puck and sends it forward again.

Before it reaches anyone's stick, the buzzer sounds. We won. Holy shit, we won. We're going to Game 7, we're not out of this yet. Our home crowd is on their feet yelling more than singing the team song as we all hug it out before lining up. Best of all, I get to sleep in my own bed knowing I'll get to play more hockey this week.

Chapter Six

Saylet

Ah, the joys of a private jet seat built for hockey players, which will be followed by a real bed. Even better, as we've been here twice before in the last week or so, it's a familiar bed in a familiar place. Game 7 may be tense, but I'm not. I get my laptop out to work, but I'm so tired and comfortable.

The next thing I feel is my computer being tugged from my loosened grip and a blanket thrown over me. My eyes flutter open to see Drew squatting in the aisle beside me, tucking the edge of the blanket around my bare knee below my dress.

He looks almost angry.

I mumble an apology—for what, I'm not sure, as I didn't ask him to take care of me—and drift back to sleep, my petite frame curled in the oversized chair.

I studiously ignore him as we disembark, file onto the bus, and check into the hotel. I'm not embarrassed, but I'm not *not* embarrassed, especially given that indecipherable look.

The guys have a light practice, and I spend the time working at the desk in my room, only noticing the time when the room gets so dark my laptop screen hurts my eyes.

I didn't have to be here; anyone from Marketing or

PR could have come to step in as necessary. And our guys haven't been arrested or drunk and disorderly, yet. But the prospect of a real bed was honestly secondary to the fact that I'm super invested in this team, and I'm dying to see them pull this off. Or be there to support them if they…nope, they'd kill me if I thought that.

The room service menu still looks uninspired, featuring bland chicken, pasta, and salads. On my last visit, I found an Italian place down the street that was quite good, and I could use a change of scenery and some fresh air.

Changing to business casual rather than business attire, I head downstairs. The elevator doors open on the main floor to a sweaty Drew and Jack chatting.

"Hey, Saylet," Jack says, as Drew's chin jerks upward in a silent greeting.

"Hi, guys. Save some for the game, will ya? And Drew, thank you for the assist on the flight."

"I'm glad you got some rest. Where are you headed?"

The elevator has been called and is gone, so Jack leans over to push the button again.

"To a pizza and pasta place I found last time."

He's suddenly serious. "Did you eat there before our win or our loss?"

"Um," I say, thinking while giving him the side-eye. "Loss. It was between the games."

"No way. Uh uh. You can't go back there. Come out with us. We're going to a burger place that has decent chicken. We went there before the first game."

Jack is nodding like a maniac now, too. They won the first game.

I manage not to roll my eyes at their superstitions, but I won't mess with them before a playoff game.

Stephen and Greg—heck, the entire city of Austin would kill me. "How long will y'all be? I'm hungry."

They exchange glances. Jack wheedles, "Ten minutes? Fifteen tops. Even if any of the other guys are coming, we won't wait for them, we'll have them meet us there. Just hang out at the bar for a few. There're pretzels."

"Okay, okay."

They're back in ten, hair wet, with Cam and Saint tagging along.

More Tornadoes pile out of the elevator as we near the front doors, so we end up at two tables of eight in the place. Someone must have slipped the manager some cash, because we're positioned in a semi-private rear corner behind a half wall.

There's no way I'll be able to eat or talk without drooling if I sit across from Drew's dark eyes and those lush lips accented by the dark close-cropped beard. So when he turns toward one table, I aim for the other one. But when a chair is pulled out to my right, I know who it is just from his light cologne and the heat of his body before he even sits.

Bracing myself, I smile at nobody as though everything is normal, and I still plan to enjoy my dinner.

Indeed, he is chatting to Mattie on the other side of him as they debate whether a player named Harju will be off Chicago's IR—injured reserve list—and play this game.

The waiter comes to stand behind Drew and me to take our drink orders. I'm the only woman present, and it's the right approach, but couldn't he just this once start at one end of the table and work around?

Drew turns, catching my eye and smiling, as the

waiter asks what I'll have.

"Club soda with lime, please," I manage. His bulging quad pressing against my knee is so distracting I'm surprised the words are coherent. When he smooths a hand over his beard, I worry for the state of my underwear.

Drew does another short chin nod acknowledging my professionalism and says, "I'll have one, too."

His baritone adds another layer of lust to my lower belly, as does the drawn-out "too" showing his Duluth roots, and I regret not ordering room service.

I stare a hole through the plastic coated menu. The words are invisible, though. I'm picturing ever-increasingly unlikely scenarios where his baritone would echo those words again. Him offering me an orgasm, then saying with a lopsided smile, "I'll have one, too." Him offering me a pillow and bed, then saying with a lopsided smile…

Fuck, if a bed to sleep on is second in that short list, then clearly I'm more sleep-deprived than I realized.

In an effort to rein my wild thoughts back to the realm of professionalism, I turn to listen to the players on my left, smiling and nodding in the right places.

After dinner, I decline Jack's invitation to the hotel bar and veer off toward the elevator. Drew starts to follow me, and Jack hollers at him, "Buzz, get your ass over here. Everything the same as Game 1. We hung in the bar until just after ten."

In the mirrored elevator door, I see him pivot back to the bar. Phew. Now I have the rear view as well as the front view to enjoy when I entertain myself in my room. On my *bed*.

I am pathetic AF, and I don't even care.

Chapter Seven

Drew

The Chicago crowd is thunderous. The plexiglass does nothing to block the sound or allow us to hear each other.

This game is going to be brutal. We're tired, we've lost more than we've won in this arena, and we're a new team. On the other hand, we're younger and fitter than our opponents. And we're hungry.

We can all taste the success of being the first expansion team in over a century or arguably ever to win the Cup in our first year. This series has shown us the odds are long, but we are determined to give it our best effort.

Cam was close to a shutout in our home game, and we played seamlessly. All in all, I won't allow myself to put anything other than positive energy out into the universe. We're going to pull this off in the Icemutts' house tonight.

One of the Icedogs' stars, Timo Harju, is on the roster for tonight, which had some of the guys on edge. In the locker room, Quasi was muttering something about the guy being fragile. When I targeted Minnesota's number 12, it was because I knew I was faster than him even on his good days, but I get the feeling Quasi's thoughts are darker. I don't say anything, though. Guys coming off the IR understand the risks, and it's up to them, their trainers, doctors, and coaches to decide when they feel strong enough to deal with body checks.

The puck drops and we're on it. I use every tool in my toolbox to get the biscuit, keep the biscuit, and put the biscuit in the basket. I slam and am slammed against the boards more times in the first period than I was in the whole last game, but I don't care.

They come super close to a goal, the puck disappearing under Cam and another player for a long minute before the ref blows the whistle to stop play. As he rises, the puck under him is dangerously close to the goal line.

That is all we need to re-energize us. We take it down the ice, where Mattie drills a snapshot that should hit just inside the goal post at elbow height on their goalie, an awkward angle to block. But block it he does. We race back to defend our net and grab the puck away almost as soon as they attempt to set up the play.

Saint speeds forward with it, and I'm only a few feet behind him in the center of the ice. He dekes then sends a wrist shot into that same pocket Mattie was aiming for. It's one we discussed when watching game tape. We know this goalie's weakest spot.

The lamp lights! We've drawn first blood, and the home team and crowd aren't happy about it.

My line changes out so we can catch our breath.

Only a few minutes later, our goal lamp lights. They've evened it up. Damn.

Cam pounds his stick, and we're back in for a faceoff.

On the next line change, I catch a gleam in Quasi's eye that doesn't bode well for Harju, who is his mirror.

Quasi keeps it clean. There are no more body checks than I've received. But whenever Harju is by the boards, Quasi skates full tilt into him to battle for dominance of the puck.

The buzzer sounds. The game is tied 1-1 at the first intermission.

We regroup, ice knees and other body parts, and cool off as Coach reminds us to own the corners. I miss Saylet's presence at the mouth of the tunnel like she often is during home games, but I don't have time to think about that now.

As our team files onto the visitors' bench, with the top six circling the ice, I'm checking who is leading off this period for the other team. Saint skates over and faces Cam as he skates backwards next to me. "Do you see Harju?"

I shake my head, still searching.

"How about on the bench?" he pushes.

"Nope. And the rest of his line is here on the ice."

"That's what I thought." He skates over to Coach and fills him in, the whole bench listening avidly. Quasi smirks. I try to temper my annoyance; this is what we all sign up for.

We win the faceoff, and the period follows from there. They are uncoordinated, off. We are like a well-oiled machine, for both offense and defense. We score midway through the second period. Remarkably, their tank of a goalie is playing better than ever, damn him, but I can't hate a guy for doing his best.

During the second intermission, we talk about the elephant not in the room.

"What the hell happened?"

"They played without him the first six games, why

are they so lost now?"

"Who cares? Let's finish this thing." Jack's comment shuts all the guys' questions up.

"Damn straight," I add. "Let's..."

My glance to Jack is all the encouragement he needs. He belts out in a long howl, "fucking goooo!"

Back on the ice, the Icedogs' mouths are tight. Will that translate into better play or worse coordination? Turns out, they are less synchronized. They trip, miss passes, and generally lose the game. I mean, we played our guts out, and we certainly did everything to win. But given the earlier games, I don't know whether that would have been enough against the version of this team we played for the last six games. Tonight, though, it's more than enough. They pull their goalie, but I get it away to take it down and make a long goal to get us the W, 3-1.

We are screaming for the last few seconds into the buzzer, the whole team clearing the bench to celebrate after the clock times out. We made it to the Conference Finals, the last hurdle between us and a direct fight for the Cup, as a brand new team.

Holy fuck.

* * * *

On the flight home, the crew keeps the plane dark for us, so we can try to nap. In my case, I check on Saylet first, but she's typing away like that little pink bunny we liken her to. We burned off our celebratory energy pretty quickly in the locker room after seven stressful games and related travel. We're also very aware that we'll only have a few days to recover before we're facing an even tougher team. So remarkably, with the exception of a few guys talking quietly in the back, most of us sleep.

The following day an afternoon practice is scheduled. Sitting in my living room rewatching the recorded games and obsessing is better done in the dark of night, so I head to the facility in the morning. My plan is to grab some food from the players' lounge then do a light workout.

I push open the lounge door and stop short. A very feminine hot little butt in yoga pants is bent over the couch stuffing something into a bag. Is that a pillow? Wait, is that *Saylet*?

I've never seen her in anything resembling leisure attire; she even dresses up for social events with the team. I guess knowing you're on call for any player needs at any time will keep you dressed for the public at all times. Except now, apparently.

Damn, those are either the best yoga pants on the planet, or that is the hottest ass I've seen in recent memory, maybe ever.

Clearing my throat, I take a step forward.

She whips around. "Drew. Sorry, just cleaning some things up for y'all."

Her adopted Texas slang "y'all" seems to slip out when she's tired or distracted, whereas the rest of the time she's uber professional. And she looks exhausted again, even more so without makeup on. Although why she'd be here without makeup and in casual clothes, I don't know. I narrow my eyes. Pretty sure she's not wearing a bra. My hockey-fried brain takes another two beats to put it together…

"Wait, were you sleeping here?"

"Don't tell on me. I worked really late and didn't feel safe driving home, so I crashed here. I'll get out of your hair and go clean up now."

I prowl closer, taking her in. "Are you okay? You look tired."

"Hmph. Says every guy to a woman not wearing makeup."

"Don't even start that. You're smokin' in this getup, possibly even hotter than that little purple dress last night. I mean it. You legit look tired, and I was voicing concern."

Her eyes go wide as I talk, making me realize I've given away that I've been watching her. *Creeper, much, Busbee?*

Thankfully, she doesn't comment on that, saying instead, "Sorry. Uncaffeinated PR Director here, hence the snark. Thank you for your concern, but I'm fine. I'll see you later."

She ducks around me and is gone.

Two days later, it's our last day home before we fly to Las Vegas for Game 1 of the Conference Finals against the Desert Kings.

I drive to the arena early. Since we won after I ate food prepped by the team kitchen before flying out for Game 1 in the earlier rounds of the playoffs, I'm following post-season superstition protocol and keeping everything the same.

After parking, I send a quick text to the other top six guys that I'm here before stepping out. Movement at the back of a car to my right has me checking.

Saylet is rummaging in her trunk.

I stroll over and spy a large suitcase, with folded clothes to one side as she searches for something. "Hey, Saylet."

She starts, then whips around and tries to look casual.

"What's up? Why do you have a suitcase in your

car?" I smile. "There might be such a thing as being too prepared for us to screw up and need bailing out."

"Oh, ah, ha ha. Yeah, maybe you're right."

I peer at her, cataloging; the bags and smudges are bigger than ever. Even her shoulders droop. "Saylet, something's going on. Sleeping in the lounge, suitcase in the car. Tell me what's up."

She straightens further and sidesteps to intercept my line of sight to her trunk. "Nothing major. I'm handling it. You worry about the Conference Finals, not me."

"I'm a hockey player, not an idiot. I can walk and chew gum at the same time, and I can worry about two things at once. Now, tell me what's wrong. I'd like to help if I can."

"You can't."

"Saylet." I fold my arms. "We can stand here until Coach comes looking for me, or we can do this the easy way."

She sighs and waves a hand in dismissal. "My apartment building has no electricity for a few weeks." She adds under her breath, "I hope."

"Where are you stay…Please tell me you have not been sleeping in the players' lounge the whole time."

Chapter Eight

Saylet

"No, no. Not the whole time." My office counts as somewhere different. Our game schedule and resulting PR schedule is so grueling it hardly makes sense to make a commute to a temporary place. Besides which, the ones that wouldn't eat too deeply into my savings are all close to an hour away.

"Where have you been staying then?" Drew is relentless.

Okay, I've tried waving it away and that hasn't worked so I'll try getting defensive. I fold my arms to match his stance. "Here and there, not that it's your business."

"Really? Do you want me to ask security to check the players' lounge every night, or would you prefer to tell me?"

He wouldn't…would he? He's trying to help, but threatening me is mean. Frustrated, I give up. "Okay, mostly the lounge. I'm hoping it will only be another week, though."

He gapes at me. I guess he hadn't really believed it, or maybe hadn't expected me to admit it. Then his head is shaking side to side. "You're going to burn out. You're killing yourself taking care of us, but not affording yourself the same courtesy."

"Look, my entire focus recently has been this organization. Y'all have each other for those long days, but my friends have different lives. Within the company, I'm sort of betwixt and between the team and the back office. Kayla's a friend, but not close enough for me to ask to couch surf for more than a night or two. And I don't make what y'all make, so I opted not to do an Airbnb or a hotel."

He frowns. "The Donovans would have helped you figure something out, like they would for us."

"Maybe, but they pay me a decent salary and might have judged me for it. My goal is to be the best, self-sufficient, efficient PR Director they've ever seen after they took a risk on me." I'm younger than most PR Directors in the league, and I'm eager to prove myself to them and to my parents. That means I'm not going to make waves when a personal crisis crops up at the most important time of the hockey year.

That seems to resonate with him. He nods, then reaches in his pocket, pulling out a set of keys, and starts working one off the ring. "I understand. I have a perfectly good two-bedroom condo, fully furnished, unlike some of the rookies. Stay at my place. We're on the same schedule after all, so you won't disturb my beauty rest."

My eyes flick between his face to his hand holding out a key. A flash of him walking around in boxer briefs—fuck, I hope he wears boxer briefs—tempts me. I consider the missed emails, falling asleep at my desk, and the fact that I'm nowhere near where I want to be on my campaign championing diversity in the NHL. But no, I'm an independent woman, and he needs nothing to disturb his routine during playoffs. I sigh and shake my head once. "Drew…that is an incredibly generous offer, and I really appreciate it. But I couldn't impose, especially now."

"I'm telling you, you're not imposing. I offered. It's a two-bedroom, two-bathroom place, and it's furnished since my grams stays with me sometimes. She couldn't make it down for the playoffs, so it's all yours. She'll come later this summer. This is for the garage. I'll text you my unit number and the code for my door." He gestures with the key he's still holding out.

I can't bring myself to take it, even though I'm so grateful for the offer my throat is tightening.

He tosses it in the suitcase. "I have a spare in my locker. Go make yourself at home, or I can come back and help you get settled."

"No," I say quickly, the idea of being with him in his space too new to deal with. "I mean okay, but don't disrupt your day any more."

"Okay. See ya tonight."

I swallow and say, "Thank you," as he turns to go.

He spins and steps into my space. "There better be no more players' lounge. You want to talk about distracting from my focus on the games? These"—he brushes his thumb under one of my eyes where there are dark circles—"are distracting. I need to know *everyone* on my team is in top form."

His touch is short-circuiting my senses, but my mind and heart melt at those words. Yep, definitely a caretaker under those playboy ways.

I work so hard, knowing they are the stars and shouldn't have to think about any of us behind the scenes. But it's nice seeing the support goes both ways. That this alternate captain includes more than just guys in jerseys as part of his team.

"Yes, sir," I say with a gulp.

* * * *

I lug my suitcase into Drew's place without waiting for his help, so I can scope it out.

The unit is immaculate but not in a cold, clinical way. There are soft accent pillows in shades of gray and purple against a slate-colored microsuede sectional. A black and white shag accent rug and a glass-topped coffee table are in front of it, with a charcoal recliner completing the seating area.

The guest room is done in neutrals, with cream, beige, and patterns of chocolate brown in the bedding and curtains.

I doubt Drew furnished this himself, so either he had a very good designer who understood his quest for comfort as well as style, or his grams helped him. Then again, I might be stereotyping with that thought.

Either way, I drop my suitcase and throw myself on the guest bed.

An extended sigh of pleasure escapes me. This is better than a massage. It's clearly a high-end bed, which makes sense if his intended guest is his grandmother. Fuck, if only I could call in sick for the day.

Hmm. I can't call in sick, but I can work from home. I scramble off the bed that is almost waist high on me and look for some sort of desk, first in my room then in the common areas. There isn't one, but as I pass the kitchen bar that separates it from the front hall and living room, I spy a jumble of cords on the end of the bar against the wall. A wall plate holds a combination of electric plugs and USB ports.

Setting myself up, I send an email telling folks I'll be remote today, and then start working.

Forty-five minutes later, I realize I didn't get to steal snacks and coffee from the lounge. I slide off the stool, and my legs go out from under me. Collapsed in a heap on the floor, I am confused until the pins and needles kick in. Stupid short legs, stupid tall person's barstool. My feet didn't quite reach the footrest, so my lower legs fell asleep. I'm so damned tired and was so engrossed in work I didn't notice.

Now I'm writhing in agony, beyond grateful that Drew was not here to witness the mess that I currently am. Forcing myself to move, I massage my legs and wiggle my toes until I can walk, clinging to the counter edge.

Must find caffeine.

The kitchen is white cabinets, a few with glass fronts, and dark gray countertops with a medium gray stone backsplash.

My lip curls when sitting on this lovely granite counter is the most basic coffeemaker. The curl nearly hits my nose when the walk in corner pantry yields the cheapest brand of coffee. I'm not a coffee snob, but as I drink it undoctored, I like it to taste good.

I scavenge for snacks so I can decide whether to be a total prima donna and order breakfast and a latte from a food delivery place. I glance left in the pantry. The coffee on the right had been my sole focus before now. My jaw drops. There is an unholy amount of canned vegetables and boxed macaroni and cheese. Ew. Worse, the only "spices" in the pantry are disposable shakers of salt and black pepper, both pre-ground.

My decision is made. I hope there are takeout menus

in a drawer somewhere, because a pro athlete cannot keep his body in top six shape on this stuff.

After placing a delivery order of breakfast food, I get back to clearing my inbox. While I'm behind on some communications regarding post-season promo opps, the email chatter has been quiet these past couple days, as though even the back office is enjoying the rest between series.

So I take a short break on my lunch hour and order groceries to be delivered later, then race north to a Korean grocery store that stocks the spices I prefer to work with when I cook my family's traditional foods.

Given Drew's appalling pantry, however, I stick with Tex-Mex for tonight. I don't know when he'll be home, but I want to do something nice in return for his generosity. Besides, the lure of this kitchen is too good to pass up. At least whoever designed it ensured he has the basic food prep and cooking tools stocked. There aren't any specialty items like a stand mixer, but the quality of the coffeemaker still stands out like a sore thumb. My guess is it predates this apartment.

I make enchiladas with my signature tomatillo sauce, erring on the side of caution and aim for a medium heat level rather than my usual incendiary. He hasn't lived here in Texas as long as I have, and not everyone enjoys setting their mouth on fire.

I've only just finished the sauce and am pan-frying the chicken to shred when the front door lock scrapes.

"Alexa, volume three," I shout over Beyoncé.

"I may never be able to look my neighbors in the eye after they had to listen to that music," Drew jokes in the resulting quiet.

I retort, "I don't want to know what you listen to.

Beyoncé is the queen.”

“Whatever. What the hell have you done to my kitchen? Are there still counters under there?”

I use a lot of bowls when I cook. So sue me. His tone was joking rather than outraged, so I reply, “Uh, yeah. And guess what, they’re there to be used. Enchiladas will be ready in an hour if you want. I figured this form of chicken and rice was safe for a playoff diet.”

“Oh wow.” He looks curious now rather than annoyed at the mess. “You don’t have to cook for me. You’re welcome to freeze those for yourself for another night.”

“Thanks, but cooking relaxes me. That said, you don’t have to eat them if you don’t want.”

He peers at the bowls and pans with a hint of unease, but says, “I’ll try them. Call me if I’m not out when they’re ready.”

An hour later, I’ve set two places at the bar and knock on his door.

He emerges from his room and ogles the enchiladas resting after their stint in the oven. “Smells spicy.”

“I lowered the spice level from my usual to be safe, but bought hot sauce in case you want to kick it up.”

“No hot sauce for me, thanks. I barely eat salsa.”

I gulp. “Uh, you may want to try a bite or two before you decide if you want more.”

“I’ll be fine. You went to all this effort, the least I can do is eat what you made.”

We sit, him with three enchiladas on his plate, a smattering of rice, and some black beans.

I have two enchiladas and a ramekin of black beans, since I tasted my way through cooking.

His first bite is exploratory. He swallows it and says,

"These are delicious. Thank you so much, Saylet."

His second bite goes down equally quickly. Then the third. He's speeding up.

That's a good sign, right?

I douse my meal in hot sauce and his eyes widen. He finishes off the first tortilla wrap, gulps his entire glass of water, and excuses himself to refill it.

I gesture to the counter and offer, "There's sour cream to cut some of the heat if you want."

"Oh, okay, thanks." Spooning some next to the second enchilada, he tries a bite. Then another, then speeds through the rest of it. His hairline is sweaty, and his face is paler than usual behind the dark beard.

"Drew, there's some leftover chicken and corn tortillas. I could make you a basic taco without the green sauce if you'd prefer."

"No, no. These are great. But, um, I might be full. Sorry, I should have just taken the two." He's talking between mouthfuls of rice and beans, appearing not in the least full.

Taking pity on him, as the sauce was indeed spicier than I intended, I grab our plates. "Okay, but if you change your mind, the leftovers both with and without sauce will be in the fridge later."

As I start placing food in plastic containers, Drew gestures to the sink and counter. "I called my housekeeper and asked her to come tomorrow. You shouldn't have to clean up after you cooked, and I need to pack."

He's also holding his stomach. If his indigestion from my food interferes with his play tomorrow night, I'll feel horrible. And the team will kill me.

"Thank you, but as I said, cooking relaxes me. The

cleanup is part of it. It's my Zen. I especially don't want you spending more money because I'm here."

He waves his hand then clamps it back against his stomach. "It's no problem. Ah, good night."

Before I can reply, he's off down the hall like a shot. Making short work of the dishes and wipedown, I look at the fridge in satisfaction as I slide the leftovers onto a shelf. There are condiments, fresh vegetables, and dairy, all making a much more acceptable living accommodation for both of us.

His deluxe guest bed beckons me, and I lounge there to call my parents. I've barely dared talk to them lately as my mother would discern the exhaustion in my voice and ask questions I'm not prepared to answer. Then, I put headphones on to listen to more Beyoncé to celebrate being able to cook *and* sleep well again.

Chapter Nine

Drew

Two hours of writhing on my bed interspersed with sprints to the bathroom have been exhausting.

Now I'm in the unenviable position of being hungry while still having a stomachache.

I creep out to the kitchen, not wanting to offend Saylet. Grams taught me to always show appreciation when someone prepared food for you, especially when they paid for it as well. But holy hell, those enchiladas were so hot they should have been smoking.

Instead of them going up in flames, my entire GI tract is on fire, with a particular area burning that could cause major issues if not resolved by tomorrow night's Game 1 of the Conference Finals.

I groan under my breath. The ribbing will be relentless if I'm still trotting back and forth to the restroom on the flight tomorrow.

Pulling out the container of shredded chicken, I sniff it warily. Then pinch a small piece and place it on my tongue. Chew. Swallow. Okay, there are more seasonings than I knew I owned, but it's edible.

Foregoing the tortillas, I grab a slice of white bread out of the cabinet, throw the chicken on, then a smattering of shredded cheese. After running it through the toaster oven to warm the meat and melt the cheese, I contemplate ketchup. Nah, too acidy and salty for my system right now.

With my stomach slightly more settled, I slink back toward the hall to try to pack and get some sleep before the team's flight. A faint beeping becomes audible.

Checking the kitchen, I can't find anything left on or making a sound. Same in the living room and the half bath in the hall. But as I near Saylet's room, it gets louder.

Damn. There was a minute-long power outage while we were away for Game 6, just long enough to make all the clocks in the condo reset and flash. Grams prefers to leave her phone outside her bedroom, instead using an old-school alarm clock. I always forget to reset it.

But why isn't Saylet turning it off?

I knock, softly at first, then louder. No answer. Dammit. She might not exert the physical exertion we do to play, but she's a midnight-haired Energizer bunny behind the scenes, and her mind runs a mile a minute. This was my fault, and she needs her sleep as much as I do; her rest in the players' lounge has been crap.

I crack the door, but I can only see the foot of the bed and the dresser without stepping in. Checking the mirror over the dresser, I spy a bare leg. I suck in a breath, and call, "Saylet?"

No movement or response.

Now I'm a little concerned. My entire focus is on her, stomach issues all but forgotten. Swinging the door wider, I step through.

Before I turn to face the bed, my eyes bulge at the more complete reflection.

Saylet is on her stomach, naked but for a pair of panties that arch over the mounds of her ass and display as much as they cover. Neither thong nor bikini, they're a goddamn tease, especially in Tornadoes purple lace. Her hand is up by her chin, the phone facedown a few inches away. And I see the issue. She's sleeping peacefully, noise-canceling over-ear headphones blending with her dark hair.

Without realizing it, I'm turned to face her now, my mouth agape and my hand on my dick that is tenting my sweats. My fingers tighten, then stroke, and it's all I can do to not jerk myself standing right here ogling her, as much of an asshole as that would make me.

My eyelids drop, then fly wide when that only cements the image in my brain. I step around the bed and turn the alarm off on the clock, not daring to reset the time. The whole time I'm muttering, "Don't roll over. Don't wake up."

I book it out of there, leaning against the wall by her re-closed door to palm my cock again. Clutching it, I take the few steps to my door, close and lock it behind me, and throw myself on the bed. I don't bother pushing the sweatpants down, just reach in and jack myself with the precum that has been leaking continuously since my first step into her room. A handful of strokes later, I'm coming in my pants like a pre-teen.

The woman is hotter than her enchiladas. How the hell am I going to share space with her now that I know what she wears—or doesn't wear—to sleep?

* * * *

The blaring of a siren forces me to consciousness, which is why I picked that alarm sound. When I take stock of the state of my stomach, all seems calm. All the same, I'm not sure I should attempt coffee.

But damn, I'm dragging. I had to jerk off a second time before my body collapsed, probably from dehydration as much as exhaustion.

With that in mind, I swing out of bed, intent on getting an energy drink to ensure I'm in game shape. In the kitchen, I glance at the coffeepot. Does Saylet partake? Perhaps I should start a pot for her.

In fact, she'll be flying with us. She should be up soon. Doesn't it take women longer to get ready than men?

Nothing short of a fire could make me open that door again, however. Shrugging, I decide to give it another fifteen minutes. I opt for eggs and toast rather than my normal protein shake; real food will be gentler on my raw stomach than the chemicals in the powder. Okay, and it's quieter than a blender, although if the alarm right next to her head didn't disturb her, I can't imagine that a kitchen appliance will.

Once I eat, brush my teeth, and throw my toiletry bag into my carryon, I hover in the hallway and check for signs of life.

Silence reigns.

An internal debate ensues. Finally, I sigh and knock, then knock louder.

Nothing.

A thought occurs to me, and I speedwalk to the kitchen, where I grab my cell phone, scroll through my contacts, and hit Saylet's name.

One ring, then a second, then as my thumb hovers over the End Call button, it connects. After a second of fumbling, her voice is strong in my ear, "Hello?"

Shit. I hadn't figured out what to say. "Uh, hey there, roomie. You're flying with us today, right?"

"Drew?" Her voice goes up. "Ohmigod, what time is it?"

"About eight. I was going to head to the airport in about half an hour. Do you want coffee?"

"Half an hour." She is distracted, moving around. "I can do that. Why are you calling me? Nope, never mind, I don't have time for that right now, but thank you. Yes, please, to coffee but not that swil—uh, I mean, I bought some so I wouldn't use yours up. Any chance you could make me two cups worth of that if you have time?"

"Seems the least I could do after you cooked and cleaned." Even if certain parts of me still burn from those enchiladas.

"Thank you. Man, I could really get used to this roommate thing. Okay, I'll be out in a few."

She emerges fifteen minutes later, dressed in a clingy belly button length purple top and black high-waisted flowy trousers that will likely look as fresh after a plane ride as they do now. Her roller bag goes by the door, a black and white checked cropped jacket folded over it. She hasn't done her makeup yet, but her hair's up in a clip, and she looks ready to take on the world. If you ask me, she shouldn't waste the time or the money on makeup; she's just as sexy and gorgeous without it.

I hand her a cup of her chichi coffee and she smiles her thanks, inhaling its aroma for a long moment before sipping.

"May I take this in the bedroom with me while I finish up?" she asks.

"Absolutely. Do you want something for breakfast?"

"Wow, this is a full service establishment. No, I'll grab a protein bar to take with me, thanks." The last words are almost inaudible as she disappears back into the guest room.

We load up my SUV and aim it toward the airport right on time. Color me impressed at how efficient she is. Still, I squirm a little in my seat when I notice a sliver of skin between purple and black at the back of her waist when she's sitting in the passenger seat. My brain leaps back to the view from the night before with just that little provocation.

I clear my throat, unsure how to raise a new concern. "Uh, do you care if people know you're staying with me? If we pull up together, there may be questions."

There will 100% be questions, because hockey players gossip like they're trying out for the high school cheerleading squad, no offense intended to the lovely girls of my past.

"Hmm. Good thought. I don't mind if people know you're taking your alternate captain duties to a whole new level"—she flashes me a smile—"but as a woman in a man's world, I'd like to maintain some semblance of independence, even if it's a bit false in this instance. Perhaps for now, if people ask, let's say you gave me a ride, please?"

"You got it."

Chapter Ten

Saylet

Away games are much less attractive when I have a lovely bed to sleep in back in Austin, even if it's not my own. And a girl could get used to her roommate being her backup alarm and making coffee.

Now if only he walked around shirtless more.

No. Bad Saylet. He's one of your players who you're supposed to protect from scandal, not encourage into bad decisions.

I don't want the other guys to know I'm staying with him, so there's no excuse to wish for him naked or even partially naked. I can't go there. He of course would get high fives and wolf whistles while I'd lose every shred of credibility. The ultimate double standard.

It's more than that, though. This is my career, and I really, *really* like working for the Donovans. The Tornadoes are a passion project for Greg. Along with that, the organization is innovative and forward-thinking. When I pushed for diversity on the team right from the expansion draft, Greg, my boss Stephen, and Coach Steele listened.

Drew has been one of my most frequent volunteers for charity appearances in the community, and a huge help getting other players involved, so we talk and text a lot. But being coworkers or friends does not equal living together, and I'd prefer to avoid even a whisper of rumor.

With that thought, I order lunch in my hotel room and work on my laptop until the bus leaves for the arena.

I check in with LaRhonda and our press liaison then stop to chat with a few of the kinder, gentler members of the media about our starting lineup and hopes for the series.

The stands quiet and the rink darkens. I take my position in the tunnel to watch our guys come out, knowing their superstitious asses need me there, but also trying to convey with my presence my belief that they can do this.

Music swells as the announcer introduces our team, and the guys clomp by, as agile on their skates as I am on stilettos. I smile, bump fists, high five, and nod as required.

Drew glances at me, his gaze not quite meeting mine, and gives the shortest nod known to mankind before averting his eyes. Weird, but we have bigger things to worry about.

I have fewer responsibilities at an away game, so I stay by the tunnel and watch from behind the glass.

The first period is a race, as though each team is attempting to skate the other into the ground—or ice, I guess. Everyone is panting, guzzling sports drinks, and sweating their asses off by the time the buzzer sounds with the score still 0-0. I'm extra glad I don't have to be in the dressing room during intermission as the stink would bring me to tears.

Instead, I use my eighteen minutes wisely, finding a seat in the currently-empty press room off the tunnel where post-game interviews happen. Slipping my feet out of my shoes, I place them on another chair and take the break. Standing for sixty game minutes is challenging in heels, but I want every inch of presence I can get.

Second period brings what I like to call a Tornado warning. The guys' mouths are slashes under their helmets and visors as they file past me out of the tunnel. There's no joking around, and only Jack is flipping his mouthguard around with his teeth, one end hanging from the side of his lips.

They're here to get things done, despite it not being home ice.

Half the team becomes enforcers, and each time one of them bangs their opposition into the boards for a puck, I cringe. I hold my breath as they chase every last pass and rebound, essentially doing everything they can to draw first blood.

They get it. Drew is perfectly positioned, and I bounce in my heels when he captures a rebound. He sends it right back into the opposite corner of the net before the Desert Kings goalie can recover, and I scream along with the crowd.

A few minutes later, Milo Petrovsky chirps just enough to enrage his counterpart, and gloves get thrown, thankfully only by the Vegas player before the whistle blows.

We're on a power play, and our strong second line is out there. My fingers dig into the rail below the plexiglass, and I keep leaning forward so far that my breath fogs the glass and blocks my view until I swipe it away.

Lukas's dark flow lifts behind him as he flies down the ice to set up the play, the front line doing everything they can to stay free for a pass. He sends it to Joon Park, our other D-man on the ice, and darts in. Joon looks left for the second necessary to distract Vegas then sends it back to Lukas in close to the crease, who deflects it to Petrovsky. Milo almost never scores, preferring to tackle guys along the boards to get it to Gauthier. So his one-timer into the near corner of the goal must take Vegas' goalie by surprise as it slips past him. It shocks me for sure. Our guys on the bench bang their sticks as the lamp lights.

The players file off the ice at the end of the second period, sweatier than ever. But their mouths are in wide grins rather than grim lines as they glance up at the scoreboard, where 2-0 is in lights.

I use the intermission to rest my feet again and contemplate who we'll need in the press room and whether it's safe to include Petrovsky in that lineup, assuming the Desert Kings aren't able to feed off their home ice energy. A hockey game is never over until the last buzzer sounds. I've seen two-goal leads killed in the last few minutes of a game, as Coach Steele no doubt is reminding the guys.

A few minutes into the last period, their offense is pressuring Cam, crowding our goal. Our guys are fighting hard, scrambling to get the biscuit out of our zone. A Vegas player takes a shot. Cam slides into a left RVH to block but can't get control of the puck. Another Desert King slaps the rebound to the right, and Cam shoots over there a second too late. The lamp lights and the other team celebrates as the stadium erupts. My fists clench.

The teams congregate at mid-ice for the puck drop. But Cam isn't getting up. Shit. Dan Murphy, our backup goalie, has gotten very few minutes of playoff time, as our games have been so tight, and Cam is young and healthy, or was.

A trainer is out on the ice. Jack is hovering like a nervous grandmother. When they get Cam on his feet, he takes Jack's offer of help and slings an arm across the "Landry" on his jersey. I see why when they start toward me, and my heart aches for the team. He's only skating with one foot, relying on Jack's blades and momentum to get him to the tunnel. From here, the trainer can help.

There's a smattering of applause from the crowd for his performance so far, and he waves a hand as Jack passes him off to a trainer at the edge of the ice.

I'm worried about how this will affect the team's focus and morale, but as PR Director I have to consider how much we share with the public. No doubt it's a dreaded groin pull, the most common goalie affliction. It will be thinly disguised on IR reports as week-to-week with a lower-body injury. No team gives specifics on short-term injuries as it can put them at a disadvantage.

As expected, the team is in upheaval, or as the talking heads say, "they lose momentum." Murphy does his best, but with the D-men adjusting midgame to the differing style of his play, the Desert Kings use the opportunity to press hard in our zone. We lose the game 2-3.

In the end, only Saint and Coach are needed for the press room. Instead, I field questions we don't have answers to yet regarding our star goalie's injury.

Breakfast the next morning is miserable. Cam and Jack are noticeably absent, and even Petrovsky, who is a grumpy self-centered fucker most of the time, is worried. Jack had texted Saint that it was indeed a groin pull. When Coach comes into the meeting room designated as our private dining space, everyone quiets without being asked.

He grimaces and says, "Prancer's out for the next game. Murphy, you got this. Guys, do not let this distract you."

They nod, but it does, which is understandable. We fly home with the series at 0-2. Not completely unexpected, but not the best way to go into Game 3 either. The guys keep muttering, "At least we'll be on home ice," as though that is the most promising thought.

Chapter Eleven

Drew

Coach calls a long practice and scrimmage on our first day home, so we have as much ice time with Murphy as possible. You'd think that as a relatively stationary figure, swapping the goalie shouldn't make that big a difference. Plus, they're usually quiet guys.

But Cam was—*is*, dammit—this team's backbone, and his stats are unbeatable. Those stats helped us mess with other teams' psyches. Now, knowing that's lost is messing with *our* minds.

After practice, I drag my ass back to my condo, torn between excitement and fear at the possibility of Saylet cooking. But she's not there when I arrive, so I text her.

Me

Ordering food in. Want anything?

Saylet

Sure. I may not get out of here for an hour.

She comes through the door minutes after the food arrives saying, "I thought I'd eat while it's hot then work from here if that's okay."

Damn. I was going to watch game tape on the big screen, but I'm a little self-conscious at how upset I get at past-me's mistakes. I'll watch it at the practice rink tomorrow instead and hope it helps me get into a winning mindset.

We eat; my chicken and rice seasoned as the restaurant sends it, hers doused in so much hot sauce I wonder how she tastes the food. I should serve her cardboard or styrofoam under hot sauce and see if she notices.

I rinse my dishes and put them in the dishwasher then excuse myself. Saylet has been notably quieter than her usual standard, and I catch a flash of sympathy in her eyes before she smiles wide and turns on the PR support. "Good night. Get some sleep, and tomorrow will bring a win here at home with a sold-out stadium."

In my room, I strip off my sweats and exchange them for a white undershirt and sleep pants, a habit I started in the AHL when we always shared rooms on the road. We see enough of each others' junk in the locker rooms. It was an attempt at privacy. Probably also because I spent most of my younger years in a one-bedroom with Grams where, despite her best efforts, privacy was at a premium.

Lying on my bed, my muscles ache. I expect to fall asleep in seconds, but instead I listen to Saylet move around in the apartment. Against my will, my brain conjures up a view of Saylet in bed the last time we slept here. The tiny slice of disgusting jerk in me that survived living with Grams and blossomed among a bunch of hockey players thinks I should have left the alarm on so I could see if that was a regular sleep outfit for her.

Rolling over I punch my pillow as my cock presses against the mattress. Refusing to make jerking off to mental images of my roommate a nightly habit, I ignore it. But it's a long time before I sleep.

The next day, I do everything I can to bolster the team's spirits, as does Saint. As we suit up, before Coach goes through the specifics of what he wants us to focus on, I stand and call, "Murphy."

Everyone stops what they're doing and turns. Murphy looks up and takes the ear buds out of his ears.

"You got this. We got this. We have your back. Do your best. All of you"—my gaze sweeps the locker room—"believe in yourselves. We made it this far. Now…" I look to Jack.

"Let's fucking goooo!!"

"Damn right."

"Fuck yeah."

Nods accompany the pledges. Murphy blinks at me, nods once, and puts his ear buds back in. That's about the reaction I'd expect from a goalie other than Cam. Whatever gets him in the zone.

Despite the extra practice and all the heart the team puts into it, we lose.

We are run ragged by our counterparts. Their two wins have given them wings, and they make every pass and every play look effortless.

I'd love to console myself that we were simply outplayed, rather than losing, but my brain won't let me. No matter how it happened, the score shows a third loss. We're one game away from our inaugural year being over, when we could all taste the beer we'd drink from the Cup. Fuck—*sorry Grams*.

Murphy is more sphinxlike than usual, refusing to acknowledge the pats on the back from other team members. I get it. Every goalie takes losses personally, but the team wins and loses games, not any one player.

Tell that to yourself, asshole. You know you'll obsess over game tape for hours later.

* * * *

I grab food to go from the players' lounge and head home. I'm not sure if Saylet is home yet or not, but I quickly sequester myself in my room so I don't have to interact. My headspace is too fucked to be a polite roommate.

My physical exhaustion is no match for my whirling thoughts. I'm supposed to be leading this team, or at least helping lead them. What could I have done differently? How could I have ensured Murphy was more confident in his netminding skills? One player, even a standout goalie like Cam, should not make this big a difference. Which means it's in our heads. Which should be fixable. But I haven't managed it.

After a half hour, I assume Saylet is in her room and it's safe to creep out to the living room. For the first time, I regret not having a TV in my bedroom. But I live alone, and a second TV was a luxury we could never afford when I was a child, spending money on a second felt excessive.

The irony of torturing myself with hockey tonight rather than visions of her ass in barely-there underwear is not lost on me. In the living room, I flick the TV on, immediately muting it and silencing my phone for the inevitable call. Pulling up the game recording, I put the replay speed to 1.5x and watch.

Almost as though she can see me, the phone rings with "Grams" on the screen.

"Hi, Grams. You're up late."

"Drew. I'm sorry. I could see you were all doing your best and fighting hard."

"If we were doing our best, we would have won."

A gasp sounds to my right, and I whip my head around.

Saylet stands there in—fuck me—a mid-thigh length floral patterned satiny robe tied tightly at the waist. Despite my grandmother still at my ear, and hockey on the screen, all I can think is, *What is she wearing under that?*

For the record, my guess is lacy panties and only lacy panties.

I gape at her.

Grams is placating me as best she can when my ears start working again. "…know you're competitive and want to be the best. And you are. You wouldn't be playing at that level otherwise. But you cannot punish yourself or your team for losses. They're always going to be part of it."

"I'm trying."

"Are you watching the playback?"

"Are you watching tonight's game?"

Grams voice and Saylet's blend.

I frown at her. "I had it on silent so I wouldn't disturb you."

Grams exclaims, "Oh, is someone there? Who's staying with you? One of the guys? Maybe he can talk you off the ledge."

"Nah, Grams, our PR Director's apartment had issues." I deliberately avoid using her name or pronoun.

It doesn't matter, Grams is smarter and has a better memory than I do. She gasps. "Ohhh. Isn't that Saylet? The one you said was super attractive?"

I close my eyes, hoping that Saylet cannot hear her through the phone.

Saylet goes into the kitchen, allowing me to finish my call.

Grams teases me, saying, "Put her on. I'll tell her about your ridiculous post-game penance and ask her to think of ways to distract you."

My cock pulses at that idea, totally on board. Despite that, my voice is quelling. "Grams."

"Don't 'Grams' me, boy. We're both grown, we can talk about things like this."

"No we can't. Ick. Besides," I cup my hand around the phone and lower my voice. "I'm not going to do that with someone I work with." Or anyone, but I prefer to avoid getting that lecture again.

"Alright, well I won't keep you with Saylet there," Grams says with a snicker. "But here's the lowdown. Murphy did a good job. You did a fantastic job, in my clearly unbiased opinion. Everyone did. The other team was simply better. They're not a better team, but things clicked for them."

"And the game before, and the one before that." My tone is bitter. Movement catches my eye, but when I turn to look, Saylet is out of sight in the kitchen.

"So? This is the team's first year and only your third year playing in the NHL. You've made the playoffs two out of three of those and should be proud, no matter what happens from here. Out of thirty…gah, I can't keep up with the number of teams in the league with all the recent expansion. Out of over thirty teams, only four get to the conference finals. Only one gets their names on the Cup. You're closer than the vast majority of the league's players. Be satisfied with that for now and work from there. Now, you need your sleep for the next game. Or maybe whatever support Saylet can offer."

"Yes, ma'am." I respond over her cackling. "I love you, Grams. Thank you."

"I love you, too. They wouldn't have made you alternate captain if they didn't think you were essential to the team's success."

I smile at the familiar words as we hang up, but then look toward the kitchen and frown. I'd prefer to avoid any questions from Saylet right now, but I'd like to go through more of the game.

Picking up the remote, I restart the replay.

"Why are you torturing yourself?" Saylet is standing between the kitchen and the end of the couch where I'm sitting.

I close my eyes in frustration at the sound of her voice. Apparently, we're going to do this now whether I want to or not.

"Look, everyone has their way of processing a loss. This is mine. As one of the team's leaders, I have to look for ways to improve."

"Isn't that the coaches' job?"

I narrow my eyes. "I'd argue that it's everyone's job, but each player has to make their own decision on when and how to do it."

"It seems like self-flagellation, especially right after the game. Wouldn't tomorrow give you a bit more perspective on it all?"

First Grams used "penance." Now Saylet with the "self-flagellation." I'm tired, sore, stressed about the next game, and fed up with yet another person telling me how to manage my career. I respond through gritted teeth. "I didn't ask for your opinion. This is my house and my career. I'll handle things as I see fit."

She blinks.

Okay, maybe it wasn't the most polite, but it beat the "butt out" I really wanted to lead with.

"Sorry. You're right. I wanted—you know what, it doesn't matter. I'm sorry. Good night. If you need the sound on, I'll understand." Putting her head down, she flees to her room.

Ugh. Another thing to stress about instead of sleeping.

Chapter Twelve

Saylet

For Game 4 of the Conference Finals, I do everything the exact way I've done for the games leading up to this. Every step, smile, high five, and nod are the same, despite still being in shock from Drew's last words to me.

The guys look grim again as they trudge out to the ice. Even Jack can't find a smile.

Drew looks tired, but maybe that's because of how late he was up last night. I stayed awake listening for him, bothered more than I cared to be by the glimpse behind the mask I'd seen, for his sake more than mine.

"You got this!" I call over and over as they go by. "Take 'em by storm!"

Finally, Jack cracks a smile. "I see what you did there, Saylet. Thanks. We'll give it our best shot."

"That's all anyone wants."

"Pretty sure most of us, including Greg, want the Cup more."

Gah. Stupid macho hockey players do not handle losing well.

They leave it all on the ice. A steady stream of sweat and occasional drops of blood adorn the ice each period. Saint scores one with an assist from Mattie Du Près, which gives the team fresh energy. But their reserves are depleted, and when Las Vegas evens it up in the second period, I can see their jaws set as they dig in, ready to fight to the end.

I usually shmooze with the invitees in the owner's box, but tonight the atmosphere is too tense. And frankly, it's hard to do any kind of PR with Cam pacing back and forth in the bar area. So I sit with Christina and Amy, and let the guys hang by the bar, hoping Greg can keep a leash on Cam.

The regulation buzzer goes and the game is still tied, prolonging the torture and our hopes. Sudden death overtime adds another layer of intensity.

The puck drops and the Desert Kings have it. Shit. Their hunger for the Cup Finals is tangible, even from up here. It's like someone fed them caffeine and uppers; they're Tasmanian Devils out there—the cartoon kind, whirling and ducking and deking.

Our guys fight. For the puck. For position. All without garnering a penalty or throwing down gloves. Probably under threat from Coach Steele. This will be hard enough.

At two minutes left in the first overtime, Coach puts our best six on the ice. The attempt to break the deadlock also lets our team overtake the manic energy of the other team for a minute, and we spend most of that time down their end. But shot after shot is blocked, and some of those rebounds are dangerously close to giving the Desert Kings control.

Finally, they get it. Jack and Scottie race back to help guard the goal, but their forwards are equally fast and it's three-on-two, the remaining players from both teams racing to catch up. Drew reaches a Las Vegas player as he gets the puck and poke checks him, but it's too late.

He gets the shot off and it slides between Murphy's stick and skate. The lamp lights.

A collective groan reverberates through the stadium before quiet descends. Vegas is in a dog pile on the ice, but after scattered applause, the audience and those of us on the bench are glued to our seats, in shock.

The Tornadoes season is over. No Cup for us this year.

As the home crowd cheers the team through the handshakes, Christina and Amy excuse themselves to the bar area, presumably to console Greg and Cam. I'd like nothing more than to console Drew, to reassure him he did everything he could, that it wasn't his fault.

The memory of his biting at me when I tried to do that last night surfaces. There will be no commiseration, no sympathy. He doesn't want it, and he's made it clear we're nothing more than coworkers, despite his sweet words when he offered me his home.

* * * *

Cam and I take the elevator down to the ice level, him to join the team in the dressing room, me to corral mourning players to talk to the press. I'm sure Greg will follow once he extricates himself from his guests.

As we emerge onto concrete in the tunnel, the three Stars of the Game are being announced. In a poignant gesture, Murphy is named, the only Tornado, given our loss.

Cam peels off from me and strides toward the ice, so I follow.

The stadium claps for all of them, but give Murphy a standing ovation.

After Murphy does his lap waving to the crowd, the

Jumbotron catches my attention, zooming in to where we stand at the gate to the tunnel. I step back.

Cam in his suit meets Murphy in his sweaty uniform and doesn't hesitate. He wraps the game's star in a fierce hug as he steps off. Even without skates, Cam is only a few inches shorter than Dan. They thump each other's back, and Cam's lips move as he says something to the other goalie that I can't hear. Dan nods and squeezes him again, and they walk down the tunnel together.

I quickly gesture to Sara to catch that with her camera. That will be a fantastic official team post, although I have no doubt the media will help us with the Jumbotron footage.

Now, though, I have to disrupt their camaraderie. Murphy's designation as a star of the game means that the reticent goalie will have to grunt a few words to the media.

He, Saint, and Coach, prepped by me, give one or two statements about the game, take two questions and excuse themselves as I run interference. Mostly the press wants to talk to the winners anyway, so we're in the clear.

I race out of there, determined to make something home cooked for Drew to have in case he wants it. Call it sympathy, call it comfort in the way I do best, but I need to try, even if he rejects that too.

Shrimp are fast which is why I almost always keep some in the freezer. I sizzle them in a sweet chili sauce that I cut with olive oil so it's not too spicy. Since that first fumbled dinner he choked down, I've learned that Drew doesn't have the chops for spice.

Tortillas and a Thai-style cabbage mix are set out for in the wraps with the shrimp or alongside them.

He won't be in a good headspace right now, and is probably regretting offering me a bed, so I sequester myself in my room after cleaning up. Remembering my thermal cup full of water is in the kitchen after I get out of my game clothes, I throw my robe on and tiptoe back out there.

Drew is standing at the sink eating.

I roll my eyes. Such a bachelor.

"Hey," I murmur to ensure he knows I'm there. He turns, looks me up and down as he did the other night while on the phone, and narrows his gaze.

I get a chin jut. He scarfs the last bite of Thai shrimp taco then rinses his hands and turns. Leaning back against the sink, he folds his impressive arms across his awe-inspiring chest. The performance fabric of his t-shirt showcases each well-defined muscle.

I swallow audibly and hope he's too far away to hear it.

"Thanks for the food."

"You're welcome. I'm sorry about the loss. I wish I could help. Is there, is there anything else I can do?"

He prowls toward me, and I catch a whiff of a sweet liquor on his breath. Bourbon, if I had to guess. He stops a few inches closer than normal conversational distance and growls, "You want to help?"

I lift a shoulder and his eyes follow the movement of my robe. "Yes."

"Usually I have ways to release tension after a game."

I swallow. His expression is tight, and his eyes keep dropping to the deep vee of my robe, as though he knows I only have panties on underneath. I'm starting to suspect where this is going, and I crave it while knowing I shouldn't. My inner devil—*he's hurting, it's just this once, the season's over*—and angel—*he's a coworker! Don't jeopardize your position with the Donovans, they'll choose him!*—are fighting.

I say only, "Oh?"

"I haven't indulged in those in a while, because none of them appealed. Now here you are, walking around my house in the tiniest robe ever in this slinky fabric"—he slides his fingers between my collarbone and the robe, slowly, as though giving me every opportunity to step back—"making me wonder how little you have on beneath it. You definitely appeal. And now you offer to *help*?"

His voice is full of gravel, and so deep it's almost unrecognizable. This is a man on the edge. Yet, here I stand, my pulse thumping in my neck and chest against his knuckles that still rest against my skin.

"Y-yes."

His eyes flare.

His phone rings, jolting us both, and when I look next to us on the bar, the display reads, "Grams."

He steps back with a deep inhale. "Saylet. I…sorry. I'm not good company right now. Again."

Unsure if I'm relieved or disappointed, I step around him to grab my water cup.

He picks up the phone and says, "Hi, Grams. You're up late."

As I turn to go, I dare to touch his shoulder.

He flinches and skates his eyes sideways at me. They're still fiery, his brows fierce. When he turns to round the bar and sit in the living room, I notice his track pants are tented.

Small consolation to know he's as confused and

tempted as I am. But holy fuck, the size of that bulge makes me salivate.

* * * *

I put my noise cancelling headphones on so I'm not tempted to listen to his phone call, shed my robe, and crawl into bed. Drew's comments about what I was wearing underneath the robe conjure a smirk when I recall my black and red paisley cheeky panties. Sobering, I wonder what he wears to bed.

Ugh. I smash my pillow. I'm not going to masturbate when he could walk past my door any minute. With my luck, that would be the money shot, I'd make some noise, and he'd come barreling in. Then we'd be right back in the dilemma in the kitchen.

Too tired to make sense of it all or decide which way I wish the kitchen scenario had gone, I close my eyes and concentrate on Shakira's uplifting feminist lyrics.

The next day I'm up and out before Drew emerges. They have one last team meeting today.

I wrap things up for the team's PR. That two-goalies-walking-down-the-tunnel-together shot is magnificent. There is also a fantastic angle of Drew racing down the ice with the opposing players behind him blurred, making it look like he is flying. That one gets downloaded to my phone, for PR purposes of course.

I spend much of my day working with Sara, LaRhonda, and Stephen planning the "new face of the NHL" campaign we are launching. It's really a thinly disguised way of showing off our team's diversity and ensuring players of all nationalities and races get publicity. This remains the whitest of the professional sports. And even now that players of color are winning awards and breaking records, they are not being chosen for sponsorships by the big brands as often, meaning they continue to earn less than their counterparts.

As a Cambodian-American, I've experienced racism firsthand, and I'm more passionate about it than I am the game of hockey, which is saying something. And after ensuring that Greg, Stephen, and Coach Steele had as many top-tier players of color in front of them for the formation of this team, I want to brag about the representation we have. We'll set up some social media posts with stills, then do much more during training camp and pre-season. I also hope to get some press coverage during the off season to build hype for us, in national sports magazines, websites, local newspapers, and podcasts. And it helps that the guys can interview from anywhere.

In the late afternoon, Kayla comes to my office, and we work through the schedule for the July hockey camps we'll run as well as a few shows Greg contracted in the arena for August.

It's after six o'clock when I wrap up and head to Drew's, reviewing the contents of the fridge and freezer in my mind.

He's on the phone when I come in, so I take a quick peek to confirm my memory and take chicken out of the fridge. He's pacing back and forth between the coffee table and the TV, then down the hall, then back. All that energy usually expelled on the ice has to go somewhere, I guess.

I close myself in my room to give him privacy. However, he's clearly not used to having another person in his place, because he gives no thought to how the pacing will affect what I hear.

"...super smart, but kind of thin-skinned...what do you mean, what did *I* do? It's *my* condo..."

Uh oh. They're talking about me. I go stand next to the door. If he's going to discuss me when I'm within hearing, I have every right to ensure I hear it correctly. And hey, he said "super smart." I'll take all the compliments I can get.

"Fine...I said I would. Yes, I'll text you if she accepts the apology."

Fist pump. Go, me.

He's back in the hall again. "Yes. Yes, okay, yes. Model-hot, but in miniature."

I gasp, but manage to stifle it with a hand. I'm not miniature, I'm freakin' petite. I rarely buy clothes in the kids' section any more.

"Grams, I know you want great-grandbabies. We've had this conversation before. You're going to have to make due with me for the time being. I'm focusing on hockey so I can cement a long-term contract and have security for the both of us."

Security? He can't possibly be worried about security at his age with the salary he's making.

"No. Hockey doesn't allow for dating. Heck, Grams, I'm barely even fuc—No, ma'am. I'm sorry. Anyway, no dating, especially dark-haired little hotties who are way smarter than me, and who I work with."

A pause. Then, "I'm taking a golf trip with a few of the guys, then I'm teaching at a couple hockey camps. After that, I'll be there to get you and bring you down here for a visit. I love you."

I'm leaning against the wall, contemplating my options now that I know he's attracted to me. If I change into my robe to cook, it would be too blatant an invitation, and frankly I haven't had time to consider the fallout from last night. I'm dying to climb him like a tree, but there are very real risks if I do. I've worked too hard to get where I am to gamble with my career. My meak's voice in my head reminds me that my career is my safety net, my jewelry for independence if I need it. I should never risk it.

In the end, I pretend I didn't hear anything and set up his boring hockey-guy meal with my twist on flavors—chicken and rice, this time with taco seasoning on the chicken and the rice is red rice and beans (really pigeon peas). Hot sauce is out on the counter for me. And salads for the both of us.

He's not watching the final minute of the last game like I expected. Instead, he's on the Pittsburgh game from early in the season, which if I remember correctly was one of their first losses. Holy fuck, he's torturing himself by rewatching every loss. No wonder his grams calls after every game to try to talk him off the edge, now I understand why he's wound so tight.

I pop open a beer and bring it to him, saying, "Dinner will be ready in five minutes."

He pauses the game and glances from the beer to me to the TV, before ducking his head and mumbling, "Thanks."

As I finalize dinner, I drag out a stepstool I found in the linen closet and now keep tucked into the pantry. Climbing it, I stretch for a serving platter on a high shelf in a cabinet.

The TV goes off. Drew's hand on my back jolts me. "Saylet, get down. What do you need?"

"The big plate, please. But I can get it."

"This?" He pulls it out with those long monkey arms,

not even going on tiptoe, the annoying guy. "You've used this before. Do you mean you've been going up and down that without me around?"

I roll my eyes. "Yes, Caveman Drew. The little woman lives alone, don't you know. I've been using a stepstool in kitchens since I was four. We can't all be goliaths."

He shakes his head and opens his mouth.

I stop him from saying whatever he was thinking by raising a hand. "Let's eat while the food is hot."

After dishing it onto the platter, I turn and nearly drop the chicken. He's right in front of me. I start to pass him the plate, thinking he's here to help carry, but his hands stay in his track pants pockets, and his head is still down. My brows lower in confusion.

"Look, I'm sorry about the other night."

I sigh. That night was not our best idea, but neither was it something I regretted. It sucks to hear that he does, especially after all the "model hot" words I just heard.

He looks up and must see that in my expression. "Not that night, the one before. Well in a way, that night too. Ugh. I'm making a mess of this."

"Why don't you have some protein? Maybe it'll help the organ in your head as well as all those muscles." Shit. I didn't mean to say that out loud.

He's grabbed the chicken and turned to put it on the bar, but glances back at me with an arched brow.

Stepping away, he grabs his beer. I have a glass of wine at my setting. With the salad bowls already dished out and the rice now on the counter, I slide onto the barstool next to him.

"Want to start again?"

"Not really, but I will." He grimaces. "I'm sorry for

being harsh with you the night before our last—" another grimace "—game. Most of us take losses hard, although Grams says I am the worst. I'm not used to having to temper my mood or at least speech."

I nod. "Just out of curiosity, what did you do when you were on the road with a roommate in a hotel room?"

"Go elsewhere and watch whatever streaming video I could find," he says without thinking, then twists his lips as though regretting sharing.

"Did your grandmother call you then, too?"

He nods, shoveling rice into his mouth. "Oh hey, this rice is different again. What are these? They're not regular peas."

"They're pigeon peas. More of a bean, but for some reason called pigeon peas. Anyway, thank you for the apology. Really, it's not necessary. I'm sorry I'm in your space. I really hope it will only be for another couple of weeks. And, since we are roomies for the time being, you—" I take a breath. I've never offered this to a guy before, only a few close girlfriends. "Can call me Let if you'd like."

"Let?"

"Yeah, you know. Short for Saylet. It's a nickname my family and a few friends use."

His eyes gleam when I say few. He respects that it's special. "Okay. Thanks, I will, Let."

I wiggle once on my barstool, a little giddy. That one change makes me feel closer to him.

We fall silent, him getting through twice the amount of food I have in half the time.

In a low voice he says, "If I made you uncomfortable in any way, then you have my apology for that as well. I'll mind my manners for the rest of your stay, no matter how long. And there's no rush. I'll be gone most of this week anyway."

I turn toward him, and the barstool swivels quicker than I intended. I throw out a hand to stop myself from spinning.

He sucks in a breath, and I look down. Holy shit, my hand is high on his thigh. If he dresses right, I could be touching his dick right now, although I don't think I am. It's a giant slab of hockey thigh, which is incendiary enough. I swallow and retract my arm. "Um, sorry. Runaway barstool."

His eyes meet mine, and they're every bit as heated as they were the other night. Gee, who needs a stinkin' robe when a barstool will do the trick?

I swallow again. Sip wine. Then say, "You didn't make me uncomfortable. At least in any way that I didn't just make you feel."

His eyes go wide, and his mouth opens and closes. In a hockey-speed move, he swivels his barstool and traps my legs between his much longer ones, cups my head in his hand, and leans in to place his lips on mine.

Heat, hot, fire. Holy fuck the smoke detector should be beeping about now. This man pushes all my buttons, without touching the most important one. My hands clutch his thighs again as he sweeps his tongue against mine. I have a new understanding of the word "swoon" from all those bodice rippers.

His hand moves from my neck to tug on my hair, angling me better. And now I know that my hair follicles have a direct connection to my pussy, because that tug goes all the way down.

His other hand comes to where one of mine is kneading his thigh. His lips are gone then, and my eyes fly open.

He's watching me from a few inches away. His voice rumbles, "Is this okay, Saylet?"

Is he kidding? It's magnificent, not simply okay. But on a whole other level, it can't be. I can never forget my mother's warning, especially being a woman in a man's world, times ten because it's a sports world. I'll always be the one at risk, even if he wasn't a star player.

I tug my hands free, straightening from where I'd leaned into the kiss. My answer is honest and complete— he beats himself up enough without me adding to it. "It was more than okay. But we can't. I'm sorry. I love my job and this team, and I won't jeopardize that."

He licks his lips once, and my eyes nearly roll back in my head, I want to taste them again so badly. He'd released my hair when I pulled away, and now he swivels his barstool farther around to stand. "I understand. I even agree. With both parts. Here, let me take your plate. I'll clean up since you cooked."

A thrill shoots through me at his confession before I shut that line of thinking down. "Thank you. I'm going to call it a night."

"Good night. Sweet dreams." I ignore his quiet chuckle after that statement, too busy planning on a cold shower…or a warm one where I can finish this myself without worrying about him hearing.

Chapter Thirteen

Drew

I replay the kiss and our stilted conversation as I load the dishwasher. Those lips, that thick dark mane of hair, and her taste are tactile memories I won't soon forget. Her handprint might as well be permanently embedded on my thigh.

"I blame you for this, Grams," I mutter under my breath as I rinse Saylet's wineglass and place it in the top rack. She put the idea of dating in my head, along with pushing Saylet at me. All because I mentioned her in a few calls earlier in the season. We work together, so of course she came up. Okay, and the fact that she's smoking hot might have surfaced. Grams and I are close, or were, until she started using those conversations against me.

She knows what this opportunity as alternate captain means to me. Most AC contracts are six plus years and over fifty million. But I'll take less money per year for a longer contract, as I'm trying to convince Grams to move closer, but she won't move unless I'm stationary. Which is why she's still in Duluth rather than Tampa where I last played. When you grow up poor like I did, stability is everything and sacrificing a couple mil is nothing if it gives Grams and me a place to call home along with a nest egg that makes us feel safe. I have one more year on my old contract that transferred to the Tornadoes from my trade here. Hopefully the team will give me that long-term contract next year. Grams would love Austin, it's the perfect size and there's something for everyone here, especially as she's still pretty active and likes the arts.

Austin also has Saylet. But no, my plan is to get myself and Grams settled first before I tackle bringing anyone else into my life.

That kiss was hotter than any I can remember, though. My hand clenches around the sponge I'm using to wipe out the sink. So much spice in such a petite package. When she said she was uncomfortable the same way I was, my brain short-circuited. Her kitten claws making biscuits on my thigh were tantalizingly close to my cock, and her hair against my fingers was almost as delicious as her mouth against mine.

Saylet's right, however. It shouldn't have happened. I don't want things between us to be awkward. And as much as she took equal responsibility, I initiated it. But she's right. A workplace romance is always a bad idea, and while it might threaten my focus, it could hurt her a lot more. Final year of my contract or not, a player is more valuable to a hockey club than a PR director. And she knows better than anyone that the public would be tougher on her than me if we were discovered.

At least Cam chose to date an owner so he was putting only himself in jeopardy. It's not fair to do that to her, especially when I don't want the romance part, just her hot body. And I'm nothing if not fair to my teammates and coworkers. Maybe if I had time for a girlfriend or was ready for kids, it would be different. But my sole focus is on locking in a big contract so Grams and I never have to worry about money again.

I spray and wipe the counters clean. Damn, that woman is a messy chef. Looking around, I take stock. Everything is away and all surfaces are immaculate, just as Grams required. I'm at loose ends, unsure what to do with myself. When I use my bathroom, I hear Saylet's shower running, as our showers back on each other.

Leaving the bathroom doesn't help, I'm already picturing her naked courtesy of that first night's forbidden glimpse of her asleep.

This roommate situation may yet kill me.

Settling down without relief is going to be impossible, so I strip down and lie on my bed, leaving the bathroom door wide open. Fisting myself, I picture her golden brown skin with water running over it, her nipples beading when the cooler air hits them. Her hair is up on her head in a clip, perfect for a hand grip or easy release to have it flow down her back.

My hand slides up and down slowly, gathering precum to ease the friction, but not letting the orgasm build yet. I'm edging myself to her shower. I'll hate myself for that tomorrow, but tonight I don't care.

The water turns off. She's toweling herself dry now. Arms, back, breasts. I draw the thought out to slow the imagined motion, but my hand pumps faster. Legs. Ass. My hips are arching off the bed now, but my speed is still a hair slower than I need to come. The towel is between her legs. Within those folds, she has to get it all dry. I squeeze the base of my cock, trying to hold off and finish the fantasy, but there's no stopping the orgasm. My hand slicks at lightning speed now, chasing the storm as my thoughts center on Saylet tugging on lacy underwear. Jizz explodes over my stomach, arm, and the sheets as my movements slow. Finally, I'm still, my messy hand beside me on the sheets that I'll change when I find the will to move.

Thank god I leave tomorrow for Myrtle Beach, golf haven of the Southeast. Seeing all of those housemates naked doesn't bother me in the least. I can only hope Saylet's apartment has electricity by the time I return. She is far too tempting.

Chapter Fourteen

Saylet

The first night Drew is gone for his guys' trip, I find a recipe that I can cook at his heat level as well as doctor for mine, so I can freeze some meals for him.

My jaw drops when I open the pantry. The highest two shelves are empty, with the lower ones stuffed.

Walking around, I open cabinets over the counters one after the other. Sure enough, the oversized teddy bear hockey player has rearranged his entire kitchen for me so I don't need a stepstool.

Holy fuck that's hot. If he was older, I'd say he has a daddy kink, he's such a freaking caretaker. With anyone else, I'd say that's boyfriend behavior, but it can't be. But damn, who said the way to a person's heart is through their stomach?

It takes me days to get used to where everything is, my heart missing a beat each time his kindness is reinforced as I grab items easily. I texted him a thank you and got a thumbs up in reply. The lack of communication is another element messing with my head. I miss him. Not just the glimpses of that bubble butt or dark bearded face with shining brown eyes focused on me. Our conversations, his expression as he tastes a new dish. I have always prided myself on my self-sufficiency and like living alone. I swear I do. But it's been nice to have someone care enough to distract me from my always-on brain and tendency to work all night. He's an easy person to share space with, even beyond the eye candy and the hotter-than-hell kiss.

By Thursday, I'm antsy and caught up on work, so when Amy Donovan and Kayla invite me out for a drink, I jump at it. As three of the more senior women in the Tornadoes offices—Christina rarely works onsite—we try to have girls' nights semi-regularly.

After the server takes our drink order, Kayla turns to me. "It's good to see the Saylet I know and love back."

Amy frowns and asks, "What do you mean?"

Kayla says, "You know how she defines the word 'vivacious'?"

I snort. "Nice word, Grandma."

She waves a dismissive hand and continues, "She hasn't been her usual self the past few weeks."

"Excuse me, playoffs make for long hours."

"You thrive on work. It seemed like more than that," Kayla says.

Her statements come from a place of concern, but my heart beats in fear I'll say something and give away my living situation. Given the length of time I've been out of my apartment, I'm more relieved than ever I didn't ask her to crash for a night or two. "I wasn't sleeping well. First time through the playoffs with an NHL team, and lots of travel and different beds."

Amy chimes in. "I get that. I never sleep well the first night on a trip. It may be part of why I'm a homebody."

Thankfully, our drinks arrive and we change subjects. We talk about vacation plans for the off season. Kayla is going to England for a week and is super excited. And of course we talk about work. Amy loves using the Tornadoes Foundation to create meaningful live/work spaces for people coming out of chronic homelessness. Her work is even more year-round than mine. As Operations Manager, Kayla's is as well. She manages all facets of the facility which includes the off season. Somehow, it still feels easier to take vacation during the summer. All of us are hockey fans, after all, and England will be less cold and wet during the summer months.

Later in the summer, Chris and Cam are hosting a week-long house party at some swanky place which Amy's joining.

As of now, I have no vacation plans. I took a couple extra days at the holidays mid-season to visit my parents, since my siblings were all going to be there then. But I'm super focused on my passion project.

I throw in that Drew, Cam, Kyle, and a few other players are coaching summer hockey camps for kids, so they'll be here at least part of the time.

"Anyone know what Saint is doing?"

"Whatever Jessica Rabbit drags him to, I suspect." Amy's voice was low out of respect for our public setting, but sarcastic. Someone on the team came up with that moniker for his beautiful but bitchy and self-centered wife, whose first name really is Jessica, and it stuck.

Holding up my margarita, I change the subject. "Anyway, cheers to a less testosterone-overridden summer!"

* * * *

The next day, my apartment complex sends an email with an update. They are waiting on the City of Austin for an inspection. After that, it should be a matter of days until we're allowed back. I have no idea how long it will take to procure the certificate of occupancy, but I'm glad Drew's not here so I have time to figure out how to tell him my estimated departure is still unknown.

I've been here over a month and have been accumulating spices as I cook more and more. This week, I've made all my favorite super spicy foods that I don't have to dilute for Drew. I also experiment with spicing up mac and cheese a few ways, since he had so much of it in his pantry. Mine is from scratch, of course.

That pantry has been bugging me. Not only because my stuff will barely fit in there, but also because the nutritional value is minimal. Then I looked at a few of the off-brand mac and cheese boxes and found they're expired.

Drew is so busy, I'm sure he hasn't had time to go through this. And of course, I'm part of the "problem," because I've been cooking, so his inventory has been sitting there unused. One evening, I can't stand it anymore. I figure it's another way to help him and thank him for the room.

Putting music on, I empty the pantry. The kitchen countertops and floor are overrun. I organize everything as I put it back in. Prepared foods on the left, cans on the bottom, boxes on the next shelf up, and so forth. All expired goods are tossed, and the ones put on the shelves have the latest expiration in the back so the oldest get used first. Hey, if I quit my day job, I guess I have a future at a grocery store.

Spices have pride of place at my eye height, his bicep height probably. Other condiments go alongside them, even if Drew's condiments are also plebeian. What millionaire buys off brand ketchup?

Even some of his spices and sauces are out of date. When all is said and done, I've cleared about a third of the pantry out, and it's much more usable.

Before he left, I started stocking his freezer with Drew-sized portions of the food I made that he'd enjoyed, labeled for his future use, and I've continued doing that in his absence. I have no idea why he doesn't use a personal chef or food delivery service oriented for athletes like so many guys do, but I can at least keep him healthy and fed for a time.

A few days after I got the email from my apartment management company, I texted Drew to apologize and warn him I was still here. He replied with a simple thumbs up.

They were due back this afternoon, but now I see a text saying their flight was delayed. It'll be coming in around six o'clock. The next one makes me smile.

Drew

Hey, are you in or out tonight?
Just wondering if you happen
to be cooking something
yummy like that Lap Khmer...

Then very quickly:

Sorry. No pressure. You
probably have plans.

Me

Actually, I don't. I can make that, although I had something else in mind for you tonight that I've been experimenting with.

Oh yeah? What?

Not telling.

I'd been planning a surprise for him and worrying about how I'd get through an evening in together without tackling him for another scorching kiss. Part of me is excited he's been thinking along the same lines, but the sane part knows I should come up with an alternate plan to avoid getting hurt.

I need to talk to Jaden and Lukas anyway. If you want to invite the guys, tell them we had plans and I've offered to cook for all of you.

Let me ask. I'll tell them I found out you cook, and you offered to demonstrate, so I called to get you access to the building. Thanks, Let.

I stare at that last text for a long minute, a small smile forming. So fucking considerate, he's even come up with a cover story for the offer I made without thinking.

And he called me "Let." The night I first made Lap Khmer for him, he asked about my heritage. I described my family and learning to cook, especially traditional Cambodian dishes such as this. He loved the dish and was ecstatic when I told him Cambodian food is a bit more like Vietnamese than Thai and not all that spicy. He asked about finding the ingredients in Texas, and I explained that there are a couple markets north of town that are amazing resources, along with online sites when needed.

And he asked about names. My last name is not Cambodian because the US Immigrations agent at the time didn't realize that we put last names before first names. She took my father's name Yeng and made it Young. She also spelled my name phonetically, so I am Saylet rather than Sreylak.

Then last week I gave him permission to use my family name, Let, but he was leaving town. This is the first time he's done it, though, and my pulse spikes in pleasure seeing it.

Jack, Jaden and Lukas are in.
Cam and Mattie are whipped.

Or maybe their better halves cook food they like better—or THEY cook food they like better?

Oops. That was a bad idea.

Thankfully, he ignores it.

They come through the door three hours later heckling each other over who had the worst shot of the week. Heaven forbid they relax and play golf for the fun of it.

They pause after closing the front door, however, staring at me.

"What the fuck?" Drew and I ask at the same time, frowning.

"I've never seen you in yoga pants. Damn, girl. You hot." Leave it to Jack to be crude and unprofessional with the first words out of his mouth.

Drew smacks the back of his head.

I blush. Then I say, "Thanks, but I've seen the bunnies you pick up. I'm sure you'll make do. Please remember I'm still the PR Director, and I can assign the smelliest promo to you at any time. Changing babies' diapers, farm animals, there are so many options here in Texas."

"Ma'am, yes ma'am." He salutes and steps into the kitchen to grab beers and pass them out. With a smirk, he asks, "Saylet, ma'am, would you like one?"

"No thanks." I gesture at my pre-poured glass. "I prefer wine."

"Buzz said you wouldn't tell him what you're

making," Lukas says.

I pinged him back to ensure there were no food allergies or other dietary restrictions. When there were none, I declined to provide any more details of dinner.

I shoo them to the bar. Drew has a bistro table in a dining nook, but there's no way four hockey-player-sized diners were fitting at that, even if I ate separately. There are only four barstools, so I'll feed them and see what's left for myself. I have plenty of other options after a week of cooking my food that I'm not worried. Plus I snacked as I cooked. Quality control is important.

I prepared a huge salad and put it out. The dinner was done twenty minutes ago, and Drew pinged me when they were on their way from the airport, so I took it out to rest, knowing hockey players are perennially hungry.

Now I dish it out into wide shallow bowls. There is hot sauce and salsa out in case other players have interest.

"As you know, your alternate captain has a child's palate, so I made a pasta bake, a sort of take on one of his favorites, mac and cheese."

They're laughing, and Drew's pale cheeks are turning red, but he's still smiling.

"Because y'all try to eat healthy, it has a little real cheese—Mexican blend—but also a vegan ricotta I make myself. It has a ton of ground turkey, seasoned with taco seasoning, and there is salsa in there as well. The goal is for you eat equal portions of salad to offset the heaviness of the meal."

They're already passing the salad bowl.

"But wait, where are you sitting?" Drew asks, his brows creased.

"I'll eat later. I want to make sure you all get

enough."

"No." He stands.

I blink and jerk back.

He skirts the bar and puts his stuff at the L of the counter beneath the bar and where it runs along the wall.

Serving me a dish, he puts my wine glass and a new set of flatware where he sat.

Then he puts his back to the kitchen counter against the wall and plants his hands on it. His triceps and forearm muscles bulge as he effortlessly raises himself to sit on the counter.

"Drew, that's not nece—"

"Yes. It is. Please enjoy the food you worked so hard to cook."

Both of us suddenly become aware of the silence around us. The other three have stopped dishing out their salad and are ricocheting their gazes between us.

To cover, I slide onto the barstool and jab my elbow into Jack's ribs next to me, saying, "He takes alternate captain very seriously."

Laughter breaks the tension, and the guys doctor their pasta and salad.

Drew tastes it carefully, watching as I douse mine in hot sauce. After a second, larger bite, he nods. "Delicious, Let."

My heart skips a beat at the nickname again.

Jack raises his brows. This guy never misses anything. "Let? As in he let you come in without him here to cook? As in you let him eat like a grownup? Can we call you Let?"

"Nope. You can stick with ma'am," I say firmly with another jab.

"Aw, come on." He places his head on my shoulder

and whines. "You love me. Admit it."

The other two at the bar barely notice Jack's antics. They're used to it and seem engrossed in their dinner.

I shrug him off as Drew's beer bottle hits the counter with a loud clack.

It froths over a little, and he holds Jack's surprised gaze for a long moment before leaning sideways to grab a paper towel from the standing holder by the sink.

Jaden and Lukas look up at the sharp sound, exchange glances and drop their gaze to their plates, staying quiet.

My mouth goes dry at the taut ab muscles displayed when the side of Drew's shirt rides up. Gulping wine, I force myself to look away, catching Jack's watchful gaze.

He murmurs, "So that's how it is, huh?"

"No. It's not anything. Stop it, please." I must look scared, because he pats my leg and gives me a jut of his chin in acknowledgment.

"You know we have a rule, right?" he asks.

"Is this another superstition or something? Y'all have a lot of rules." I roll my eyes.

"This is a good one: what happens in the off season stays in the off season." His eyes gleam.

"Jack, please. Behave. I wanted to talk to Jaden and happened to be texting Drew. Don't make anything more of it. We work together."

"So do Cam and Christina."

I retort, "Yeah, and the one lower on the totem pole is at risk."

His brows raise, and I realize I'm protesting too much. I quickly tack on, "Anyway, it's not like that."

"Okay."

Fuck. Thinking these few guys that Drew is close to were safe to see me in his space was a big mistake. Although it was still better than being home alone with Drew all evening and trying not to remember how good a kisser he is.

Chapter Fifteen

Drew

From my vantage point on the counter, I can see everyone's reactions to Let's delicious meal. The mere fact that all of them are quiet is testimony to its quality. Except Jack is down there whispering to Let, irritating her.

Thankfully, Lukas interrupts them by moaning as though someone is sucking his dick under the counter.

Let's head whips around Jack to look at him in concern.

"Ohmygodthisissogood," he mumbles through a second heaping forkful of Mexican mac and cheese.

Jack starts, "You know they say stirring mac and cheese sounds—"

He's cut off by a wallop to his head by Jaden. "Fuckwit, there's a lady present."

At which we all howl. Leave it to a hockey player to use foul language to berate a teammate for being impertinent in front of a lady.

"Thank you, Jaden. Not that I haven't heard it all before from hanging out with hockey players," she says with a grin.

"It's delicious. Thank you for feeding us," he replies. "I can do my interview any time this week if that works for your team."

"What interview?" I ask.

"How come you're not interviewing me?" Jack gripes at the same time.

Always the biggest baby in the room, Jack believes he should be the center of attention at all times.

She ignores him and looks at me to answer. "My biggest focus this summer is to get a series of articles and social media posts put together showing all the ways this organization is the future of hockey."

"You mean like because we're the youngest team? Because we made the Conference Finals?"

"Nope. Because we have at least six nationalities and ethnic groups represented on our roster, instead of the usual Canadian and American mix with a few strays thrown in."

Lukas perks up. "Does that mean I'll get an interview?"

"Geez. I can barely get you guys to string two words together when I interview you after a game, and now you're excited? I can't keep up," she jokes. "And maybe. Czech players aren't quite a dime a dozen. However, I'm focusing on the groups with less than a 2% representation in the league."

"What percentage is Czech Republic?" he asks.

"About twenty, last I looked."

He grunts.

"Seems like a low bar," I throw out there.

"As of the end of last season, there were over seven hundred active players on NHL rosters. After you take out the measly *six* countries that have more than two percent representation, you have at least fifteen other nationalities. But it's more than that. It's time to show that the faces in hockey are not just toothless North

American white guys with mullets."

Damn. She's giving me another boner with the statistics. She's so freaking smart, she's intimidating. Every time I think I understand how her brain works, she unveils another layer. I'm starting to see why Mattie was worried about Nicole getting a graduate degree because he doesn't have a Bachelor's. But hey, they ended up together, so all is not lost.

Wait, I am not going to end up with Let. We've already established this. I wish my cock would get the message. On the other hand, I understand more why she is still single. Here she is cooking for us, having no plans on a Saturday night same as all the nights she's stayed with me. Her big brain never shuts off. Even cooking, which she says is therapeutic, is another somewhat frenetic activity from what I've seen. And she used the time I've been gone to try out recipes she thinks I'd like. When does she take care of herself?

Jaden brings me back to the conversation, stroking the sides of his hair shaved close to his skull, back into his thin braids that peek out under his helmet when he's playing. "You want the brown guys with mullets, too, yeah."

Another round of laughs circles the room.

He adds, "I should count twice, since I'm Afro-French. Maybe three times because I'm not white."

"And that's why you definitely get an interview," Let says with a smile.

* * * *

The next morning, the condo is quiet when I wake. I neglected to ask Let what her plans for the day are. Mine are boring, consisting mostly of the gym.

In search of coffee, I round the wall into the kitchen and stop short.

She's bent over in the pantry, doing who-cares-what, and her robe is no longer mid-thigh. It's mid-ass, showing off yet another pair of lace-trimmed panties cut high on those cheeks.

Saliva pools in my mouth as I dream of biting that spot where her ass meets her thigh. I stifle a groan but she hears me and whips upright, twirling to face me.

I'm frozen. The front view in that robe is as delicious as the back view. My sleep pants are tenting, and I can't make my legs move to sidle behind the bar. Instead, I stare. I think I'm panting.

"I, uh, dropped the coffee. Sorry, did I wake you?"

"No. It's fine." My voice is several notes lower than normal. Hopefully she'll attribute that to sleep.

Her gaze drops to my cock then flies back to my face.

I take a couple steps toward her, hoping if we both ignore my hard-on it will wane. "I can pick the coffee…What the hell happened in here?"

She flaps her hands, wearing a big grin. "Don't you love it?"

I step closer and blink grimly at the neatly arranged shelves, the reduced quantity making my heart beat a mile a minute. For a second, I'm ten and hungry again, looking at a bare shelf where I'd hoped there'd be food.

She continues, "I organized for you. So much easier to find stuff. And there was a bunch of expired food."

I grip the pantry doorframe so hard it creaks. Only someone who grew up privileged abides by expiration dates. Especially on dried goods. Shit, she should see the dates on some yogurts I've eaten. They're bacteria cultures to start with, after all.

My teeth are clenched as I turn and enunciate each word carefully so I don't scream them and ask her, "What did you do with my food?"

Her chin retracts and she blinks. "I threw them out. They were beyond their use by date."

"That was not your decision to make," I say, my voice rising on each word. I'm nearly roaring as I add, "Leave my stuff alone. That is the one rule of you staying here. Do. Not. Touch. My. Food."

I stomp out of the kitchen, throw gym clothes on and street clothes into my gym bag, and stomp out. Saylet is still standing there between the pantry and the coffeemaker, clutching the coffee bag, still in that f-ing tease of a robe.

I can't go to the gym like this, where I might run into other people. The condo gym could potentially have fans, and the practice facility gym will almost certainly have coworkers.

Instead, I toss my stuff in the car, drive down to Ladybird Lake, and find a spot to park. The ten-mile hike and bike trail around the lake is crowded, especially midmorning on a Sunday. Austin is a surprisingly fit place, despite sharing a state with five of the top twenty-five most obese cities in the US year after year. So the walkers, bikers, and runners commingle respectfully. Looking down, I realize I am wearing Tornadoes gear and I forgot a hat. I strip off my shirt, knowing my physique will garner interest, but hopefully not as a player, and don my sunglasses and ear buds. Then, I run.

My running music, like my gym music, is calm and soothing. It's basically yacht rock mixed in with some acoustic guitar or piano renditions of songs like you'd find in an elevator. Usually it's to offset my pounding thoughts driving me to get better, do more, be faster. Now, it's a backdrop to memories.

As my muscles warm, my pace quickens, my thoughts stepping through history to the cadence of my footfalls. When my mother took off as soon as I started first grade, Grams stepped in. She was still working, and had to take on more hours to ensure she could pay the bills and keep me fed. I have no idea where she found my first pair of skates, but after that, I worked every hour I could around school and practice to ensure I could buy my own. When I couldn't, my coach found other ways. Even so, there were weeks that were leaner than others, when Grams couldn't get the hours she wanted, or I grew out of clothes too quickly as I shot up in height.

I've hit my stride, passing slower joggers and walkers, and my teeth clench again as I consider this morning. Grams taught me to take expiration dates as discount opportunities, looking for things that were close to their use by date and bringing them to the grocer to ask for a drop in price. We scoured the shelves for clearance items that were marked 50% off because they expired the next day. That's not to say we used them within the day, but we froze them if we didn't. Cans and boxes of dried goods we used for months after.

By mile five, I'm clenching my arms and legs to stop myself from all out sprinting or stopping to recheck my investment account balance. Doing that reassures me when I start to spiral.

When I was drafted, I spent a couple years in the AHL building muscle and speed. I worked harder than anyone else on my team and my coach noticed, working with the Tampa Bay coach to send me up as soon as he thought I could keep up with the more experienced pros.

Grams urged me to get a meal service at that point, but I couldn't bear the cost.

Other guys have ginormous houses and multiple vehicles, simply because they can. I own my condo here, despite being in the last year of my contract, as I did in Florida. That's because home ownership always seemed like the end game of security. I kept them modest so I could pay cash for them, avoiding debt, since that would have ruined the feeling of safety. The Florida one is now being rented out by a property management company. I drive a mid-level SUV and own the latest video game console. Those are the extent of my extravagance. Even those have set my cash nest egg back further than I'd like, which is why I'm gunning for the big multi-year contract.

I've gotten this far on the food I grew up eating. Splurging on rotisserie chicken and fresh vegetables when I'll be home long enough to eat them is as extravagant as I get. No longer do I go out of my way to look for clearance items, but there was no damned reason to throw perfectly good food away because Corporate America wants you to buy more. And there damned well was no reason to pay more for a name brand when the store brand tastes the same.

Rationally, I know I can afford the loss of that food. And it was a nice gesture on Saylet's part. Grams will tell me I should apologize again.

My footsteps slow. Dammit. Yeah, I have to make this right. I know that without Grams having to tell me.

I accelerate to finish my loop.

Chapter Sixteen

Saylet

I'd planned on going to the Tornadoes gym, but when Drew slams out of the house with gym bag in hand, I rethink that idea in case he's headed there. He clearly needs space from me, and I want to think this through without visual daggers being thrown at me. After a quick stint in the condo's basement gym, I shower and throw my robe back on, unsure of my plans for the day.

Drew seemed more upset than the situation called for. I mean, some of it was expired. Coming from a hot country where their home wasn't air-conditioned, my parents were sticklers for food freshness. However, it's his house and his food, so while I don't understand his reasoning, I need to apologize. I take out ingredients for Lap Khmer, hoping he'll be willing to dine with me. I haven't had a chance to tell him about the meals I've stored in the freezer. Perhaps he'll forgive me when I show him those.

Unsure whether I should wait to talk it out or make myself scarce, I make coffee and perch on a barstool to check email. As too often happens, an hour and a half flies by unnoticed as I work, still in my robe.

I'm flipping through calendars for the various organizations using the arena this summer when the door opens. When I whirl the stool around, the hem of my robe catches air for a second, and I bat it down.

Drew pulls up short. Muttering, "Hey," he swallows hard and continues past me into the kitchen to grab a huge thermal cup and fill it with ice water. Sweat drips down his temple, neck, and back. His t-shirt is tossed over his shoulder, and there's a smattering of hair from his nipples to a line down the center of his body to the waistline of his shorts. Everything glistens. After gulping down a quart of water, he uses the discarded shirt to mop his face.

Ho.Ly. Fuck. As a professional woman, my dates are always either suit-attired or business casual, and while they're fit, their day job takes most of their time. I had no idea a sweaty man could be attractive, much less as hot as Drew is right now. I want to lick the sweat off him, to sniff his neck and tug on the silky hair in his armpits. I want to grasp his muscled ass and have my hands slip on perspiration.

Drew and I were casual friends during the season. He and Saint helped match promo events with the best suited players and corralled said players when needed. My respect for him increased when he insisted I stay with him, and his close relationship with his grandmother is yet another layer that shows what a good man he is.

All of that allows me to tell myself that my feelings are friendship and respect. This, now? It's lust. Everything about this man is tickling all my pleasure spots.

No one should *ever* take relationship or hookup advice from Jack Landry, but here I am contemplating his Vegas analogy and thinking of creative ways to apologize.

Refilling the water glass at the fridge door, Drew

says, "Let, I should probably—"

I'm leaning sideways to admire his ass in nylon shorts when his words cut off. Glancing up, I realize he's staring at me. I shoot straight on the barstool.

His gaze drops.

I close my eyes, knowing my nipples are pointing at him, beckoning him.

"Let," his voice sounds like tires crunching over a dirt road. "I would like to talk to you. And I'm trying to respect your wishes and not kiss the life out of you. It would really help if you'd get a longer, thicker robe or something."

Oh. I bite the inside of my cheek to contain my smile. Knowing I affect him as much as he turns me on is somehow comforting.

"Give me a minute." I slide off the barstool and go change. Tempted to forego a bra, I choose to behave. I'm in the man's home rent-free, for fuck's sake. A cute t-shirt and capris will do for the office if I have to go in, or for working at home.

The kitchen is empty when I return, so I slide back onto my barstool.

Two minutes later he's back with a clean shirt and shorts, hair wet from the shower.

That's disappointing. I didn't ask him to put more clothes on as the view was thoroughly enticing. Shaking that thought off, I jump in, wanting to clear the air before we discuss whatever's on his mind. "I'm sorry. I shouldn't have thrown anything away without your permission. I was trying to help but it still wasn't okay. If it's any consolation, I made you a bunch of meals and froze them."

He opens the freezer and whistles. Plastic storage

containers that I bought are stacked four high and four deep on one side.

"Dang, roomie, I might keep you around. This is great." He turns and gestures at my laptop. "How the hell do you have time to do all that when you work all the time?"

I shrug one now-properly-clad shoulder. "I told you. Cooking is a hobby; it's how I unwind."

He shakes his head as he pulls out ingredients for a protein shake and starts loading the blender. "I cannot imagine."

"Now you don't have to. But I'm still sorry about the pantry."

"I over-reacted. I'm sorry for that. I'd appreciate you checking with me before you do something like that again, but there was a nicer way to say that. It's just…my grams worked her butt off, but it's hard to feed a growing boy who plays hockey every minute he can." His mouth goes to a thin flat line, and he turns the blender on high.

Now I get the gist of it. Food must have been scarce in his past, so he goes overboard on having enough on hand now. My gaze softens on his rugged profile, all dark accents around ivory skin and plush lips, and I wonder what he looked like back then. If I could go back and hug that boy and bring him to our house for a home-cooked meal, I would. Since I can't, I'm dying to meet his grandmother.

When the blender stops, I say, "Your grandmother sounds really special."

"She's the best." He pours the shake into a tall cup and comes to lean on the counter by me.

"I hope I get to meet her one day."

"She wants to come down to visit, maybe later this

summer, then again next season." He tilts his protein drink toward me, offering me a taste.

I scrunch my nose. I tried it the first time he offered, and once was enough.

He shrugs.

"Let me know when she comes. Oh wait, is that trip delayed because I'm here? I can move out any time." Alarm snakes through me.

He reaches forward and covers my hand where it lies on the bar, squeezing once. "No. She says she's not ready quite yet. She's only been on a plane once to see me play in Florida. Mostly I send her tickets when we play closer to her, and I go see her during the summer."

"Please let me know, even if my apartment is not ready."

"It'll be okay, Let."

But now, on top of wanting to cook unending amounts of food for this man who is already a leader of his team despite the hardships of his youth, I feel a new degree of urgency to get out of his space so he can enjoy a visit from his beloved grandmother.

Chapter Seventeen

Drew

In the few days before the youth hockey camp starts, I work my way through the first dozen losses of our season, taking notes on what the team should work on. My harshest criticism is reserved for myself.

Let goes to the office, comes home and makes us dinner then works some more. I try not to review the games too much when she's around, after her comments mirrored my grandmother's. When I do, I keep the sound muted.

She works so hard all the time that I want to help her relax. My game reviews can wait for one evening. As I stand to do dishes after dinner, I ask, "Would you like to watch something on TV?"

"Are you asking me to Netflix and chill?" she says with a laugh, playing off the team's teasing of Mattie and Nicole about how they started.

I chuckle. "Nah, just Netflix."

"Sure. Got something in mind?"

"No, but we can surf the new releases if you want."

She's thumbing her phone screen. "I keep a list of shows that sound interesting for when I have time. Maybe we can see if one of these appeals to you?"

"You keep a list." This woman. So much brain power and energy packed into that tight little body, but she never schedules time to relax. She needs someone to ground her. I may not be able to be that person long term, but I can help now.

She looks up and tilts her head. "Yeah, so?"

"Of things you want to watch when you have time."

She nods slowly like I'm a dummy she has to help through a simple sentence.

"Have you ever crossed something off that list?"

She glances down at it. Twisting her lips, she scrolls a little. "I've started a few?"

I bark a laugh as I close the dishwasher. "Are you asking if that counts? No, Let, it doesn't count. Come on."

She follows me into the living room, surveys the setup, and says, "Wait a minute!"

There are rustling sounds in the kitchen for more than a minute, then she returns with her customary evening mug of chai, a glass of water for me, and a plate of Nom Kong, Cambodian donuts which are each the size of my palm but are delicious enough I consider them bite size. They're so yummy that I have to be careful even in the off season; they do not belong on a professional athlete's regular diet, only on his cheat meal list. But she knows this now and only brings a plate of six. The question will be whether she gets more than two.

She's still in her work clothes, a pretty hot pink blouse and dark pencil skirt while bringing me snacks. This woman still hasn't taken care of herself. "Go get into your pjs or something."

She glances down, and belatedly I remember she doesn't wear pjs. Biting my lip, I wait to see what she'll do. If she comes out in that tempting robe, all bets are off on the "only Netflix" promise.

She returns makeup-free in a tank top and yoga pants, as gorgeous as ever. When she sits, her tits bounce a little. Hot damn, she's braless and sitting right next to me with those gorgeous mounds freeballing it. How the hell am I going to focus on the television?

Sniffing in a deep breath through my nose, I let it out slowly, reaching for my Zen. But that's a mistake; I get a big hit of her sweet, spicy, floral scent, and my Zen is cowering in a corner as my cock takes over. I grab a throw off the back of the couch and spread it across us to disguise the bulge in my gym shorts.

She smiles and grabs the remote, referencing her phone. "Ah ha, I think you'll enjoy this one."

When it's up on the screen, I try to read the description, but it's gibberish to me. All my senses are focused on her. Her hair brushing my arm as she leans forward and back. Her breasts jiggling as she tucks her feet up under her. Her thigh pressing against my much-larger one. And that scent. I'm a goner. I might have to excuse myself in five minutes to toss one off just to be coherent.

"I'm fine with anything," I say when I realize she's been staring at me waiting for a reply.

"Cool. We'll try it. If you don't like it, my list is long."

That list is long because she works so damned hard she doesn't take time to even sit and watch a show. A couple nights this week she was still on her laptop at the kitchen counter when I went to bed, and then grabbing coffee to race to the office when I got up. I'm actually starting to feel a little lazy, though my rational brain knows the off season is our regrouping time, physically and mentally, given the pace when we're playing.

Five minutes later, she snuggles closer, and we're pressed together from shoulder to knee. My hard-on is going for records with the amount of blood in it. My hand rests in my lap to hold it down, as track shorts are useless at containment. Her hair swishes against my triceps, and within a few minutes her head rests there.

Her scent is stronger now, and my hand itches to squeeze my cock for some relief, but she's *right there*, plastered to my side.

I glance down to see how she's enjoying the show. If she likes it enough, she'll want to see more episodes, and I've lost the thread. Scratch that, I never found the damn plot line. I can't see her face, though, that thick black hair and the tilt of her head obscuring it from my height. Glancing around, I notice that my stereo equipment on the shelves next to the TV reflects our images. Let's eyes are closed.

So now I sit, my dick literally in my hand dammit, torn between sleeping with her against me all night for the sheer pleasure of it, or getting us to our beds, after which I can get a different sort of pleasure.

Instead, I sit there staring at our reflections as I slide the remote out of her limp grip and slowly lower the volume of the TV. My admiration for her continues to grow. I'm amazed how she keeps all of us, every last one an alpha male or we wouldn't be here, in line the whole season. At the same time, she juggles investors and whales and our public image. Who knows what all she handles during the off season with so many groups using the arena and practice facility week by week. Worse, when our second season starts, Cam learned from Christina that Greg and management are bringing in other entertainment for the nights we don't play at home.

As if that's not enough, Let champions diversity for the team and the league.

* * * *

I wake up feeling better rested than I have in a long time. There was no way I could sleep on that couch then coach peewee hockey the next day, so eventually I carried Let's limp form to bed. Tempted as I was to strip her leggings off, I left her to fend for herself, although she was so deeply asleep I doubt she did. I did, however, steal another quick sniff of her hair for that flowers and spice scent.

I didn't bust a nut before falling fast asleep. The sense of satisfaction at giving her the chance to relax was pleasure enough.

Every time she mentions something new she's working on, I'm impressed. She's so damned smart and organized. And driven.

Says the pot about the kettle. Yeah, yeah, but I only have one task—to play the best hockey possible.

Maybe it's the good night of sleep, Let, or the kids I'm looking forward to helping. Whatever the cause, I'm finally free of the dark cloud from our aborted Cup run and ready to coach.

The first day is spent understanding the kids' capabilities. With only so many coaches and one practice rink, we had to group ages together, and some boys and girls at seven are taller than others at ten. Same goes for skating prowess.

A couple volunteers from the office have helped us get them outfitted with gear, and the other coach and I get them on the ice as soon as we can. Everyone gets a puck to take around the ice for a few laps so we can see their stickhandling skills, and we go from there. This is work I love, whether or not any of these children decide to pursue hockey further. I want as many kids as possible to have access to a sport that is otherwise expensive.

One thing I'm going to have to train myself out of, though, is checking the suite level for signs of a particular dark-haired siren stopping by from the offices behind them.

Hockey camp days are longer than our non-game days, but leave plenty of time for the gym and for me to watch the season's games reviewing my errors so I can work on fixing them. And bonus, I can do that for almost two hours each afternoon before Let gets home, since camp ends at four o'clock and I never have to worry about foraging for dinner these days.

She and I end up in the Tornadoes' gym at the same time a couple of days because I'm going before the kids arrive, and I'm amazed all over again at her fitting in workouts with her schedule. She doesn't talk about friends or hobbies other than cooking. I'm starting to see that she's as career-focused as I am, which makes sense when she's made PR Director by age thirty-ish or however old she is.

We've gotten a routine down for the weekdays. The first weekend, I'm back out on the golf course with some of the guys, and she goes out Saturday evening. Apparently, she does have girlfriends, and I'm glad. At least, I'm happy until she walks in close to midnight.

I'm sitting on the couch watching game tape when the door opens to her in a white lace dress that barely covers her ass. The white against her skin is mesmerizing. It's got different lace edging at the deep vee neckline and bottom hem, drawing the eye. Her hair is piled up on her head, escaped tendrils curling and touching her shoulders. When she turns to put her minuscule purse on the bar, I see that the top ties at the nape of her neck. The white lace has patterns of transparency in it. I squint, looking for nipples to see if she is wearing a bra.

Pissed, I stand and prowl closer, ignoring the fact that there's a larger-than-normal bulge in my gray sweatpants, the only article of clothing I'm wearing. Every guy in the bar or club she was at was doing exactly what I just did. Followed by looking for panty lines. Which I check also.

"Hey. You're still up. Did you find something to eat?" she asks, as though I'm not about to reach for the tie at her nape and strip her down. She leans over the bar to snag her thermal water cup and her boob mashes against the counter, nearly coming out of the dress.

I gulp. "Where did you go dressed like that?" The words come out harsher than intended.

She turns, arm still in the air, brows raised. "Excuse me?"

"I mean, that dress is see-through. I worry about your safety walking around in a scrap of lace." I'm barely able to sound placating.

She laughs and brushes past me to get into the kitchen, having been unable to reach her cup.

Prick that I am, I didn't pass it to her. My cock is at full strength now, and I stay at the end of the bar. She has to walk past my ass, but it allows me to hide my inappropriate reaction.

She glances over at me as she fills her cup at the sink. "Not that it's your concern, but there's a lining."

"But guys don't know that, Let. They're all staring to

try to see what's under there."

Turning toward me, she asks, "How do you know?"

Surely she knows what a typical guy's reaction would be. She's baiting me. She wants to play? I'll play. I pull away from the counter, strolling past her to get a completely unnecessary glass of water myself. I already have one on the coffee table. But this way, she'll see the tenting of my sweats in profile, followed by them draping low on my hips over my ass. The other day I caught her checking out my ass, and I'm pretty proud of it, so I'm happy to give her a repeat show.

"The same way I know you're checking out the gray sweatpants." I don't look back as I pull a tall glass from the cabinet.

She gasps behind me.

I grin, but keep my back to her as I turn to the fridge to get ice, so she doesn't see my expression. Finally, I glance over. Her nipples are poking through the dress, lining or no. I grind my teeth. Neither of us wants a relationship, but it's getting harder and harder to avoid the attraction between us. Living together and seeing all sides of her and the similarities between us, as well as— let's be honest, here—having her cook for me, add to the temptation.

Of course she comes out with, "Glad to see it worked."

I bark a laugh. Let is never going to be a shy, retiring flower. She calls the hard-ons as she sees 'em. My hand squeezes the handle on the fridge door. Taking a deep breath, I exhale and turn to her. "You're playing a dangerous game. This dress, like the robe, is a red flag to a bull. Yes, you're against getting involved with a player, but my internal voice saying 'what happens in the off season stays in the off season' is getting louder. I'm starting to think I can convince you of that."

Her pupils are dilated, her legs are crossed, and she's hugging herself.

I can't read whether her posture is defensive or if she's attempting to hide her arousal. When she licks her lips, I stop trying to resist. I trust she'll tell me no if I cross a boundary. Stepping into her space, I grab her hips to tug her closer, forcing her to uncross her legs. My cock nestles against her flat stomach, pointing at her cleavage where I'd like to slide it.

When her glass clanks on the counter and her arms wrap around my bare middle to play with the waistband of the sweats, I have my green light. My hand slides around her neck to cup her head. Bending, I say against her lips, "I'm adding licking your lips to the list. You're so damned sexy, you're killing me."

She presses forward and our tongues chase each other in the warm cavern of our mouths. Her hands roam my bare skin. When I bring my other hand to her back, I enjoy her naked back as well.

Holy hell, I'm harder than I've been in my life from a kiss. There is no doubt a wet spot on my sweats from my cock leaking with excitement.

The lace of her dress abrades my stomach, and knowing that is the only thing between me and her gorgeous breasts makes me burn hotter. I need to touch them, see them.

Tearing my mouth away, I lick up her neck. Bringing one hand forward, I show her the tail of her dress's halter tie in my fingers as I toy with it.

"Drew," she whispers.

I don't know what her plea is, though, and I need it

spelled out. "Tell me now if you want me to stop. I meant what I said—this can remain between us, short term. I understand your concerns about your job. But Let, I want you. Your smokin' body is just another layer after you've spoiled me with cooking and conversation. All of you is too damned sexy to resist."

Chapter Eighteen

Saylet

Drew bare-chested across the room makes me drool. Against me, telling me all the aspects of me that he finds sexy, is irresistible.

I fold my hand over his where it holds my dress tie, and step back, keeping our hands in place.

The bow unties and the top loosens, but the single knot at my nape still holds it in place.

His eyes are black, his cock straining toward me with a dark gray spot spreading at its tip. His voice is guttural when he says, "I need your words, Let. Please."

He might be begging for my words, but the way he groans the last word makes me think he's specifically asking for the *right* words. Either way, he gets them. "Yes. Secret. Finished when I move out. But yes, please. The temptation of you isn't so easy to withstand, either. As you know."

His teeth flash white in the dimly lit kitchen, and both hands scrabble with my halter straps. "Thank god."

My breasts bounce free and he pauses to admire them, licking his lips. I blink, and he's on me, one hand cupping a breast, thumbing my peaked nipple. The other slides behind my head again, angling me for his searing kiss.

Weeks ago, our first kiss left me weak-kneed and

overheated. This one is incendiary. My blood roars through me, my heart pounds, and I cling to him.

His shoulder muscles roll and flex under my grip as his hands roam my body.

Since he asked me to voice what I wanted, I manage to breathe one word against his mouth, "Bedroom?"

His pecs leap against me, his biceps going taut, and in the next moment, I'm scooped into his arms. His bedroom is a whirl of blue shades, with teal and white accents before I'm set down on my feet. My dress is skimmed down me, leaving me in nude lace cheeky panties. He pauses in a deep squat where he was tugging the dress away from my feet and inhales.

Holy fuck, is he smelling me? I try to step backwards and lose my balance against the edge of the bed. Lying prone, I see him stand, smirking.

Determined to give as good as I'm getting, I jerk to a sitting position and skim one hand along his waistband, looking for a drawstring. The other tightens on his hip. Plucking the tie open on his sweats, I shove them downward, first over his butt, then drawing the front out and over his cock before releasing them to pool around his ankles.

It's my turn to swallow as his cock juts up at eye level. Proportionate to his height, the thing appears massive up close, and I've never felt more petite. I gulp. Well, there's nothing like testing it. I return one hand to his hip to hold him in place while I play, and the other grips the base of his stalk.

He groans and gives me a gentle shove. "Not this time. I'm too close. Ladies first."

WTF? Yes-fucking-please. Apparently I should have been dating hockey guys all along. Half the corporate types considered it a race to see who orgasmed first, winner take all, and the other half negotiated. If I gave them a blow job, they'd give me a few minutes of lackluster oral. Yet this man, younger than almost all of them, is insisting I come first. I wonder if I could send his grandmother flowers without having to explain why I appreciate his upbringing so much.

Thankfully, I don't have to justify my grin at that thought, as this situation offers plenty of reasons to smile. So I let myself be urged back to lying down, while he scoots his sweats out of the way and kneels.

I can't decide if Drew standing over me, cock pulsing and eager, or Drew kneeling before me, shoulders forcing my inner thighs into a stretch, is hotter. The best part is that I don't have to choose, I get to enjoy them both.

His hands grasp under the back of my knees and yank me closer to the end of the bed, and his breath wafts over my swollen pussy.

Ahh, this is happening.

I reach above me and grab a pillow so I can watch without craning my neck, and he chuckles.

Sliding his hands up my inner thighs, he strokes my outer lips with his thumbs before pressing them inwards, squeezing my clit. It has the unintended consequence of pushing my wetness to roll down my perineum. I close my eyes in embarrassment, jolting when his tongue flattens against that rivulet and licks upward. My eyes fly open as I gasp.

He's grinning at me. "Yum. More, please."

His thumbs reverse their movement and slide in to spread my pussy open as he lowers. Warm breath tweaks my sensitized clit before his lips and tongue land.

I relax and enjoy, my eyelids drifting closed only to fly wide at his precision. Fuck, of course he's as good at this as everything else he does.

Tongue swirls alternate with sucking. A thumb teases at my opening and when I jog my hips toward it, he laughs quietly and slides it inside.

Yes. That fullness.

"Do you want more?" he asks against my flesh, his close-cropped beard teasing the line between soft and scratchy and amplifying the pleasure.

Oh, I must have said that out loud.

"It's all good. Please, carry on," I say through gasps.

He chuckles again. What is with this chuckling? Seriously, no guy I know actually enjoys this. They do it if they're good lovers and their partner wants it.

Then his thumb glides in and out of me as his lips clamp around my clit. He tongues it at the same speed as his digit, speeding both up a bit at a time until I'm writhing and clutching his hair with one hand to shove him against me. He goes one degree faster, and I'm there.

"Drew…!" I draw the word out, unable to form any more words to warn him I'm going to come on his face. Stars burst behind my eyelids as they slide closed, my nipples ache for his touch as every nerve and muscle he's touching between my legs spasms in pleasure. I can feel every inch of his thumb as my internal muscles squeeze it with all their might. Shards of pleasure zing out from my clit slower as my stomach muscles unclench.

He lifts his head, that dark beard shiny with my juices. My clit pulses against his hand from how hot he looks wearing my essence. Remembering he likes verbal encouragement, I request, my tone urgent but words polite, "I need your cock now, please."

Those hockey thighs come in handy as he's on his feet in a microsecond, rounding the bed to grab a condom from the nightstand and don it, before leaning over to scoot me up the bed, pillow and all.

He passes a tissue over his face in a couple quick swipes, then lowers himself over me. Knees between my haphazardly spread legs, elbows by my ears, he buries his face in my hair for a minute, making me wonder if he wiped his face specifically to do that without ruining my hair. Would a twenty-six-year-old really think of that? This one might, I concede.

His voice is rough in my ear as he rumbles, "Damn, Let. You're a dream. You taste delicious."

"I get to taste you next time," I mutter.

His cock has been probing at my entrance, and at my words it bucks against me and slides in. He groans and shoves his hips to fill me. Lifting his head, he meets my eyes. "All good?"

I'm out of patience. Raising my legs to cling around his hips, I glare. "I'm fine. *Move*, please."

He laughs again, the madman, and withdraws then glides forward, watching me the whole time with a smile.

"Faster," I demand.

The smile widens as I tighten my hold on his hips and dig my nails into his biceps. But he complies, so I don't have to kill him. He tries different angles of thrusting, widening his thighs, kneeling up, on his hands, back on his elbows, watching and listening to my gasps and sighs with each change.

The thought that he might want game film of this to study flits through my brain. I don't know if that would be a good thing or bad, so I let it go and focus on the rising crescendo in my body.

Only once have I come twice in a night, which is a sad statement on the men of Austin and my schedule. But damn, I am down for this. I angle my hips a fraction differently, and he sucks in a breath.

"Yeah?" I ask.

"Oh, yeah."

His hips piston now, as fast as his skates move chasing a puck. His bent knee, hands braced position offers me unfettered access with my hands and my eyes.

I feast on his young, virile, athlete's body. The view plucks at my pleasure center as much as a vibrator to my clit, and I go over.

Clutching his biceps, I tighten my legs around his butt and keen. Every part of my pussy contracts around him, and electricity shoots from there to every corner of my body. Even my toes feel singed. Trailing off to a moan, I realize my eyes had closed so I reopen them to find him watching with a clenched jaw.

"All yours," I manage.

His teeth flash in yet another grin and then he's pounding into me, extending my ecstasy. Three, four, five slams and he stills, groaning. His eyes shutter, and one arm collapses to an elbow as he makes micro-thrusts that send aftershocks through me.

He drops to his elbows and threads his fingers through my hair before clutching me and ducking his head. "Let."

The nickname that no one here in Austin uses rings through me, reminding me I'm playing a dangerous game. He's so damned nice, such a caretaker, and hotter than any man has a right to be. He checks all my boxes, except the really important one of not interfering with my career. If only I can remember that until the end of the off season.

Chapter Nineteen

Drew

Today is Thursday. I have one more day with these kids and then a break between camps. Which is great, because I'm exhausted.

Not from the camp, though. Let and I have been having the best sex of my life every night for nearly two weeks. I can't seem to stop touching her, even after sex.

We're approaching our arrangement as rational adults. But the short-term nature of it all makes me want to make as many memories to hoard as possible.

So we've been snuggling and staying up until all hours learning about each other, like we're kids at a sleepover. I tell her about juniors and my struggles in Tampa, being new to NHL-level demands on my time and my body. She shares more about her family and the pressure she feels to keep up with her siblings, who all have higher degrees than she does.

Eager to finish this camp and be at Let's beck and call, my attention is only half on the camp while the rest is several floors up on the executive offices level.

My phone rings from the bench. I stare over in surprise—it's Grams' ring. Only she, Coach, and Saint have emergency bypass status. My co-coach, a local league hockey coach, looks at me in question, and I gesture to him to take over. Grams knows my schedule and would never call during the day unless it was important. In fact, she's never done this.

Gut clenching, I try to keep my voice neutral. "Hi, Grams, this is a wonderful surprise."

"Drew, I'm sorry to call you during your work."

Shit, her voice sounds frail, unlike her usual domineering tones.

"Grams, you know you can all any time."

"I'm—" she sucks in a breath "—First, I'm *okay*, I promise. But I'm headed to the hospital. I fell. I'm sure it will all be fine, but they think I might have broken my hip, so I may need your help navigating health insurance and whatnot."

"Grams!" I whisper-shout on a sucked-in breath. She is my world—my mother, father, and best friend all rolled into one incredible human after whom I strive to model myself. "Holy shit. Where are you now? I'm pulling flights up on my phone. Shit! I'm teaching this hockey camp."

"First, watch your language."

Seriously? Only she would interject that at a time like this. I snort, but apologize. "Yes, ma'am."

"Second, I know you're coaching. You don't have to come up here. I'll make sure they give you all the status updates. I'll be fine. I *am* fine. You live your life."

"Don't talk crazy. I can't go about my days knowing you're in the hospital. I'll lose my mind. Let me talk to a few people. I'll be up there as soon as I can, whether you approve or not. Now what hospital are you at?"

"I'm actually in the ambulance, but since I was awake and alert, they didn't put the sirens on. Even though I asked." Her voice is pouty. Only Grams.

I shake my head, safe doing that on the other end of

a phone call. "Good, put me on with a paramedic, please."

A sigh gusts through the line. "I warned them. Here ya go."

"This is EMT Jackson," a woman's voice states. "Your grandmother is doing great, all things considered. All vitals are stable, she just goes green if she tries to sit up. Between that and the position she fell in, we suspect a break. We're headed to St. Mary's."

"Good. Thank you so much. Take care of her for me."

"We always do, sir."

I'm already unlacing my skates. Let will know how to get me out of here today. The other coach sees how agitated I am and comes over.

"I need to step away for a few minutes." Time enough to tell him I'm bailing on him when I get management's approval. "You okay here, or do you want them to take lunch break early?"

"I'll be fine, thanks. Everything all right?" he asks.

"Family emergency." My sneakers are on, and I'm striding away as I answer.

Upstairs, I beeline for Let's office. Damn, it's empty. Her purse is there, though, so she's likely onsite. I pull out my phone and text her, my fingers shaking as I try to spell the words out.

Me

> Do you have a minute please?
> Grams fell. I'm losing my shit.

Staring at the screen waiting for the three dots to

appear, it occurs to me that I'd never send one of my prior bed partners such a vulnerable text. Hell, some of them had no idea that Grams raised me or where she lived, if they even knew she existed.

At that thought, I'm freaking out about looking like a loser to Let. Before I can hit full-blown panic, she walks into the room, closing the door. Stepping into my space, she drops her laptop on the desk with a clatter and throws her arms around me.

I inhale. Exhale. Everything is marginally better. I can deal with it all now. I drop my head to the top of hers and hold her tight. "Thank you. I needed that."

"Any time." She leans back to see my face. "Now tell me what happened."

I relate the phone call, getting agitated again until she sits in a visitor's chair and tugs me into the one next to it, keeping my hands in hers when we're seated.

"Wasn't there a substitute coach list?" she asks.

"Maybe?" I try to focus on that rather than imagining my grandmother in pain. Thank god I made her get a cell phone and taught her how to use a few apps on it. Finally, the list of backup coaches swims into my brain. "I think the first guy said this was the one camp he couldn't cover, and the second one was the guy co-coaching with me already. He's willing to sub in for other camps this summer as he's a college coach full time so he's between seasons earning extra money."

"Damn." Her brow is furrowed. Let is in full problem-solving mode. I take another deep breath. "What's left for the camp?"

"Today and tomorrow then a game on Saturday for the parents to watch." I recall something from the paperwork for the class. "Shoot. Even if he could handle all the drills, my co-coach can't cover these last two days alone. We put a minimum child-adult ratio in the contracts the parents signed."

"Oh?" Her brows lift. "Child-adult or student-coach?"

"I think it was actually student-coach."

"Shoot. I was thinking someone from the office could cover, or a few someones."

"Not unless it's the GM or Greg, and I'm not asking them, even for Grams."

"Nor should you." She thinks for a minute more. "I've got it. Someone from the office can't cover the coaching, but they could cover helping your grandmother."

I frown and open my mouth to say I'd never let a stranger step in for me.

She stops me by squeezing my hands. "I have plenty of PTO. I can go, and you can join me Saturday evening. Maybe earlier if you can drag one of your teammates off the golf course or the lake to sub for the kids' game."

The word no reflexively comes to mind, but Let continues before I can say anything.

"You helped me when I needed it most. Family is important to both of us. Let me help you, too."

I start to refuse but the words die in my throat. Instead of anger and fear, there's peace in my chest. This could work. I trust her. Besides being so damned smart, she knows me and understands my relationship to my grams. She'll do things the way I want them done.

I'm nodding before I finish the thought. "*Yes*. Please. Thank you. Are you sure it'll be okay for you to take off so suddenly?"

She rolls her eyes. "You've seen how much I work,

no matter where I am or what time it is. They know I'll do whatever's needed to keep things running around here."

"Doesn't sound like PTO to me, but I'll take it. Thank you. Thank you, thank you, thank you."

She doesn't wait for approval. Instead she flips open her laptop and pulls up a travel site to search flight options.

"Uh, if you'll allow me?" I slide the laptop over and within a minute I'm on the airline site that has the most direct connections. "It's 11:30. Can you make a 2:50 p.m. flight? If necessary, I'll send a credit card with you so you can buy clothes there."

"I can make it. We'll worry about more clothes later, but I'll run by the apartment and grab what I can."

I book her in first class and pay with my card, then shove the computer back toward her. "Let. Holy shit. I can't thank you enough. I knew you were good at your job, but this takes the cake."

Her lips firm, and something I can't read flashes through her eyes. But all she says is, "Text me the remaining details, and I'll call you when I'm there."

"I'll arrange a hotel on my phone before I go back downstairs. Damn, I can't imagine how I'm going to coach, but I'll do my best."

She has her laptop packed and her bag on her shoulder and races out the door before I can hug or kiss her again. That's okay, Grams is the priority right now. We can get back to hugs and kisses later.

* * * *

I land in Duluth late Friday night after Kyle agrees to coach the Saturday game. My conversations with Let last night and midday today felt stilted. She answered all my questions, put me on video chat with Grams who was groggy from the hip replacement surgery, and was doing everything I asked. But I'm missing something, and I have no idea what.

A taxi ride later, I'm at our hotel room.

At my knock, she comes to the door in that hot-as-hell robe. What would she have bought if she hadn't had time to pack that?

She frowns at my suitcase. "I assumed you'd get a separate room."

"What? Why?"

"Was I supposed to do that for you as part of being good at my job?" She tosses the question over her shoulder in a bitter tone as she walks away.

"What?" I'm lost. Realizing I'm still lingering in the hall, I step in and close the door. "Let, what are you talking about?"

She whirls, and I suck in a breath as her robe gusts out from her thighs. But I have to focus on her words right now.

She crosses her arms over her chest and frowns. "I thought we were friends. Apart from the fucking."

"We are." Still lost here.

"Then what was with that comment in my office?"

"Let, the last two days have been a blur of trying to get here. I need a little help understanding what comment you're referring to, please."

"You said, 'I knew you were good at your job, but this takes the cake.'"

I review what she's said tonight against what I said. Dammit. I'm an ass. "Oh no! I didn't mean this was an extension of your job. I know you're doing this as a friend, and it truly goes above and beyond. That's what I meant—your willingness to jump in and problem-solve in all situations, not just your job, takes the cake."

"Hmph." Her mouth is set. She doesn't quite believe me.

"Seriously." I close the gap between us and hold her hands in mine. "You've always been great, organizing our charity appearances, running between us and the suites at games, etc. But that's all work. In our personal lives, due solely to the circumstances, it's been me helping you. For you to turn around and fly to help a woman you've never met at the drop of a hat is amazing and wonderful. I didn't have the words to say all that clearly because I was freaking out."

Her head tilts as I speak, hair rustling over one side of the silk of her robe as the black curtain dips toward her breast. I blink, refocusing. We need to be okay before I let myself focus on what's underneath that fabric.

"Oh."

"Oh? That's all you got? You've been mad at me for a simple miscommunication for two days," I tease her.

"You sort of took the wind out of my sails." She shrugs and her boobs jostle. So sue me. I'm a guy, I notice. "Sorry."

"I get it. I'd say ask next time, but I know I was super distracted and we were in a rush when I said that. How about a hug to finish getting past it?"

When I hold out my arms, she steps in and smashes her face against my chest. I stroke her hair. Leaning down, I murmur, "I could not have made it through these couple days without you here. Thank you again."

"So…you're staying here? In this room?" she asks, wiggling against me.

"Unless it's a problem. That is always your call."

"The only problem is that something is poking me in the belly."

I huff a laugh. "Pretty sure we can do something about that, but I'd really love a quick shower first."

"K," she lets me go with a yawn.

I toe my shoes off and step into the bathroom. By the time I'm through the shower, she's asleep, lying on her stomach in a tiny scrap of lace over her perfect ass. I turn the bathroom light off, grab sleep clothes, and slide into bed. Plastering myself to her side, I sink into the peace that comes of knowing I'm with her and only a few minutes' drive from my grandmother, and drop into sleep.

Chapter Twenty

Saylet

When I first arrived at the hospital, Drew's grandmother was ecstatic. She was already on a first name basis with most of the nurses, and her room had at least a dozen decorations sent by friends; flowers, balloons, teddy bears, you name it.

However, when I introduced myself, I swear she almost tried to get out of bed. The creases in her forehead and the sporadic clenching of her hands suggested she was in a lot of pain, but she ignored that to ask about my friendship with Drew, insisting that I too call her Grams.

Once I got her off that subject, we had a lovely visit. When she started fidgeting, I suspected she needed more pain meds but didn't want their side effect of making her sleepy. So I insisted I had to step out for an hour or two to check in with work, but that I'd be in the hospital cafeteria and would come back up before dinner.

Yesterday followed the same pattern, allowing me to keep mostly caught up and for her to rest and heal. I am amazed at her resilience and energy, and slightly daunted by the idea of her at full health.

As we round the doorway, Grams gasps, holds out her arms, and tears up. No one could doubt what a strong bond they have. These two amazing independent people clutch each other, rocking and whispering. I hear a distinctly male sniffle as well.

I sit back in the visitor's chair, as Drew is cross-legged on the foot of the bed, and watch their obvious love for one another manifest itself in chastisements about eating right, taking care of one's self, and calling more. All the usual ways family shows their care. It feels like my family when one of us kids is sick, with Ba reviewing the patient chart and Meak fussing. Mine has more technical jargon, given my parents' professions, but otherwise it's the same.

He asks about what the doctors have said, and I'm able to help fill him in on that, as he made sure I was authorized to hear everything. Despite it being the weekend, her surgeon will come by on afternoon rounds to check on her, and has already given me the name of the doctor covering on Sunday.

Drew gets up to look at the cards with all the gifts, asking after each friend and neighbor. He comes to one without a card and glances over at his grandmother. "Who's this from? Have you had many visitors?"

"The first day, the hospital suggested waiting. So I told people to come starting tomorrow since I didn't know if I'd be up for visitors. That lovely arrangement was hand carried in by your wonderful girlfriend."

We freeze, our eyes meeting for a second before simultaneously deciding to ignore her word choice.

"Oh wow. Let, thank you. You've done so much already."

"Well, as I didn't know your grandmother, I thought she might need something to brighten her room," I say, laughing through my words as I gesture around the room.

They both chuckle.

"Drew, what about the hockey camps?" Grams asks.

"Next week is off because of Fourth of July, but I do have to go back mid-week to gather the gear together and plan the schedule with my co-coach," he says.

"Really?" Grams' voice is high with excitement. Then she frowns. "Wait, does this mean we can't have a visit later this summer? I hate wasting my time with you stuck in a hospital bed."

"I'm keeping that week open, but let's see how this goes," he reassures her as he returns to perch on the bed.

I clear my throat. "I have some work to catch up on, so I'm going to head down to the cafeteria for a bit."

Drew glances at me then narrows his gaze looking at Grams, whose fingers are clenched on the blanket. "You know, I could use a cup of coffee. I'll wander down with you."

Grams perks up. "Why don't you show her around town a bit? Spend some time together."

Uh oh. I'm starting to smell wedding flowers rather than hospital flowers. The odor is cloying, strangling me and my career goals.

Drew smooths things over. "Grams, we spend plenty of time together back in Austin. I'm here for you. So I'm not going far."

"But—"

"Tell you what. When your friends visit tomorrow, we'll take an hour or two. Now, you rest. I'll be back in a bit and be right there in that chair with coffee and perhaps a deck of cards if you want to kick my butt in rummy as usual."

She grins and nods.

As I show him the way to the cafeteria, he strokes his beard, looking thoughtful. "Let, you're so observant. You told me what to look for, and I still didn't see it until after you. How the hell do I anticipate moves so well on the ice and miss this stuff, eh?"

"You're focused on her words, and maybe see the grams you've always seen. It'll be fine."

He slings an arm around my shoulders and tucks me against him. "I sure hope so. I feel better now I've seen her. And knowing she's been in good hands."

* * * *

Drew steps out with the surgeon after she's been by on rounds. Grams is likely to be here for a few more days. Because she lives in a third floor walk-up apartment and doesn't have help at home, the surgeon says she'll need to go to a rehab facility. At her age, it's helpful to keep her weight off the hip as much as possible until she's had some physical therapy.

She already hinted as much to me yesterday, but I hadn't told Drew because I hadn't wanted to worry him without some solutions.

So as soon as the doctor leaves Drew alone in the hall, I grab my laptop from the room and join him. Setting it on a corner of the counter keeping visitors out of the U-shaped nurses' station, I open my spreadsheet of rehab facilities that the hospital recommended and are on Grams' insurance, and some of the positive and negative feedback I'd been able to find on them. Ah, the power of the internet.

"We should take this all with a grain of salt and go visit the places," I say.

He's mute, staring at the screen with mouth open. Finally, he turns to me. "Let, when…damn."

I grin, pleased with myself.

Running his hand over his beard, he manages to

finish the thought. "When the hell did you have time to do all this?"

I shrug. "Last night. This morning."

He's shaking his head again. "You are a force to be reckoned with. Sort of a sexy Energizer bunny. We could use you on the ice."

"Ha! I could probably just skate through the opponent's legs. I don't think I meet the minimum height requirements for the game."

He laughs and smooths a hand down my hair. "A compact but combustible package."

His words remind me of how skilled he is at igniting my fire. My breath catches and my back arches, pushing my chest toward him.

His hand drops from my hair and slides around to cup my nape, and he bends to fuse his lips to mine. The beeping machines, ringing phones, and conversations around us fade away. Cognizant of where we are, we keep it closed-mouth, but linger in the embrace. I anchor myself by gripping his wrist next to my chin because any kiss from him makes me lightheaded. He lifts his mouth an inch and murmurs, "After Grams eats supper, we'll head out and I'll take you somewhere nice, okay?"

I nod, only letting go of his wrist when he steps back.

"I don't know how to convey the magnitude of my thanks, Let. You're amazing."

"I'm good at this stuff, and I'm happy to help. Dinner works as a thank you, especially if there is wine."

"I'll make sure of it."

We run by the hotel to shower and change, and I choose a clingy silk sweater and lightweight trousers in an effort to be cute and warm. I've lived in Texas long enough to have lost my Colorado tolerance for cool nights. He looks amazing in a patterned crew-neck sweater and black pants.

The restaurant is lakeside, with much of its indoor and outdoor seating providing excellent views of the evening sun on Lake Superior. He's scored a corner table and sits facing the corner, letting me having the view. I pretend I didn't see him slip a bill to the host. This is hockey country, far more so than Austin, and while he doesn't play for the local team, he's a local boy. Someone new recognizes him in the hospital almost hourly.

Snagging a wine list, he offers it to me, but I wave it away. My brain is off for the day. He shrugs, flips it open, skims down a couple pages, then closes it.

The waiter is there in a moment. "Have you decided on cocktails, Mr. Busbee, ma'am?"

I wince at the ma'am. I thought I left that behind in Austin, too. Gone are the days I'm a "miss" apparently, even out of the South.

Mulling that over, I miss what Drew says, but a minute later, the sommelier is here. "How can I help you, sir?"

"We'd like three bottles to try please. Different varietals, but at least two must work with spicy food, and one must work with—what was it you called my taste, Let? 'Midwestern bland,' I believe?"

He's laughing, teasing me. Thankfully, he's also lying. I play along, gasping with a hand to my chest. "I would never!"

"She didn't," he reassures the man. Phew, there's at least a fifty percent chance no one in the kitchen will spit on my food now. Maybe I'll order the same thing as Drew and switch plates with him to be sure. I snort, and he glances over.

"Do you have a preference for red or white, sir? And may I ask if you're open to our reserve wine list?" The man's eyes may as well have dollar signs in them.

I jump in, saying in a firm voice, "Red, please, and only one from the reserve list."

Drew smirks at me. "Whatever the lady says."

He hands the wine list back to the sommelier. "Thank you."

The man is barely ten steps away when I lean in and mutter, "Three bottles? Who's going to help us drink those?"

"I wanted you to have choices, and I figured we can take whatever we don't finish back to the hotel. I don't drink wine as much as you, but I hardly ever find good choices in the wines by the glass."

"You're nuts."

"Nah, I'm incredibly grateful, and if giving you a miniature wine tasting is a way to show that, then I'm going to do it."

Well, fuck. This guy rushes to his grandmother's side, hangs out to play cards with her, eats whatever I put in front of him at least once, and gives me the best orgasms of my thirty years. Now he's thanking me by creating a wine tasting in a romantic restaurant. I don't think there's any coming back from this.

Reality and my career are going to suck come the fall. For now, I'm going to enjoy this while I can.

Chapter Twenty-One

Drew

The sommelier is a good sport, clearing half the table and setting out the bottles and a pair of glasses. "Would you like me to decant?"

I glance at Let.

She responds, "Only if you think it's necessary. Otherwise, we're happy to give them time to breathe in the glasses."

He bows his head in her direction. "And did you wish to taste all three now?"

I step in, in case she's going to try to be thrifty and not end up opening one. "Yes, please. We'd like to do a mini-tasting, if you will."

"Ah, a flight. Certainly."

He speedwalks off, returning with four more glasses and two pieces of paper and pens. "In case you wish to take notes."

Let's smiling, but I'm lost. Am I supposed to write about notes of wood and tobacco and all the other silliness? Her happiness ensures I'll do whatever she wants so she has a fun evening.

He pours two half-glasses of each wine and leaves us to it, suggesting the relish platter starter and some bread, which we accept.

It's early in the off season, and I'm relieved enough

to see my grams alert and on the mend that I indulge in more drinks than I usually have. Sharing our thoughts on each wine devolves into making up silly reference notes. I smack my lips after another sip of our least favorite. "Definite notes of seaweed."

"You think? Maybe a bit of leather, in the form of an old shoe," she retorts with a giggle.

We're halfway through our entrées and sharing bites off each other's plates. As I steal another forkful of seafood tortellini, she leans over and says, "I'm pretty sure they didn't spit in my food after you told them I called your taste 'Midwestern bland.'"

I choke, and shove my napkin in front of my mouth.

She's rocking in her chair, wheezing with laughter in an effort not to disturb other diners.

I glare at her. "Why would you tell me that after I've eaten it?"

She shrugs, widening her eyes as though the little terror could be innocent. "You said it, not me. I figured if I had to live with the consequences, so should you."

Grimacing, I look at the remainder of my plate. I haven't worked out in the past two days so I'm not as hungry as usual. I can't eat what I normally would, drink all this wine, and not be miserable at the end of summer when it comes time to get in shape for the season. Nutrition statistics run through my brain for every bite of food I put in my mouth; it's part of being a professional athlete. Well, unless you're Jack Landry, but that's another story.

"Are you going to finish that?" I ask, looking at a few scattered tortellini on her plate.

She shakes her head. "It's delicious, even with their wimpy hot sauce. But I'm full."

"Shall we ask them to pack it up? And do you want a dessert to go? We can see which wine holds up to sweet food."

She smiles. "Thanks, but I'm good. I picked the seafood out when I started to fill up. This was so much fun, Drew. Thank you."

"We're definitely taking the wine. I'm curious as to which was the reserve." We shared a least favorite, but were divided on which of the other two we preferred. That could have been because of what we ate—my steak to her creamy pasta, or it could have been that her palate is more sophisticated than mine.

The sommelier comes back, seeing our knives and forks down, and asks how we enjoyed the wines.

I point. "This was nice, but didn't wow us. This I loved, and that one Saylet loved more."

He turns to her and nods. "Ah, madam, you have excellent taste. That is the one from our reserve list. And you can see the vintage is several years older than the others, but well preserved."

She smiles, but her mouth twists. After he steps away for the check at my request, she says, "Figures I like the reserve when you're the one with the budget for them."

"You liked the other ones, too. And I'm happy to buy you wine any time. How comfortable are your shoes? Any interest in a walk along the lake before we head back?"

"That sounds great. I'll tell you if my feet hurt, but I'd love to walk some of this meal off."

We tuck the wine bottles in the rental car and stroll. The wind off the water keeps throwing Saylet's hair in her face and she doesn't have a hair tie with her, so I throw my arm over her shoulders, trapping her hair. It's a great excuse to tuck her close to me, and I angle my head to sniff her spicy floral scent.

She elbows me. "You're sniffing me again, weirdo."

"I can't help it. You smell yummy. All deliciousness and none of the calories. I want to eat you up."

She stops and turns to me. Her eyes are hot. "It sounds like you're ready for dessert. Hotel?"

"Yes, please." Damn, I'm going to have to drive with a hard-on again.

Thankfully, the hotel is only a few minutes away.

In our room, I strip her down, her barely-there underwear taking my breath away like it does every time. Still squatting from removing her pants and shoes, I grab her hips and twirl her so I can sink my teeth into one taut cheek.

I don't bite down, but she squeals anyway. "Drew!"

"Tasty, but not the dessert I was hoping for. Lie down." I rise and shuck my clothes as she climbs onto the bed. I command, "Stop."

She's on her hands and knees, and the sight is frying my brain. She flips her hair to look over her shoulder, questioning.

I grab her lacy panties and skim them down her thighs, waiting for her to lift one knee then the other to rid her of them. Then I slide onto my back between her thighs.

She looks down.

My hands come to cup her hanging breasts, and her eyelids slide closed on a moan.

Adjusting my hold to her hips, I lower her to my face to nip at her outer labia before pointing my tongue and licking a circle on top of her clit.

She shouts a wordless cry, and one elbow gives

before she stabilizes herself. Tugging her down another fraction, I set to work with my lips and tongue, as my hands return to her sensitive breasts.

"Drew," she breathes. "Holy fuck, Drew."

Let loves oral almost as much as I love giving it to her. Her hips start to slide forward and back on my face, so I firm my mouth and let her ride over my chin, mouth, and nose.

"Ah!"

Placing my hands around her hips, I'm able to hold her open further so I can reach as many of those nerve endings in that tight little clit as possible. It's swelling against my mouth, and I swear I might come with her. My cock is pulsing and jerking and weeping precum against my belly. Yes, alcohol loosens inhibitions, but coming from her taste alone would be embarrassing, even if she finds it flattering.

In desperation, I stop and drag her town my torso. Holding her over my cock, I grab a condom and roll it on before impaling her. *Yes.* That tight wet heat clenches around me and I nearly spurt there and then.

She whines, "Drew...move."

I grit out through clenched teeth, "Give me a moment."

It's been days since I've been inside her. We went cold turkey from at least one round a night to separation when Grams called. Which sucked because it was—*is*—the best sex of my life. Now after a couple glasses of wine, my pump is primed.

Apparently hers is too. She grinds against me.

I gasp. "Let, wait."

She shoves forward and back to maximize friction against her clit. When I lift her off me, she slams down, then repeats it. Let is clearly done waiting.

My orgasm coils in my balls. After two seconds of trying to beat it back, I realize it's not going to happen. Reaching for her clit, I get my thumb on it as I pound up into her, doing my own grinding as my cock empties into the condom. "Fuuuck."

At my groaned curse, she pauses, her hands still balancing herself on my chest. Tilting her head, she says, "Oops. Did you just come?"

Since I'm still pulsing inside her, I simply narrow my eyes. "Dammit, I told you to wait."

"Don't give me attitude when you're inside me, hockey boy." She squeezes her internal muscles, making my cock pulse.

"Sorry," I mutter.

"It's okay." She pats my chest and climbs off me so I can deal with the condom. "I'm probably ahead of you in orgasms anyway."

Is she crazy? She's so matter of fact, like she actually thinks I'd be done now. Like "too bad, so sad" for her. She really has dated some shitty guys.

I tie the condom off and toss it toward the bathroom. I'll deal with that later. Rising over her, I nudge her from her side onto her back.

"What are you doing?" she asks.

"I'm not leaving you hanging because I couldn't control myself. I'm not a stupid teenager, despite all recent evidence."

She snickers and lies back. "I'm not going to look a gift climax in the mouth."

I skim my hands down her sides, pausing to cup her breasts as my mouth meets a nipple. Sucking, I plant one hand on the bed and kneel over her, following her hip bone with my fingers to where her pussy is still swollen and open from my dick.

I slip two fingers in.

She grunts and grabs fistfuls of my hair.

I try to circle her clit with my thumb but it's so engorged I end up flicking it from side to side. Raising my head, I watch her to see if that's going to cut it.

She is biting her lip and returning my stare.

No. I need her mindless, and since her gaze is focused on my mouth, I'm going to read that body language.

Shifting down, I slide my fingers in and out while my tongue traces her drawn-back clit hood. Those edges, normally hidden behind that protective shield, are what she needs stroked. Or sucked. I close my lips around it and pull, tapping with my tongue as my fingers glide out, then in, then curve on that super-sensitive spot on her front inner wall.

Her fingers tighten in my hair, and her walls clench around me as she nears her peak. Within minutes, she keens a wail as her body milks my fingers and the kernel of flesh in my mouth vibrates as though it's battery-operated.

I lick her slowly down from the high, my fingers retracting.

She pants, her arms now thrown wide, having left at least most of my hair attached to my head.

I go up on my hands and knees to kiss her. *"Now, we're done."*

Without opening her eyes, she grins and pats my shoulder with a limp hand.

* * * *

Two days later, I'm hanging with Grams playing rummy. Kyle Scott showed up on some fan's social media feed, drunk off his ass, thankfully not the same day he substituted as a coach for me. But there goes that option for the rest of the summer. No parents are going to want him around their kids.

Let's dealing with the fallout at the hotel, as it wasn't something she could discuss in the hospital cafeteria.

I've reached out to Scottie, but so far, have received only radio silence in return. I hope one of us—teammates, coaches, Saylet, anyone—can reach him before he goes off the deep end. Saint is out of town visiting his wife's family, and as much as he sounded like he'd welcome the excuse to return to Austin to help, it seemed like a bad idea. There's been some weird tension in that marriage, and no one on the team understands it. But even in the most supportive relationship, in-laws trump teammates during the off season.

I reached out to Coach to see if he was in town. He is, and was already very much aware of the incident. When he indicated he'd be on Saylet's conference call, I left it in their hands and headed here.

Grams fans her cards on the table, face up. "Gin."

"Dammit, Grams. Can't you let me win one?"

"Do you ask the opposing teams to do that, too? Where's your competitive spirit?"

"Hmph. If I lost every hockey game like I am cards, I wouldn't need a competitive spirit. I'd need a new job."

"I wouldn't recommend applying as a card shark," Grams says with a shout of laughter at her own joke.

I roll my eyes. She's been told she'll be released Friday, but I fly out this afternoon. If it was anything else, I'd call off. But Greg set these classes up for underprivileged youths, and all gear is provided, as is transportation to and from the rink when needed. The only reason I'm playing in the NHL today is because of a similar group that ran camps in Duluth. I could never have afforded the camp and league fees, much less the gear that I grew out of every six months.

Grams understood why I wanted to get back to Austin, but she was frustrated when the doctor told her she'd have to transition to a rehab facility. When Let told us she arranged to work remotely for a second week, Grams perked up noticeably. Then we showed her the websites of the places we'd visited so she could pick where she wanted to spend the next few weeks.

Suddenly she was excited and texting her friends pics. The nicest one is pretty close to her apartment complex so her friends can visit, and it has some pretty swanky amenities, including an indoor pool.

Now, she shuffles the deck again and asks, "When are you going to show Saylet around your hometown? Are you ashamed of us?"

I press my lips together. "Please stop. I've told you, she's not my girlfriend."

"So? How will you make her your girlfriend if you don't open up to her? And don't tell me you don't want to hit that."

I close my eyes. I'm not shocked, because this is Grams. But nor do I wish to give away that yes, I want to hit that, and in fact already have, repeatedly.

To no avail. This woman can read me like an open children's book with large font. "Ah ha! So she *is* your girlfriend. Or at least a fuck-friend."

Now I'm groaning. "Please stop watching TikTok.

These phrases should never be used by a sixty-something-year-old woman to her grandson. Not to mention that if I'm not allowed to swear, neither are you."

"How can you not want to lock that in?" she asks, ignoring my comment.

Grimacing at yet another phrase that sounds strange in her mouth, I choose to give her a hard time right back. "We work together. If shit goes sideways and we break up, then I get in some bar brawl and end up in prison, I'd have to worry whether she'd bail me out or not as the team's PR Director."

Grams frowns. "I better *never* hear about you getting arrested, or bail money is going to be the least of your problems."

"Yes, I know. It was hypothetical."

Let walks into the room carrying her open laptop. "Drew, if you got arrested, do you think Coach Steele would bail you out?"

We turn to stare at her wide-eyed. Brows raised, she looks between us, confused.

Grams slams her hand on the overbed table, spilling the card pile. "Drew better not get arrested, or he'll answer to me!"

Let swallows. "Sorry, bad example. If anyone on the team got arrested, would you expect Coach to cover bail?"

"Hell, no. That would set a terrible precedent. Plus, not to sound ignorant, but isn't that more in line with your job?"

"Yes. Which is why I'm confused as to why he bailed Kyle out."

I stare. "He did what?"

She nods. "Anyway, he's out. The buzz is already dying down. Given that it's the off season, we're going to let it lie for now, although I'm sure he'll be penalized by the team. We won't make a big deal of it. Hopefully, that won't lead to other players thinking they can get away with that kind of thing."

"Yeah, I'm not sure how deep Coach's pockets are," I joke. She gives me an exasperated press of the lips. "I'm sure Kyle reimbursed him, but still. Anyway, I'll check on Kyle when I head back."

"Thanks. Oh, and I probably shouldn't have shared about the bail thing, but I figured as alternate captain you should know."

I nod.

After lunch and being beaten in several more rounds of rummy, I have to go. As I sit in the cab to the airport, I heave a sigh.

I'm confident Grams is in good hands with Let there. But damn, I'm going to miss the heck out of them both.

Chapter Twenty-Two

Saylet

Grams and I roam the halls of her hospital floor. I'm used to stepping double time to keep up with long-legged hockey players, so the glacial pace she needs for her recovery has required an adjustment. I have no doubt she could walk circles around me if she was healthy. We share the same energy level, hers is just temporarily on simmer.

My phone buzzes and I check it for work messages, but it's my meak. At my smile, Grams asks, "Ah, someone fun?"

"My mom." My grin is still wide, thinking of talking to her and my father later if their shifts at the hospital allow.

"You are close to your parents?"

"Definitely. And my siblings."

She nods, and as we meander, she tells me stories of Drew's childhood. "I was the thrift store queen. I would stop in at least once a week, and the staff knew I was trying to clothe and entertain a fast-growing boy. So they'd put stuff aside for me if they thought I'd want it. One September, they had a pair of rollerblades. He was seven, and these were too big. I was so afraid he'd fall and lose his teeth, and there's no way I could afford dentist bills. But he was growing so fast, and I knew he'd love them, so I bought them anyway."

"Did you have him stuff socks in the toes?"

"Nope. I held them. If you ask him now, he'll probably tell you they are still in his top three Christmas gifts ever." Her voice holds pride. "And by the time December rolled around—haha—they were only a teeny bit big. Much safer."

"I'm pretty sure I wasn't coordinated enough for rollerblades at seven."

"He was athletic, already playing any sport he could talk his friends into. Even then he had captain energy. But of course winters in Duluth are unpredictable. When the sidewalks were clear, he sped around the neighborhood on those. He knew how far he was allowed to go. Heck, it made him eager to buy our groceries. But oh lord, when it was snowing or raining or too damned cold, he'd race up and down our apartment building hallway. Every once in a while he'd go full bore into the wall at the end."

"Sheesh. Why?"

"I asked him that. He'd seen hockey on TV and was playing an imaginary game in his head. That was him being pummeled against the boards. His words." She's shaking her head, grinning.

With that understanding, I see it. He wasn't simply a kid burning energy. Drew wouldn't only play a game, he'd need imaginary competitors and obstacles to beat, even as a child. "Ah. He's told me a little about you finding the junior leagues and scholarships for him. This was the start of that, eh?"

She cackles. "You've been up here long enough to start ending questions in 'eh.' You fit right in, like I knew you would."

I blink. Huh, I hadn't even noticed.

She continues, "I kept telling him to show you our neighborhood. I swear the boy is embarrassed by his humble beginnings."

"My family immigrated to the U.S. and had to start their lives over, so I understand humble beginnings. And he knows that about me."

She shrugs. "Will you be allowed to drive me to the rehab place?"

"I don't know, but I can find out. Why?"

"Perhaps we can take the scenic route. I'd love to show off Drew's...coworker to my friends."

* * * *

Grams has come so far this week, but today was the transfer to the rehab, and it's been a lot. Drew is due back later today so hopefully a nap will rejuvenate her.

I was not allowed to transport her, but she did ask me to get clothing and toiletries from her apartment as she might be there a few weeks. If only she'd agreed to move when Drew started making NHL money. But she'd insisted that the old neighborhood was fine, and she didn't want to move away from her friends.

She claims her third floor of a walk-up keeps her fit. But that means she has a higher threshold than most before she can be released—two flights of stairs. Nevermind that it's her right hip, so driving is an issue, as well.

Her doctors say she's progressing well, but she's still nearly seventy, so they're being careful.

I look around the neighborhood. Even if one were available, I don't love a ground floor apartment for an older woman living alone. I bring up a real estate app on my phone and do a quick search using my current location. There are a few homes on the market a short walk from here. Only one of them is a single story, and even that has a flight of stairs to the basement, where the laundry is. But she's likely to have home help for a time after she is released, so they could do the laundry for her. Or if she's as stubborn as I suspect, help her up and down the stairs occasionally to do it herself.

But will she move that far, and will Drew be amenable to buying this house? It's tiny and old—a 1920's build. Not what he'd choose for Grams. But if it's something she wants, to stay close to her friends, then perhaps he'd be cool with the idea.

Her small roller bag in tow, I depart with a plan. When I arrive at her new temporary abode, Grams is settled in. She wastes no time directing me in unloading her clothes and then arranging the flowers and gifts I had to carry out of her hospital room in batches. Finally, I bring her a fantastic trio of photos in a single frame. Horizontally aligned, they depict her and Drew at various ages. I suspect he's about five in the first one, ten in the second, and fifteen and towering over her in the third.

I desperately want a copy of the set, despite berating myself that childhood pictures of Drew have no place in my life. I'll be back in my apartment and my career, happily single, by September at the latest. I promise myself I'll create things like this for my kids, and perhaps ask for a few more of the many family photos my parents have on their walls.

After she brushes a hand over it, she places it on her bedside table. A huge yawn escapes her, so I tell her I'll stop by after her dinner, and I return to the hotel where I enjoy the lounge while I catch up on work.

When I return to the facility and enter her room again, Grams still looks tired.

"Did you get to rest?" I ask.

"A little, but people kept coming in to tell me I was scheduled for this, that, and the next thing. They're going to keep me busy here. I already told my friends not to come until I know what my days look like. But hey, at least the food is good."

"Excellent," I say, pulling a chair up with tablet in hand. "I have something to show you. I haven't said anything to Drew yet, because I wanted to run it by you first."

"Thank you," she says with a nod.

"Look at this. It's not the biggest, and it's older. But the house is only four blocks from your apartment complex, and it's one level with a basement. I know you want to stay close to your friends, so while this might not be your forever home, it might be worth looking at for the near term to get you away from having to climb two flights of stairs all the time."

For the first time, Grams looks scared. "You don't think I'll be as good as new within a couple months?"

"I do. The doctors have said so, and I see the progress you're making already. But here's the thing. Just like houses, cars, and appliances, as people get older, things break more frequently. You're in great shape, but if you roll an ankle, or stub your toe, or hell, get out of bed with a sore back here and there, do you want to face those stairs to get anywhere?"

She stares into space, thinking.

"You don't have to make a decision right now. And I can keep looking. I wanted a condo, where there wouldn't be an exterior to maintain. But there aren't any close to where you and your friends live."

"You think Drew would buy that, though?" she asks. "You should see where and what he tried to offer me."

I smile. She's at least considering the idea. "I think Drew would buy you anything you asked. Sure, he'd prefer you in something new and fancy and likely gated, but if you told him this is what you want—or whatever else we find—he'll come around."

She cackles. "Especially if you are on my side."

I raise my fist to bump knuckles. "Girl power."

Drew's voice from the doorway pulls my head around. "Girl power? Should I be worried?"

Chapter Twenty-Three

Drew

When I stepped off the plane in Duluth, I had an afternoon text from Let waiting, saying Grams was resting and she was returning to visit after dinner, so I came straight here and walked in hearing, "girl power."

I'm suddenly rethinking my comfort level about leaving these two troublemakers together for days.

Grams squeals and stretches her arms out. "Drew!"

I hug her, allowing my question to go unanswered.

She draws back. "What are you doing here? Don't you have a hockey camp to teach?"

"Not on the weekends without games. I had to scope out your new digs."

"Mi casa es su casa." She spreads an arm wide like she's displaying a prize on a television game show.

"Not bad. How was dinner?"

"Surprisingly good."

I nod and glance over at Let. "Have you eaten?"

She nods.

"She could probably use a glass of wine after today," Grams interjects.

We turn to look at her. She attempts to look innocent, all wide-eyed and "who, me?"

Giving up, I shrug and turn to Let. "How about it?"

"Sure."

I lean down and hug my grandmother, assuring her I'll be back bright and early in the morning.

"With a Duluth Coffee for me? Please?"

They haven't limited her diet as she's in good health other than the fall, so I agree easily. "Of course."

Let comes over to hug her as I linger by the door. Grams whispers something to her about a text and she nods. Something is definitely up with these two, but I can't see Let as a bad influence, so I'm confident that all will be revealed eventually.

Duluth isn't a hub for wine connoisseurs, but there's an Italian restaurant right on the water that boasts it's also a wine bar. I'm dubious as you can't pull up the wine list on their website, but we'll try it. It's not as though I ate at any of these places I've taken her to when I lived here before. We were on a sneaker laces budget, nevermind a shoestring one.

In short order, we are seated at a high top in the bar.

"Ohh, they have wine flights. You won't have to do your BDE thing and buy multiple bottles."

I laugh. "If the choices are up to madame's tastes. Otherwise, I'm happy to whip it out and swing it around."

She slaps my arm.

I raise my brows at her. "I was talking about my credit card. What were you thinking?"

She shares her flight with me—three small glasses of the same varietal which come with tasting notes—while I nurse a beer from my favorite local brewery. I was underage when they first started, but I'd just signed my contract with the Tampa Bay Storm. Grams made me see a financial adviser who set up a few investments for me and gave me a certain amount to play with. As Grams wouldn't move, I used the money I'd put aside for a house for her and bought into Ursa Major brewing. They've grown a lot, although there's an older, more popular brewery in town that continues to dominate. But Duluth hosting a beer festival every year really helps. This is and always will be a beer town. Austin, on the other hand, paints a wider swath, sitting on the edge of a burgeoning wine region in addition to having excellent microbreweries and distilleries. So even though Let's told me she doesn't love Texas wines, at least she's among her people there.

"Grams told me a few stories about your younger days."

Oh no. Thankfully, my grandmother doesn't know all the stories to tell. The times I crammed my feet into donated skates that were too small only three months later, because it might mean another kid didn't get a pair. Or the duct tape in my pads to hold them together longer that the coach pretended not to see.

"She wanted me to drive your neighborhood to see where the magic happened, so when I went to pick up some clothes for her, I did. Is that the apartment you grew up in?"

"Yep. She let me buy her a new couch, or you'd have been sitting on the very bed I slept in. Stubborn woman."

Let tilts her head. "Can I ask you something? You don't have to answer if you don't want to, of course. What happened with your mother?"

I nod. I should have expected the question. In fact, I probably should have shared more without her having to ask. "My grandmother had my mom pretty young. Early twenties, I think. They struggled financially, but so did a lot of people. And as I can attest, Grams is an excellent parent." We both smile before I continue. "It's the age-old tale. Mom fell in with a bad crowd in high school. She dropped out and worked for her dealer for a while before her addiction became too much. Grams helped her get straight when she came home pregnant, and for a short while after I was born. But the draw of getting high was too strong. She was in and out of the house by the time I was in kindergarten and gone for good by first grade."

"That must have been hard. You had Grams, but she had to watch her daughter struggle and not accept help."

"Yeah. We don't talk about it much because I can see it still hurts her to think about it. Especially since a few years later, the police came and asked her to identify my mom's body."

"Drew! Oh my gosh I'm sorry. That's terrible."

"It feels abstract to me. I barely remember her and what I do recall is more from photos than true memories. I've always had Grams, and she was all I needed."

Let hops down and comes around to hug me.

As she climbs back up on her seat, she yawns. "I'm tired and all I did was move a few clothes and flowers. You must be exhausted."

We've both finished our meal and drinks. I watch for the waitperson to get our check. "Let's get you to bed then. Come on."

In the hotel room, I reach behind my head to drag my shirt off. Toeing my shoes off, I turn and catch Let licking her lips as she stares at my stomach. I clench my abs just to mess with her, and her pupils dilate. Someone's gotten a second wind. But I need to have a better showing than last time we had sex after several days apart.

With that in mind, I face her to undo my jeans and peel them down, leaving my boxer briefs on.

She's sitting on the bed, already in that robe of hers, and I come around to stand over her knees, straddling them.

"See something you like?" I joke.

She glances up at me with a wicked smile, and I barely step back in time to avoid her grabbing my waistband.

"Nah. You first." I give her shoulders a playful shove back onto the bed and gesture for her to scoot upwards. I grab the ends of her belt before she moves though, so it naturally unravels as she slides away from me.

Grinning, I separate her robe, the rest of the tie unwinding with the motion. Hot pink lace and satin bikini panties pop against her warm skintone, but they need to go, too.

Then it's me and my favorite snack. Let starts to say something, but I hold up a finger. "Shh. We're having a moment here, this pretty pussy and me. Don't interrupt."

She snickers and quiets.

I feast. My tongue, lips, even teeth on less sensitive parts like her outer lips, all enjoy the hell out of Let. My hands grasp her bottom and knead it before one joins my mouth in a power play.

Her fingers loosen and tighten in my hair as though directing my cadence. I follow their lead, speeding up when she tugs faster. Her hips raise, her stomach muscles mound, and I move into the slot, two fingers in her slit and my tongue on her clit, strumming it at top speed.

A whine comes from above me indicating I'm about to score. "Ahh, Drew."

I hold my mouth firmly against her quivering flesh

as my fingers rub inside, finally slowing as her hips drop to the bed and she pants.

Only now do I dare remove my boxer briefs and grab a condom from my wallet.

Chapter Twenty-Four

Saylet

The next morning we're back in Gram's room at the facility, and I'm nervous. Drew is not going to love the house I found. Bringing him around will take some finessing, and I set Grams' expectations that we'd succeed. Rolling my shoulders, I give myself a pep talk. I'm in PR, for heaven's sake.

As soon as our butts hit the chairs, Grams starts talking about the house.

"Look at this, honey," she says, passing her phone over.

"Okay." He scrolls through the photos in the listing, his expression neutral. "Is one of your friends buying it? Where is it? Maybe I can buy you something nice nearby."

"It's only a few blocks from the apartment. I was thinking it might be better than all those stairs."

He jerks his head back, a look of horror crossing it before he can stop it. "For you? You want me to buy this old house for you? Can I buy it and tear it down and build you something nicer?"

"No." She crosses her arms. "You may not. You're lucky I'm caving on you buying me anything. I can just stay in my apartment."

I almost have to leave the room because I'm not sure

I can contain my laughter. I daren't sip my coffee to hide my face, because I'm going to spew it everywhere if she keeps talking. Worse, when he ducks his head to look at the phone again, she winks at me. I widen my eyes and shake my head, then get up and walk to the window.

"Grams. Come on. I'd be worried it'd be a fire hazard. Are the outlets even grounded? And what happens when the plumbing bursts during a hard freeze because the pipes are so old?"

"Frankly, I think they built houses sturdier in 1920 than they do today. You probably have less to worry about with this one than you would with a new build."

He rolls his eyes.

"Okay, never mind. I seem to remember you saying you'd buy me anything I wanted." She reaches for her phone.

He passes it back, and narrows his eyes. "You really want that house? Have you looked around for any other options?"

I pipe up before I've thought it through. "Everything else in that area is multiple stories, with no bedrooms on the ground floor."

"Ah." He leans back in the visitor's chair, folding his arms. "Now I know how she found it when she's been in a hospital bed this whole time."

I try to look innocent, avoiding his aggravated gaze.

"Seriously, I can't believe there aren't better options," he says, looking between us.

Since I did the research, I answer. "Not within a short walk to her friends in the apartment complex, the stores she knows, etc."

"Look," Grams says. "Is it my dream house? No. But does it make sense for the time being given my age and this recent fall? Probably."

"What about moving to be near me when I get a long-term contract. That's hopefully next summer."

"I've thought about that. I'm still young and active and have so many friends here. I think you're going to have to sweeten the pot, hon."

He frowns. "With what? I've offered you a car, trips. You won't take them."

"Great-grandbabies."

This time, I do spew the coffee I'd just sipped, all over the window I'm thankfully still facing. "Uh, excuse me. I'll be right back."

Drew catches my wrist and strokes down over my hand as I walk by, to reassure me. "Grams. We've had this conversation. Those will come later, when my career is more certain, eh."

I listen from the bathroom as I run water over my hand and get a hand towel to wipe the window.

Grams says, "Really, a longer contract is good enough for *me* to move but not for children? Hmph."

"Come on, even with one of those, they could trade me. You're an adult; I can't move a kid around like that. Or won't. And hockey is more than nine months of the year of intense focus. I won't do that to a kid—leave them alone to rely on someone else for their care. But I can't compromise my value to a team and the longevity of my career by splitting my attention."

My heart twists hearing that. It shouldn't even be reacting because Drew and I aren't close to anything permanent. My own rules still apply: secret, finished when I move out. And yet, on one hand, I love that he's so thoughtful about parenting, so responsible. On the other, I want a family one day despite being focused on my career right now. My parents may have focused too much in one direction and not enough in the other, but they made it work. And my one day is a lot closer than Drew's given our age difference.

I can't help wondering if Grams threw babies in the mix deliberately. One of our conversations this week was about my family and the fact that I want children. And she's been less than subtle in her desire to see us as a couple.

Regardless, he and I don't have a future. Apparently I might need a reminder here and there, since I guess some small part of me hadn't been convinced.

I stare at my reflection. This is casual. There's no reason to care what Drew wants or doesn't want. *CAS-U-AL*.

Except he's so fucking perfect in every other way.

Chapter Twenty-Five

Drew

Grams has physical therapy and occupational therapy on Saturday, so after we have coffee with her she tells us to come back in the afternoon.

There are hiking trails along Lake Superior that have gorgeous views, and it's a nice day. Austin summers—and Tampa summers before that—are almost too hot to hike by ten am, and I want to enjoy the moderate temperatures.

Let agrees to let me buy her hiking shoes then we're off, with me tempering my pace for her much shorter legs. Balancing on three millimeter wide blades gives me the agility of a goat. I step over streams and miniature waterfalls mindful to reach back and offer her a stabilizing hand.

One is wide enough that I swoop her up in my arms and step over the gap, placing her carefully down.

I'm rewarded with a kiss, but we need to talk about her inciting Grams' interest in that tiny old house.

I have a foldable day pack that has water and snacks in it. Near the top, we find a flat rock to sit on and enjoy the view. The foliage is different here than in Austin, the trees bigger. The rocks have red and pink tones versus the ubiquitous white limestone in Austin. I offer her an energy bar and the insulated bottle. "You think I should buy that POS house?"

She shoots me a side glare.

Okay, perhaps not the best lead-in ever, but still. I'm concerned.

"I think she'd be better in a place with fewer steps, and since she won't move away from her friends, that's the only choice. I also think that y'all can have every kind of inspection known to man to ensure it is safe for her." She sips water. "And I don't disagree with her about the construction. They built them to last back then, even if the insulation and/or wiring has to be updated."

"But I'm hoping to get a longer contract with the Tornadoes next year, then she'll move down."

"Maybe. She's already backing off that, as you saw. You don't know what the future will bring. What happens if she has another mishap during your season and you can't get up here to help her, and she can't do stairs?"

The wind rustles the tree branches and Let's ponytail while I consider that. "There was nothing for rent?"

"Ground floor apartments are the least safe, no matter how nice the area. There are too many unknown faces coming and going. In a house you can put a top of the line security system in, and surrounding owners are more vested in neighborhood watch." She's nice enough not to mention the fact that Gram's apartment building's pay-based-on-income rent might be a factor.

A bird caws as it glides over our heads, and I glance up as though it will offer answers.

"I'd do anything for Grams. And I've offered to buy her a house." I gulp. "I think the combination of that house not being one I'd ever pick for her, and the reality of spending that type of money is hitting me."

"How much was your condo?" Let asks, then blusters, "I mean, you don't have to tell me, but it had to be a decent chunk of change."

That's true. I was so excited by the opportunities with a new team, then being named alternate captain, I splurged, and she doesn't even know about the one I own in Tampa. I also knew the location was very easy to rent if I'm traded, or a great choice for Grams and me should she need or want to come live with me.

But another significant outlay like this makes me sweat. I've never been so grateful for one cool perk this team offered—financial advice, from an owner, no less. "I'll call Christina and ask her about it."

She leans back on her elbows on the rock, her hair swishing over it. "Great idea. I hadn't thought of that. She'll be able to project your income into the future so you see how you can recoup this, as well as talk about investment potential for the house. Of course, you probably won't get back any upgrades like a high end security system."

"I'll talk to Grams about it, make sure she's really going to move, and not regret giving up that apartment. There's a two-year waitlist for that building."

"If you were anyone else with your income, I'd say hold it for a couple months of overlap to ensure she's happy, but I understand you may not be comfortable doing that."

We've shown each other our tender underbellies— her concerns about being a female professional in an industry focused on men, and mine about money from my childhood. Yet I'm comfortable with her knowing because of comments like that which show her respect and compassion. Given all that girl time she's had with

Grams, it's probably good that I'm okay with it, as I suspect more of my young antics have been shared.

"Any chance you'll show me more of what you did when you lived here?" she asks.

Yep, now I know for sure Grams has been bending her ear. She's so proud of me climbing my way up, avoiding the struggles she faced, that she likes to brag to everyone. What she doesn't realize is that while I'm super proud of her, the rest I hate thinking about, much less discussing. Even as a kid, I understood those were challenging times. I did everything I could to avoid asking Grams for new clothes, gear, or hockey fees, because she worked so hard and struggled so much. It's what drives me to ensure Grams never has to live through that again.

Let has seen a hint of it with the pantry cleanout snafu, and what I shared about my mother. But what am I going to show her? I could start with the alley my friends and I used for street hockey with two dumpsters framing the "goal" at one end. Maybe move on to our favorite thrift store, where most of my school clothes came from. Then the hospital that served the uninsured, which had a waiting room the size of a bus terminal, where we spent many long nights waiting our turn for one issue or another.

A gust of wind tries to grab my energy bar wrapper. Grabbing it, I start packing up our trash and water bottles.

She reaches over and takes my hand. "Hey, no pressure."

I search for something, somewhere, that won't dredge up all the bad memories. Junior league hockey was better. Sure I was a scholarship kid and some of the kids sneered at that, but I wasn't the only one. And ultimately, when I proved myself on the ice over and over, they learned to respect me. Finally, trying to give us an out, I say, "I can take you to my first hockey rink, but don't you have enough hockey in your life?"

"It's not about the rink, it's about what y'all tell me you did there. What I see through your eyes. But only if you're sure."

"It's okay. We'll do that tomorrow. I plan to spend as much time with Grams as I can. And right now, I'm starved. These bars aren't doing it for me. I'm used to being fed by a gourmet chef." I stand and offer her my hand to haul her up for the hike back.

She laughs and takes it, and the mood lightens. Phew.

Chapter Twenty-Six

Saylet

We return to the facility to hang with Grams, happy and tired from the fresh air and exercise.

Who knew hiking with Drew would be relaxing. I'm usually so competitive I race up the paths, either to keep up or to beat my companion. Or the guy leaves me in the dust and I'm walking alone and irritated.

There was no way I was keeping up with his giant strides, but he never complained or sped off. I barely dated guys in their twenties when I was in my twenties, because they were in their "take on the world" phase and were all about themselves. But Drew is remarkably balanced and ever the gentleman. His manners have always been impeccable with me, the fans, and the press. But when he carried me across that one stream, I almost melted on the spot.

Every time he shows the traits I look for in a forever partner makes it harder to remember what we have is very, very temporary. I should be thankful Grams brought up the subject of kids which gave me a necessary perspective, but I'm not.

Instead, I'm making myself crazy, especially today. My performance at the card games Grams loves reflects my distraction, and Drew almost manages to win one game.

Every hold of the car door, every deference to me to place my lunch order first, every thoughtful choice of restaurant with extensive wine choices gets absorbed and added to one column. In the other, only kids and career sit. Yet those two items tip the scales so heavily that even "best sex of my life" tossed on the other side does not equal it out.

I wish I could let myself relax and enjoy our time together, but I'm coiled too tight. My job requires me to plan for anything that could go wrong, and it doesn't turn off for my personal life. It never has. Everything in my life has been planned with precision. School activities, college, now career. Success came because of careful planning. So here I am, anticipating my agony when we end this rather than enjoying the experience. Ugh. I hate my brain sometimes.

After eating an early dinner with Grams in the facility's dining room for a guest fee, we head back to the hotel.

But instead of the hotel, Drew pulls into a strip mall.

"What are we doing?"

"Just hang tight. I'll be back in a second," he says as he unwinds himself from the driver's seat.

He steps into a liquor store and returns with a bottle of wine and six pack of beer.

I grin. Tonight, we're drinking in. Hopefully naked.

"Do you drink beer at all?" he asks when he's back in the car and starting toward the hotel.

"Yeah. I like beer. I just like wine more."

"I'd really like you to try this local beer, then. It's my favorite, although they don't distribute to Texas."

"Sure, I'd love that."

"If you like it, I'll take you to the brewery next time

we're here. They have wood-fired pizza that is delicious. If we're playing up here, I reserve a table for the team and we chow down. They make sure they have extra veggie toppings and salad for us so we don't go completely off our nutrition plans."

"Pretty sure pizza is a central focus of Jack's diet," I say with a snicker.

"Yeah, well, that's going to catch up to him one of these days. But in the meantime, I'm fucking jealous."

I laugh louder.

In the room, he grabs our water glasses and pours me a glass of beer. "It's a pale ale. They have some cool IPAs too, but I love the balance of this one."

I sit on the loveseat and sip. Contemplate with a mock gravity. Sip again.

"You're killing me here. It's not a wine tasting, Let." He's across from me in the rolling chair at the desk.

My façade breaks and I laugh. "I'm totally teasing you. It's really nice. Can I have the whole can? I like ales better than that mouthful of hops in IPAs, and this one has a hint of lemon, almost like a Hefeweizen."

"Oh my god, you can't even drink a beer without making tasting notes?" He laughs, his eyes crinkling, and holds out the beer over his other forearm as though offering a bottle for review. "Of course you can have the can."

I take it, and he grabs one for himself, skipping the glass. He's still grinning, and the starkness of his teeth against his dark beard makes me melt, as always.

I stretch, feeling tired but not in pain from our hike. I've been using the gym at the hotel while I've been here, in between work and visits with Grams. Raising my arms over my head, I roll my shoulders, not considering the effect until Drew's gaze drops to my chest, now arched forward. Liking that, I leave my arms overhead as I straighten my legs along the couch cushion and flex my feet then point my toes.

My calf knots and I fall out of the pose, grimacing and clutching my leg to my body. A long moan of pain escapes me.

Drew sets his beer down and is up and hovering over me as he asks, "What is it? Cramp? Where?"

"Calf," I grunt. The muscle won't relax.

He grabs my leg and tugs it straight.

I whine, "Ooww."

"Shh. I got you." His fingers run lines down the sides of my calf. Then with one hand he uses his thumb and index finger to squeeze the muscle a little as he lengthens it. His other hand holds my foot in a flexed position, trying to force the muscle to elongate. The knot unwinds, a little at a time. His strokes increase in pressure, and he flexes and points my foot.

"Fuck, that hurts still," I say, then quickly add, "But it's so much better now, thank you. Well done."

"Many of us get them during training camp no matter how prepared we think we are. We learn from the physical therapists. Stretch it last thing before you go to bed and first thing when you wake up, and it should walk off."

"Yeah, I know, but it's always hard to believe when it's agony and won't stop. Especially when I'm alone and have to work it out myself."

His hand finally gentles, running up and down my leg in a soothing motion. "Happy to help."

My beer is getting warm, but his hands on my leg are giving me other ideas. "Could you help me with another ache?"

"Of course."

I snicker. He's in gentleman mode, and while it's sexy as hell, that's not what I'm looking for right now.

"It's farther up my leg."

He brings my foot to his chest and puts both hands on my thigh.

"Higher."

My tone and the smirk I've allowed to show finally clue him in.

"It aches, you say? Sometimes smacking it can resolve that," he mock threatens with a raised hand.

"Nope, it definitely needs a gentle massage. Maybe with your tongue."

"I feel like you might be using me for my massage skills."

"So?"

He shrugs. "I like it."

We break into laughter. Scooping his arms under me, he gestures with a nod. "Grab our beers. We might want a post-coital beverage."

I laugh and grab them as he transfers me to the bed and proceeds to massage me to yet another mind-blowing orgasm.

Another check in the "I wish this could last" column.

* * * *

Drew has been texting the realtor about the house purchase. Apparently, Christina reassured him it's a solid investment and affordable without jeopardizing his safety net of savings. I got the feeling she tiptoed around the subject—no one says "injury" or "retirement" to hockey players—but also made him realize it might be good to have two housing options without renters for him and Grams should his horizon for playing change.

We've made a plan to talk Monday evening once I'm back at the hotel. However, my laptop has been on the fritz all afternoon, and our IT department can't seem to figure out the problem. If I was in the office, they'd switch it out for a loaner or a new one. Instead, I'm here, trying to get shit done by phone and email on my phone, without access to any files, slowly losing my mind.

So when Drew calls, I'm barely coherent. "Hey."

"You okay?" He's apparently fluent in Saylet because he can tell something's up from one stinking word. "What's going on? Is it Grams?"

Fuck, I didn't mean to worry him. "No, no, she's fine. And I am too, other than this POS laptop and this POS VPN."

"Huh?"

"I can't connect to my files on the company's shared drive. And IT has been working on my laptop for like five hours and still can't fix it."

"Do you need to come home?"

I'd already been contemplating that, and the idea of Drew being on hand to talk me off the ledge played a bigger part than I'd like to admit. Meanwhile, we're both referencing his place as "home," and my apartment's management company has gone radio silent on me about the inspection. But once that's done, the building will reopen and he won't to be there to soothe the savage beast in me, so I better not get used to having him around.

He's still talking. "I probably can't get you out tonight, but first thing."

"I don't know. But seriously, Drew. Five fucking hours? Are they paid by the hour or something to drag it out?" I'm pacing the hotel room.

"What can I do to help?"

I almost scream, *Stop being such a nice fucking guy. It's making it harder to contemplate stopping.* "Nothing unless you're an IT expert as well as one of the best hockey players around."

He chuckles. "Do you have email on your phone?"

"Yes. I've been trying to work via that. But for so much of it, I need to reference data, and that's behind the firewall."

"Do you want me to go into the office and download stuff and overnight it on a zip drive?"

"What? That's crazy. You have enough on your plate. I'd never ask someone to do that." *Ohmigod, please stop.* First, it would feel like I was taking advantage of our friendship when he's been working all day. Second, *too fucking nice.*

"You didn't ask. I offered."

I think I hear him mutter, "kind of like with the apartment, stubborn woman." But I'm distracted by my laptop screen coming back to life, and the tech's voice over a videocall on the computer asking if I'm there.

"Thanks. They might have solved it, so I gotta go. If not, I'll call you back."

After hanging up, I realize I never asked him about next steps on the house purchase or anything about his day. I'm a selfish bitch on top of being a stress case.

He deserves better.

* * * *

They did indeed fix my computer. I ended up working until midnight, which is one o'clock in the morning for Drew, before I thought to let him know.

Even with my self-absorption, I miss him like crazy, despite him having only been here for two days and gone for two.

Grams is walking amazingly well on flat ground, so I think her discharge will come sooner than later, but she still struggles with stairs. Her therapy sessions are focused on that now.

On Tuesday, I'm working in the care facility's dining room when my next meeting pops up. Kayla wants to talk about new contracts that have been signed with vendors for the mezzanine, and what promotion we'll be required to do for them.

It's mid-morning and no one is around, so I turn on video for the call, happy to see my friend's face. "Hi! I miss you."

"Hey there. I miss you, too, stranger. When will you be back? We should get drinks. It'll be hockey season madness again before you know it."

"That sounds great. I should be in the office next week, at least as far as I know." I've already told her I'm helping a friend out with a family member who needed support.

"So where are you, anyway?"

"Up north. The weather is fantastic." As I say it, I raise the coffee cup I brought in when I delivered Grams's favorite coffee.

Kayla gasps. "You're in Duluth?"

Shit. "Duluth Coffee Company" is on the paper cup. My eyes close in a long blink. Recovering, I say, "Yeah. Like really north."

Her brow furrows. "Wait, hasn't Drew been flying up there to help his grandmother after a fall…" Her eyes go wide. "Saylet—"

"Please," I say over what she was going to say. Every last fear I've entertained about risking my job by getting involved with a player will come true if someone in the office hears her. "Are you in a conference room? Am I on speaker?"

"Shit. No. Yeah. Hang on." She works in an office like mine, but we all keep our doors open, and when we really want no interruptions, we use one of several conference rooms that are farther away from curious ears.

I get an unfocused view of a dark keyboard jogging up and down as she partially closes the screen and walks. I attempt to get my heartrate and breathing back to normal, although dread still pounds through my body. My meak's warning echoes in my ears. My career is my path to independence, and I should never jeopardize it.

Then she's back, putting ear buds in as she holds a finger up to ask me to wait. "Okay. I'm in the little conference room in the corner now, and I have ear buds in. Sorry."

"Look," I say in an urgent tone, hoping I can make her believe what I'm about to say. "There's nothing nefarious going on. But I'd rather not start any more office gossip than necessary. He's a friend. I'm helping him. His grams is fantastic. End of story. I promise."

"Nothing whatsoever to do with the fact that when we ranked the players as they were signed, you put him as sexiest, then?" she muses.

"Nothing. Stop it." I mock glare. "The eye candy makes for a nice reward for helping."

We both laugh.

"I still want to know what that beard feels like," she says.

I bite the inside of my cheek so I don't get lost in contemplating how it feels—against my mouth, my breasts, my pussy. Moving the conversation to safer ground, I say, "I'll keep you posted about my return date, but it should be Monday. Now, let's talk about promotions."

I manage to hold it together for the call and take really good notes, since nothing is sinking in right now. But this sort of thing I can do in my sleep, so I'm not worried.

What *is* concerning me is the fact that Kayla knows. I'm ninety percent sure she won't tell anyone. However, if she could find out, someone else could as well. My computer left open, a receipt from a store falling out of my bag, Drew describing an experience too similar to my own.

We're playing with fire, and we have to stop.

Chapter Twenty-Seven

Drew

I just walked into my condo and am contemplating what is left in the freezer to eat when my phone rings and "Let" shows on the screen. Sliding my thumb to answer it, I say, "Hi. How was your day?"

"Busy. Listen, Drew, Grams is doing great. I'll give you details in a minute, but I wanted to start by telling you I have to get back to Austin. I'm sorry I can't stay longer."

We originally talked about her staying the week then me coming up for one more weekend, but that was already subject to change if I'm buying the little old house. Anyway, I'm beyond thrilled with the amount of time she's already put in to help someone she'd never even met, so I'll happily flex to her schedule.

On the other hand, I can't help wondering what's changed. She seemed ready to stay if the tech guys were able to fix her computer last night, but she sounds tense now. I daren't ask what's wrong again for fear of sounding like I'm trying to push her to stay. "Hey, no problem. I'm super grateful for everything you've been able to do already. You've saved me a lot of stress and sleepless nights."

"Thanks. Grams' next door neighbor showed up this afternoon with a bottle of bubbly she smuggled in," Let says.

I bark a laugh. Only Grams.

"I left them to it, but asked a nurse about alcohol and her meds, framing it as for when she goes home. When I went back two hours later, her neighbor was leaving and Grams was asleep. There was still more than a third of the bottle, so they didn't go too wild. And the neighbor was taking the bus home."

"Ah, thanks for thinking of all that."

"I can stop in to see her tomorrow with her favorite coffee delivery and look for a flight midday. They're talking about her getting out early next week, she's improving with stairs so much."

"Okay. I'm not sure I can have the house purchase finished by then, but I'll do my best. And I can talk to them when I'm there this weekend. Now, let me grab my computer and book your flight."

Five minutes later, we've found a flight that works for her. She'll be home around six.

Fuck. Sorry, Grams. I correct myself. She'll be at my place around six.

But I refuse to dwell on the negative future. Grams is in good hands, I'll be there this weekend, and now I get Let's company back. I might even get a home-cooked meal tomorrow night. All is right with the world.

* * * *

Of course today's schedule is backloaded. It should have been a light day, meeting with the reps for donated gear and spending some quality time working out. But they requested afternoon appointments. After that, I'll need to guess at who needs what, based on which kids were in the earlier camp and the clothing sizes their parents gave which invariably change, given how fast kids grow. But having a starting set for each child to try on will expedite the administrative portion of the first day.

The few players in town tend to work out in the afternoons, but now I have to fit mine into morning hours. I run for stamina, but ideally when I can't be on skates, I choose rollerblades. Grabbing mine, I head to a 3-mile loop south of town where I can race the cyclists and rollerbladers while weaving between the runners.

On the way home to shower, I arrange for a private car pickup for Let so she's not out of pocket for a rideshare. I text her once she's in the air, so she can't argue with me about it. Satisfied I've managed to take care of my prickly pear of a friend, I start my meetings on a high but become frustrated when they run long.

Finally, I walk into the condo just before seven. The spicy tomato-y tang of Mexican food hits my nose, making me grin. Let's phone is once again paired to Alexa blaring her feminist anthems. We'll never agree on music—the one con to having all the pros of Let in the kitchen.

Striding around the bar, I grab her in a hug, getting my fix of her hair fragrance as I sniff her like a hit of cocaine.

"Hi. I see you're happy to have your personal chef back," she says with a laugh.

I smack her ass with one hand, still clutching her to me with the other. "That's not it, and you know it. I missed you. I like having you here."

"Aw, thanks." We studiously avoid the fact that her apartment could be ready any day. I'll never ask about that; I like her here with me too much.

"Um…so what's for dinner?"

She laughs and shoves me away. "You've eaten half the stuff I froze for you. Feeding you on a permanent basis would be a full-time job."

I wince. She said "would be" as though it's purely hypothetical, reminding me that this relationship has an end date.

Wait, since when is this a relationship? We've always been temporary, and my career is as important to me, so I have no right to criticize, even in my own head.

She fits me so well. A fireball to meet my intensity. An organizer who thinks as far ahead off the ice as I do on it. A soother to my stress. A partner. However, I'm keenly aware of the no fraternization policy at work for both of us and would never jeopardize her future with the organization.

I set our places at the bar, pouring two waters for us and wine for her. I drank too much in Duluth, but enjoying my time with Grams and Let was important.

But we're only weeks away from training camp now. It's time to focus.

"Here ya go." Let slides a plate in front of me. Enchiladas are one of my favorite dishes of hers. Even better, she goes out of her way to make tomatillo sauce—who makes that stuff when you can buy it?—and pours a small batch into a separate pan partway through to spice it up. Her plate is doused in sauce that looks radioactive, although most of that's in my head.

"Delicious, as always. Thank you," I say through a mouthful of yumminess.

"Is your camp next week the same as the last one then?" We'd talked about the vast range of interpretations of the "knowing how to skate" requirement parents applied in putting their kids in the Intro to Hockey class. Some of them couldn't have had more than three lessons.

"No, this will be for kids who took one of our beginner weeks or have played some amount of hockey elsewhere. Hopefully, we'll have enough to run some scrimmages. We do on paper, but you never know with people's summer schedules."

I clean up dinner as she puts leftovers into the freezer. In no time, we're on the couch debating what we're going to watch, with her lamenting that she should be working.

"Fine." I give in. "You have half an hour to work."

"I need at least two hours." She groans as she considers that.

"One hour. That's it. Just enough time to digest."

"Oh?" She looks at me, then it registers, and a grin spreads across her face. "Oh."

I make her a chai and set a silent alarm on my phone. An hour later, I power the TV off, stride over, and slide an arm under her knees and another around her back. "Last chance to save your work."

She hits a button, and it's dessert time for me.

Chapter Twenty-Eight

Saylet

Kayla and I are back in our office routine, meeting for coffee in the kitchen.

"You look well rested," she comments, looking around. "You sure you and the hot player are just friends?"

I slant her a withering look from the coffee machine. "First, that makes no sense. If he was keeping me up all night, I'd look tired." Might as well throw her off the scent. "Second, yes, I'm sure."

Her words resonate, however. I'm not only better-sexed, I am better rested, because Drew forces me to stop working when I'd otherwise be typing away until I drop. And Drew is better fed, making it a fair trade.

If only we didn't work for the same company. But her comments also prove how unsustainable my situation is.

As I return to my office, my phone pings with a notification from my apartment's management company.

Thumbing it open, I skim the email, then reread it.

"Fuck." My apartment has passed inspection and is habitable again. This should be good news. In fact, it is great news. I'll have all my things, my own space, and can watch what I want on TV without a debate. Yeah.

It's good news. Maybe if I say it enough times, I'll believe it.

Swallowing hard against the urge to cry, I set my jaw. Temporary was fun. But it's over now. That thought hurts way more than it should after we've been clear on the limits of our situationship. But somewhere along the way, it became a relationship. Maybe because it was rooted in friendship. Maybe because he's such a nice fucking guy, who is easy to lov—

Double fuck. Falling in love with Drew would be incredibly stupid. Nevertheless, the more I examine the unique combination of attraction, fondness, and comfort I feel with him, the more I realize just how stupid I am. I am in love with this amazing guy. Of course I do this; I find the perfect guy in a place that jeopardizes the independence I've fought so hard for. Unfortunately, my newfound knowledge doesn't change anything other than clarifying how much the next season is going to suck.

It takes everything I have to focus on work and remain productive the rest of the day.

At home—*no.* At Drew's place, I abandon the laptop and cook three different meals, freezing individual portions. Drew texted he was hanging with a few team members for a beer because he leaves tomorrow for Duluth.

I'm sweaty and tired from all the cooking when he walks in. He stops short by the bar, looking surprised at the trail of pots and pans I've left across the counter from stove to sink. But he only raises his eyebrows for a moment before entering the kitchen to kiss my cheek and wash his hands.

I let out a breath at his acceptance. I've debated all

day whether to tell him or not, but I think I'm going to do that in the morning. No reason for him to be miserable all night too.

What makes you think he'll be miserable?

My devil's advocate is in rare form today. Shutting down the voice of doubt, I plate two portions of chicken mole and set them out on the bar at our usual places.

"Thanks, Let." He waits for me to sit before lifting his fork.

"I'll do the dishes. I got a little carried away."

"Like hell you will. Dishes are unskilled labor. I can do that. What I can't do is make anything anywhere near as tasty as this food."

After dinner, I go shower. All my stuff has migrated to his bathroom, so I head in there. Afterward, I grab a fresh pair of underwear and my favorite robe that Drew loves to hate. He's still finishing up in the kitchen, and I should go help him, but I slip into his bed instead to rest for a minute.

* * * *

I wake to Drew sliding into bed behind me and drawing me close. Shit, I fell asleep.

"Sorry," I mumble.

"Hey, it's okay to be tired sometimes."

"About the dishes."

"Shh."

But I'm awake now, and I don't want to waste time sleeping. This is probably the last time I'll be in Drew's arms and bed. I'll be damned if I don't enjoy my friend, who is also the best lover I've ever had, while I can.

I roll over, shedding my loosened robe as I go.

"Let," he groans in a half-hearted protest as he stares

at my breasts.

"I'm suddenly re-energized. And I thought we talked about you wearing too many clothes to bed." I'm tugging at his t-shirt and cotton sleep pants.

"I thought we were going to sleep," he says.

"Well, we're not. Off." I abandon the shirt to untie the drawstring at his waist and snake my hand inside. The hot pipe of his hardening cock feels like it's made for me, despite its vastness and my short fingers.

He groans again, this time in pleasure, and makes short work of his clothes.

I slide over to straddle him.

He skims his hands over my skin, touching all his favorite parts but also all the bits in between. I love when he does this—my nerve endings come alive, suddenly noticing the waft of the ceiling fan and the coolness of the air conditioning.

He crunches to suck my nipple, and I enjoy his ripped abs under my fingers almost as much as the pulls of his mouth and the spiraling pleasure they produce.

Planting a hand behind him, he rises higher to kiss me as his other hand splays low on my belly, his thumb toying with my clit.

My hands roam all over him. The velvet-covered granite sensation against my palms makes me ache. No, not ache. I crave more, so I slide forward and back a couple times.

He lies back and grabs my hips. I lock my leg muscles against his thighs, leaning sideways to grab a condom. This time it's not going to be about me. While he says he enjoys feasting on my most sensitive flesh, I want us to climb the mountain of ecstasy together tonight. My only need tonight is to watch him every second so I can sear the memories into my brain.

He protests with a mumbled, "Let me taste…"

Ignoring him, I roll the condom on and position him at my entrance. Two nudges and he's inside. Two deeper ups and downs and my butt rests on his rock hard thighs. A smile of temporary satisfaction is on my face.

"Damn, Let. You are so gorgeous." He brushes my hair back from my face.

"You're not half bad yourself," I gasp out as I bring my feet under me. I'm squatting on him now, and the angle is incredible. I raise myself and then drop down.

"Be careful, Let. You're so tiny; I don't want to hurt you."

I almost wish it would hurt, just a little. It would better reflect my feelings right now. But no, instead, this angle has him sliding against a spot inside that makes me see stars on each glide out, each slam in. "Fuck, Drew."

He's holding my hips to help me raise and lower myself, but can barely keep up with my new pace.

I'm at double time, the pleasure making my eyes roll back in my head. "Drew…Drew, I'm close."

His answer comes through gritted teeth. "So am I. Come, Let. Come on my cock."

The words push me over as much as the continued passes on my G-spot. I lose all sense of coordination and on my next drop I can only manage to wiggle on him for friction. Rapture bursts like fireworks, hot and sparkly and delicious, over and over with each scrub of my pussy against his groin.

When my squirming slows, he holds me a couple inches aloft and pistons up into me, his mouth in a grimace of concentration, his eyes still on mine. His lids droop and his mouth softens as his release pulses against my walls, sending aftershocks through me.

Fuck, how am I going to live without him? His concern even when I'm controlling our pace and the ever-fucking-lasting gentlemanliness making sure I get mine are only the tip of the iceberg of what I'll miss about this man.

After he cleans us both, he pulls his t-shirt and loose pants back on and curls his body around me.

As his breathing evens out, I contemplate and discard all sorts of crazy schemes of how we could continue this. No matter whether we do it openly or secretly, the truth would eventually come out, and it would hurt my career. As for the rest of me, I should have let him give me that first orgasm with his mouth, to last me longer.

I'm already hurting from the loss of him even as I lie in his arms.

Chapter Twenty-Nine

Drew

Let is gone from the bed when I wake up, which is unusual. Curious, I wander out to the kitchen. She hands me a cup of coffee, but her good morning smile is missing. Something's up.

"Any big plans for the weekend? Maybe a crazy drunken bash here while I'm away? Don't do anything I wouldn't do," I say, trying to keep it light.

"Actually, my apartment management company sent a note yesterday. I'm free to move back in. So I figured I'd get my stuff transferred back without disturbing you, while you're up north."

Shit. No wonder she looked grim. I probably do as well now. I clear my throat. "You know, if you wait, I could help you."

She looks into her coffee, a curtain of black hair falling between me and her expression. Her response when it comes is quiet. "Waiting would make it harder."

Part of me perks up. She doesn't seem to like the idea of moving out any more than I do. I'm at a loss, so I try teasing again. "Nah, it'll make it easier. Check out these muscles."

She doesn't glance up. "Thank you for everything. Before I leave, I'll finish restocking your freezer."

"Let, I'm a grown man. I can feed myself, I promise."

"Not on those canned vegetables and boxed pastas." She shudders.

"Okay, I'll try to do better. I can stir fry. And I know how to make salad."

She snorts. Progress!

"You've also expanded my order-in options quite a bit. Anyway, I'll be fine. Take care of yourself."

"It's the least I can do after staying so long." Her tone is wooden.

"Are you kidding?" Now I'm mad. Not only does this woman have problems asking for help, she won't accept it when offered. "What the hell were the last few weeks about? You helping me. In a way that took far more effort than offering an otherwise-unused bedroom and bathroom, and getting all sorts of delicious home-cooked meals in return. Trust me, we're not even, but not in the way you're thinking."

She says to the wall, "Speaking of, say hi to Grams for me."

"Say hi to her yourself. Are you going to drop both of us like hot potatoes because of an address change? I thought we were friends."

Turning to face me, she replies, "We were—are. Will be. But I might need some time to readjust."

"I need a minute." I pace into the living room. When that's not enough to calm me down, I stalk down the hall and back.

When I hit the intersection of the hall, kitchen, and living room, she steps into my path, having read my thoughts. Another way she's a perfect partner. "I wish there was a different way. But Kayla already guessed and is teasing me. I trust her to keep it quiet, but the threat is real. You said you understood when I told you my career is the one that would suffer. And then where would I be?"

With me. The words are a roar in my head, but that's not fair to her. I'm not willing to walk away from my career to be with her. Not after how hard I fought to get to the NHL. So I can't ask her to. I say the only thing I can, my voice flat. "I did understand. I still do."

She nods once and turns toward her bedroom, for the first time in weeks.

"But, Let," I say, my voice rough. She turns. "Please don't take too much time. I miss you already. Even if I can't have all of you, I need my friend."

Tears well in her eyes, and my throat is so tight I couldn't say another word if I tried, so we leave it there.

* * * *

Grams of course notices how despondent I am. I lose at rummy faster than normal, I'm so distracted.

Finally, she sweeps the cards into a pile and reboxes them. "What's up?"

I attempt a smile. "Nothing."

"How's Saylet?"

I shrug one shoulder. "Fine. She got the all-clear to move back into her apartment."

"Ahhh."

I grimace. "Don't start with that."

"I said one syllable." She's innocence personified.

"You always start a lecture that way."

"Now, boy, we've had this discussion before. I do *not* lecture. I impart wisdom. Sometimes it takes more words than others, because you don't listen well."

I manage a chuckle at her oft-used refrain, although mine is short-lived.

She settles back in the recliner across from my visitor's chair. "What's the one rule I taught you to live by?"

Oh man. That's a trick question. She's given me dozens of rules to live by, but she likes to make me guess to justify her lecture—I mean, imparted wisdom. I start with my favorite because it butters her up. "To respect my elders?"

"That's a good one, but no. Although, given Saylet is older than you by a few years, it also applies. Where there's a will, there's a way."

Dammit, I wish there was. I shake my head.

"Don't shake your head at me. You've given up. You've thought about it and couldn't figure out how to make it work, so you've given up and you're wallowing. Where would you be if you did that after your first missed shot in hockey, your first loss, or your first losing season?"

"But—"

"No buts." She wags her finger. I hate it when she does that.

"Fine." I'll say it without the "but," but the statement stands. "Hockey is something I can control. Saylet is not."

"This is what I mean. You don't listen well. And it's why you torture yourself after every game. You think you should have done better, because it's all within your control. I keep trying to tell you—it's not. Sometimes the goalie *is* that good. Sometimes the team as a whole can't close the deal. Yet you persevere. You do what you can and hope they'll do the same. Do that with Saylet, and you'll find a way."

"I can't push too hard, because it's not my job at

stake. Saylet has so much more to lose, and she's as career-oriented as I am."

"Right, just like you can't send the puck down the other end too fast, or you'll get called for icing. Work within the parameters of the relationship you're in, like hockey."

"You always amaze me with your hockey analogies."

"It's my love language," she jokes.

I laugh for real this time. "Okay, okay, I'll keep thinking. So I hear you're doing really well in here."

"Yes! I can already do one flight of stairs. I'm working on the second one. Although I'm not entirely sure I could do the one flight plus walk to the store and back."

"You're going to have to give in and let me order groceries for you, just for a few weeks."

"I suppose."

"I have some good news for you, though."

"Oh yeah?"

I've been working the phone with the realtor the past week for the old house Saylet picked out. "I'm doing a walkthrough of that little house this afternoon. I'll take a bunch of pictures and bring them back to you this evening."

She grins at me. "Saylet's such a smart young woman. I'm so excited she found that for me."

I huff. "Oh, sure, she gets all the credit. I'm the one making sure it's safe and buying it for you."

She rolls her eyes at me. "You're such an 'only child.' Of course, you get credit as well, along with all the other times you offered to buy me things I don't need. This particular thing was her idea, so you'll have to share. You know, like when you pass the puck instead of taking a shot."

I laugh. She can't resist. "You're definitely feeling better. More good news—the doctor says you can be released as soon as the house is ready. Given that there are only a few steps in and out of the house, and I'll get a housekeeper/helper to do laundry, you'll be free to go within days."

She claps her hands. "Drew! That's fantastic. And my friends are going to be so jealous of me having a house. I'm so happy about going home that I'll wait to argue with you about a helper another time, even though you know no one does my laundry except me."

I shake my head, grinning. I love making the most important woman in my life happy, but a pang of despondency hits at the thought I can't do that for the newest most important woman.

* * * *

My condo is unnaturally silent, empty. It never felt that way before, but Let changed things. Oh sure, she added sports magazines to the coffee table which are still there. And a few new spatulas and whatnots in the utensil holder by the stove. But it's the lack of *her* that makes it so empty.

I could live without her delicious meals if I got her.

Frowning, I tell myself to get over it. Pursuing her wouldn't be fair, given how far she's already come in her career.

Where there's a will, there's a way. Grams' voice is in my head.

Staring at the living room, I realize I'm weeks behind on watching last season's game tape. Even before Grams' fall, I spent most evenings watching shows Let picked out on TV or eating her pussy until she came before pounding into her.

Ugh, now I'm hard, recalling her delicious taste. I have to refocus. We broke up because she wants a career, yet here I am pining for her instead of studying ways to improve.

When we lost our last game of the post-season in May, there were three relaxing months stretching before me. A little golf, coaching kids at my favorite pastime, and time with Grams. Then a little dark-haired whirlwind ended up in my apartment. June's golf was eclipsed by nightly sexcapades. July started fine with the first camp until Grams fell. Soon, I'll head to Arizona to join a few members of the team at some vacation rental Christina and Cam decided to rent for a week around Labor Day. So between finishing the kids' camps and buying Grams her house, the rest of August is going to be a blur. Which I'm grateful for because I have too much time in this place missing Let right now. But also I'm starting to sweat because I haven't done my homework.

So, hockey. Not Let. If I want a long-term contract, I have to do better. I have to be as close to perfect as any player can get. No more comments from broadcasters about my shooting percentage not being worth what I'm paid, like I got in Florida. No more complaints about me hogging the puck. I have to find the perfect balance of shooting and passing. Or—I run a hand over my beard— as Grams would put it, maintaining control and giving it up.

I sit down, hard-on thoroughly erased, and cue up a game from January. It's going to be a long few weeks before the season starts, getting through four months of regular season games, never mind the playoffs. And I'll have to do it around Christina and Cam's week-long house party before training camp. As generous an offer as it was, the only reason I agreed to join them was to get out of this condo and the memories of Let. And Christina promised to ensure we'll get a decent amount of ice time.

After one period, I get up and heat one of Let's meals. Her note on the container reminds me to make a salad for some fresh vegetables with it. I grab the bin of prewashed lettuce—she knows me—and throw it in a shallow pasta bowl. When the meal comes out of the microwave, I just dump it on the lettuce rather than making an actual salad. That'll work.

After eating and finishing the second period, I lean back. Her spicy fruit smell tickles my nose and plumps my stupid Pavlovian dick. I turn my head. The throw smells like her. Damn. I toss it away from me onto the chair, and relax against the couch again.

My half-hard cock is uncomfortably bent in my boxer briefs, and I leave it that way, punishing myself for stupidly wanting Let while I do the same for my past performance on the ice.

After a couple hours of self-flagellation, and not the good kind, I head to bed. Ten minutes later, I come out, grab the fleece throw, and go back to bed, clutching it to me like I would a stuffed animal, glad no one will ever see this version of me.

The following night progresses the same way, except for my phone ringing mid-viewing.

My agent's name lights up the screen. Holy shit. Sweat breaks out under my arms. *Please let this be good news, or at least the start of good news.* "Hey, Charlie. What's up?"

"Buzz!" We go weeks without talking when there

aren't negotiations for contracts or sponsorships going on, and I always forget that he's as high energy as Let. "How's the off season treating you, my man?"

"You know me. Coaching, Grams, and kids—uh, not necessarily in that order." He met Grams once and laughs at my mock fear of having said that out of order.

"Good, good. We went to the beach back in July, but I was on the phone most of the time." He owns not one, not two, but three sets of earbuds so he has one charged and ready to use at all times, so this is not a surprise to me.

"I can imagine." Impatient, I repeat my greeting. "So what's up?"

"Guess who called me?" he says.

"Don't play coy with me. Tell me."

"Aw, all of you ruin my fun. I'm hearing that the Chicago Icedogs might be interested. Apparently, they approached Tampa Bay about a trade when you were with the Storm, and now they like the way you looked in the playoffs. They may be working on a trade offer with the Tornadoes."

Dammit. I really want to stay with the Tornadoes. The team has come together in a single season, and I enjoy being a leader. To be traded would mean building my reputation all over again, unless the Tornadoes don't intend to renew my contract after next year. On July 1, several of us became eligible for contract extensions, but the Tornadoes have been quiet on most of the bigger contracts. As an expansion team with only one season of us playing together, it's not unexpected for the Tornadoes to slow their roll on player negotiations, and the coming season will be a tightrope of deciding how long to wait for them to make their move while Charlie puts feelers out to other teams.

"Chicago asked what you're looking for beyond next year and seemed amenable to what I tossed out."

"Well, there's not a lot we can do. Thanks for letting me know."

"Okay, separate question. What happens if the Donovans only offer a short-term extension. We need to hash out responses to all the possibilities we can consider."

I'm dizzy with fear. What I want for my career is suddenly intertwined with what I want with Let, and I hate feeling this out of control.

"I don't know. You know the devil is in the details, Charlie."

What I really want is for Texas to offer that big long-term package as a contract extension early in the season and avoid the whole summer scramble of figuring out where I'm going as a free agent.

Three months ago, I'd push for all money and not care about a trade. Now, I'm wondering how to stay with a woman who doesn't want me.

"Buzz? You there?"

"Yeah. Just thinking."

"What would you want if the choice was yours?" He and I have gone over my priorities in the past for team location when I get a choice, money, and other terms. But for every contract, whether with a team or a sponsor, he always asks again.

"I'd prefer to stay in Austin. I'll take less money if I have to. On the flip side, the price goes up for me to sign anywhere else." The words come out without thought, from my gut—or my heart. But they feel right.

"Unless you're traded."

"Yeah," I say, my tone flat. "I mean for the next contract."

"If we hold out the Tornadoes could run into the salary cap."

"Yeah." My neutral answer sends the message that I still want what I want.

"Got it. I'm on it. I'll keep you posted. Keep in mind that because Chicago wants you doesn't mean the Tornadoes are willing to let you go." And he's gone.

No sooner do I set the phone on the couch beside me than it rings again. "Hi Grams. You're up late. How's the partying at the rehab?"

She laughs. "Saylet is a tattletale. Never mind my celebrating my health, what are you doing?"

"Just watching TV." I debate telling her about Charlie's call, but it's too early. I don't want her to ride this rollercoaster of hope and fear with me. I'll share when or if it's looking more likely.

"TV, or last season's games? Are you back to your old habits without Saylet there to give you something better to focus on?"

"You'll be happy to know I'm not watching every game from last season."

"Hmph. Does that mean you're running them on fast forward instead?" She's rightfully suspicious. I'm skipping the ones we won and consider that growth on my part.

"Nah. I'm completely skipping some."

"You're hiding something, but I can't figure out what. I wish Saylet was there."

"Me too, Grams." Maybe she could bounce ideas around with me regarding how hard to negotiate on this contract. No, that's what I pay an agent for. But maybe she could distract me from this ball of stress in my belly that won't resolve until the next contract is signed.

"Have you given more thought to my excellent advice?"

No. I've been too busy wallowing. "Yes, but I haven't found a way. Yet." Or I can't see a way. Hence the wallowing. And now the conversation with Charlie is creating chaos.

"Okay, well let me know about the house. And turn that TV off. Go read a book."

"Yes, ma'am. Love you."

"Love you too, Drew-boy."

Chapter Thirty

Saylet

Exhausted, I slump back in my office chair. People in the halls have been giving me strange looks for a couple weeks, and no wonder. I'm not this quiet, tired person. I'm the hyper-efficient, always upbeat…hell, just hyper PR person. Always ready to jump in and make things happen.

I was able to fake it when I first moved back into my apartment, figuring the strangeness would pass, and things would return to normal. Missing Drew was expected—a knife to the gut—but I thought being home would soothe me.

Instead, my apartment feels strange, wrong. The kitchen I loved and pined for when I first had to leave is now unfamiliar. I ended up spending an entire evening rearranging it to mimic Drew's as much as the layout allowed, which is beyond fucked up. My bed is too hard some nights, too soft other nights, and feels inferior to both mattresses I experienced at Drew's. Of course, even at the hotel in Duluth, I slept better when Drew was there than when he wasn't.

I've tried cooking my favorite foods, ordering super spicy meals of all cuisines, and not eating at all. None of it appeals, and all of it seems far lonelier than it did before I lived with Drew. How could two short months change my perspective so thoroughly?

Kayla pokes her head in. "Coffee?"

I nod. Then, finding I can't muster enough enthusiasm to get up, much less walk to the kitchen, I shake my head. I'm glad the heavy lifting for my diversity campaign with the long form interviews and initial promo are done. That deserves better than my current energy level.

"Ah. It's gotten to that point, has it? I'll be right back."

Before I can unravel her comment, she's back with two coffees, mine as black as midnight, the way she knows I like it. "Bless you."

She smiles, closes the door, and plops into a visitor's chair. "Talk to Mama Kayla."

I'm too tired to prevaricate. "Did I tell you about my apartment building being shut down?"

"What? No! Where did you go? You always have a spot with me if you need it." She rolls her eyes. "Not that you'd ever be willing to ask, you self-sufficient nut."

I smile. "Thanks, but this wasn't for a night or two. There was an electrical issue, and they had to close the building for weeks that then turned into two months."

"Holy crap. I can't imagine. I have an aunt a ways out in the suburbs, but I don't know that I could live with her for that long or do that commute. And your family isn't local. What did you do?"

"I couch surfed here for a couple weeks. It was at the beginning of the playoffs so I was out of town half the time anyway, so there were beds. But I couldn't drag weeks worth of stuff in and out of hotels here in between. And I couldn't find a short-term rental that was within my budget and commuting distance."

She's nodding. Housing costs in Austin are no joke these days, whereas a decade and a half ago it was one of the more affordable cities in the country.

"I was still figuring things out when Drew caught me rummaging in my suitcase in my car and insisted I use his guest room." I shrug. "We knew each other well enough from PR gigs that I figured it would be okay for a few weeks. Then it took longer, and his grandmother fell."

Kayla gapes at me for a moment before finding her words. "You were living with Tall, Dark, and Handsome for the past two months?"

I nod. "When I wasn't in Minnesota with his grandmother."

"And you're still going to tell me you're just friends after that? Come on. I don't believe you." She sits back and crosses her arms.

I blush. Gah. I think the last time I blushed was in high school. "We're just friends *now*, in any event."

"Why?"

"You know why." I press my lips together and gesture around us. "I worked my ass off to get here. They like my work and all, but if they had to choose between me and their alternate captain who took them to the Conference Finals in their inaugural year? This is a *hockey* organization. Which means all decisions are made to further the hockey team. I'm expendable. Drew is not."

"Wait, I'm confused." Kayla blinks and shakes her head. "Why should one of you be expendable?"

"Because he's five years younger than me and he doesn't want kids until his career is finished, and he's out of my league, plus a million other reasons. And no one wants to work with an ex." The reasons pour out of me in a jumble and feel just as overwhelming as they have every time I've tried to find a way around them.

"Wow. Okay, that covered a lot of ground. First, you're being cynical and assuming it won't work. Five years is physical. Maturity-wise I think y'all are closer. You're both leaders, driven, excelling in your careers, and obviously compatible in other ways." She wiggles her brows.

My hand flexes on my coffee cup. She doesn't need to remind me of our compatibility. Our sexploits are on repeat every night as I try to sleep alone.

"He's not out of your league at all. When we go out, you get a ton of interested looks and often get a guy or three asking to buy you a drink. That's like the non-hockey equivalent of puck bunnies. As for kids—have you even had a conversation with him about that?"

"No." Grams pretty much took care of that for us. I wasn't going to beat myself over the head with another painful reason we don't work. "We agreed the…affair would be short-term because neither of us is willing to jeopardize our careers."

"So you ended it when you moved back to your apartment?" At my nod, she continues. "Why not enjoy the rest of the off season?"

I fidget with the sticky note pad and pen on my desk, unable to meet her eyes.

"Because it isn't casual to you anymore." She leans forward and squeezes my free hand. "Oh, babe. I'm sorry. I really think you should see where it goes. We've seen that the no-fraternization rules aren't enforced—"

I interrupt her. "For an owner."

"And a player. And you're both professionals."

"I won't risk it. Don't you remember us talking during the season about him and Kyle Scott and Jack Landry all being playa' players?"

"Yeah. But there was less of that toward the end of the season, at least by two out of the three."

Now that I think about it, she's right. The biggest player, Jack, doesn't seem to have told anyone about his suspicions around Drew and me. And Kyle's struggles have gone quiet after the arrest. "True. Sometimes all it takes is the right woman. He's close with his grandmother?"

"Very." The fact that she raised him from a young age is not my information to share.

"So what are you going to do?"

I shrug. "Get over him."

"How's that going for you?" she asks with a laugh.

"Okay, I paid you back for the coffee with way more gossip than I should have. Out with you." I jokingly shoo her. "But please, don't say—"

"Anything to anyone. Of course I won't. Maybe drinks one night this week?"

"Sure." Anything beats being in my too-quiet apartment.

* * * *

On Thursday, we head to a new bar in North Austin that someone in the office recommended to Kayla.

There are a few women I don't know that well, since I spend much of my time with upper management, the team, and investors. But Sara and LaRhonda are there too, and everyone is sharing their summer vacation stories.

By the second drink, we've moved on to discussing

how well the "new face of the NHL" campaign is going. The interviews have been in the local paper, local cable news, and on a hockey podcast, but I'm still gunning for *The Hockey News* or even *Sports Illustrated*. We will continue to build material for the project until the season, at which point hockey itself will rightly take over.

It's my turn to get a round, so I scoot to the edge of the stool and do a little jump to get to the floor. I pivot toward the bar and stop short.

Drew is there with Cam, Lukas, and a couple other guys I can't see clearly through the crowd. He's facing me and smirking at my hop to the floor.

Inhaling, I close my eyes to gather my courage, open them again and stride to the bar. When he slides to one side, I'm forced to be polite and use the gap he's created to place my order.

His gaze sweeps the length of me, stopping at the V neck of my white short sleeved sweater. A second later, a sidelong glance catches him visually tracing my curves down to the black four inch heels I wear to give me extra height. I'm suddenly conscious of the thinness of my bra and the skin on display because of my short skirt. It's as though his mere presence shifts the air around me and beads my nipples, giving me goosebumps. Fucking too-hot hockey player doesn't have to touch me. Hell, he doesn't have to say a word.

I nod and then lean forward over the bar to place my order.

Tilting his head, he says, "How are you, Saylet?"

My jaw clenches. He's back to using my full name. Although maybe that's because the other guys are around. "Fine, thanks. How are you?" I am nothing if not professional. After all, that was the point of this agony.

Now, it'd be helpful if I could avoid picturing how good he looks under his black t-shirt.

"Good. The last kids' camp finishes tomorrow, then I'm headed up to check out Grams' new house, courtesy of you, then off to some vacation rental Cam and Christina found for the group."

The group. Not one I'm part of, but he's in with an owner as well as the other stars of the team. Another nail in the coffin of my career should anyone find out we'd been together. However, I'm excited to hear about the Duluth house. "Oh, you bought it?"

"Bought it, updated the appliances, and installed a security system. Grams is being released tomorrow, so the moving company should have moved her stuff today. Then I'll have to stop her from trying to unpack and place everything herself. Not what we envisioned for our summer time together, but I think she's looking forward to it."

"I don't think she cares what y'all do, as long as she gets time with you."

"I feel the same," he replies with a soft smile.

Our drinks arrive and I gather them to carry over to the ladies' table.

"Do you want help?"

I can't refuse without seeming rude, so I nod and slide three over for him to carry.

Kayla arches a brow when he follows me to the table, but he waves hello to everyone and then heads back to his friends. Ever the fucking gentleman.

What would you prefer, dumbass? That he take you to the bathroom and bend you over the sink for a quickie? Fuck. I should probably stop drinking now. His proximity and that vision have me way too hot and bothered to censor myself.

Sara fans herself and says, "That man is hot enough I'd risk the beard burn on my thighs."

"Eh, the hot ones never do that. They're all about themselves," LaRhonda says with a dismissive snort.

Kayla, ever the annoying friend, asks, "What do you think, Saylet?"

I stare her down while I respond to Sara. "I think if it's long enough, it won't burn. But it depends on the hair, too. You should ask to touch it."

"Imma need another drink for that," Sara says with a little wiggle on her barstool.

Kayla arches a brow and shakes her head, but stops pushing.

I gulp my drink down and decide I don't want to hang around and wait for Sara to find the courage to pet Drew. Excusing myself, I ignore the fact that I've got a little too much of a buzz to drive safely and head out.

I'm almost to my car in the parking lot when Drew's voice calls, "Let!"

He catches up in another second, using his long, strong legs. The ones that would hold him when he drove himself into me. The muted sun in the dusky evening sky makes him look fierce. Like some ancient warrior. He's a threat and a protector, although he would never mean to be the former.

"Are you really safe to drive?" he asks.

"Probably," I reply with a pouty lower lip. Really, it's not his business any more. Although any friend would be concerned.

"How about a bite to eat first? There's a Chinese place near here we haven't tried yet."

"That's not a good idea."

"Why not?"

"Did Sara pet you?"

His head retracts. "Um, what?"

I'm definitely not safe to drive if that came out. My internal filter gets switched off after a couple drinks. "Okay."

"Okay what? Let, you're losing me. Can you give me a few more words please? You've got that big old brain and mine's just a hockey-sized one."

I giggle. "Or mine's slightly pickled so I'm not as coherent as normal."

He smirks. "I was trying to be nice."

I smack his chest with the back of my hand. "Well, don't. That doesn't help either. But fine, we can get food. Just stay on your side of the table and don't let anyone pet you."

He takes my arm and leads me to his SUV. "Come on, then. You can explain the petting after you've had some scallion pancakes. It sounds fun."

Chapter Thirty-One

Drew

I'm dying to find out where this concern about petting came from. Mostly, my snake brain wants to see how I can use it to my advantage.

As always, Let looks smoking hot, and I've been half-hard since I saw her across the bar. Now I get to have dinner with her. Sure, it's under the guise of friends, but fuck I've missed her.

I can't even think about the coming season. All I can concentrate on is the image of Let with that dark hair loose around her spread out on my sheets for me to feast. Grams' words come back to me. I just need to find the way through this.

At the restaurant, we get seated in a corner and place our order. I get our usual: two waters and one glass of wine. If she rejects it, I'll drink it, but I figure it's worth a shot to keep her loose. No way am I going to let her drive home anyway.

After she's had a couple sips of water and a couple bites of food, I lean forward and ask, "So…who is petting me, and where and when?"

She grimaces and shakes her head. "I'm sorry I said that. It's nothing, just girl talk."

"Come on, if it was about me, and you've already told me the petting part, I deserve to know."

"Fine. One of the girls made a comment about beard burn, and we discussed the type of hair and length of said beard as to whether it would leave marks or not."

"Okay…and I was to be tribute in this quest?"

"Well, yeah."

I frown as a thought occurs to me. "Have I ever scratched you? Did someone say something at work? Dammit, Let, you should have told me."

She reaches over and pats my hand. "It's fine. Once when you'd trimmed it recently there were a few scratches, but they weren't where anyone would see them."

"Oh!" Now I have to shift in my seat to unbend my stiffening cock. "Sorry."

"Totally worth it." She sips the wine the server left in the middle of the table. My ego takes a victory lap, waving and smiling. Then she stares at the glass. "Oops. Now I need more time before I drive home."

"I'll drive you. I can give you a ride to get your car in the morning."

She narrows her gaze at me, suspicious.

I hold my hands up. "It was a friendly offer."

She shrugs and sips again. "You ready for training camp?"

"Mostly." If you count late nights trying to watch old games while wrapped in a throw blanket that distracts the heck out of me.

"Anyone else's contract get finalized?"

"Not that I've heard." Cam's contract had been locked in before the end of our last season, to no one's surprise. A few other players had been offered bridge deals, and still others have a couple years left on their existing contracts which the Tornadoes assumed, including Saint. Only a handful of us are going into our final year. A low level hum of stress has taken up space in my stomach since July 1, and it ballooned when my agent called the other night.

Trying to keep things light, I say, "I'm happy for Cam and Christina. I'm also glad he didn't rake them over the coals and use up more than his share of the salary cap."

She laughs. "How could he? There must be a no-move clause in that contract."

"I don't know. Why would he need a no-move if he and Chris are getting married? Heck, he could be a SAHD."

"A sad?"

"Stay at home dad. The team thread blew up with how 'sad' we'd all be if he did that."

"Hockey boys' humor leaves something to be desired, but yeah, I suppose he could. So Grams is getting out of rehab, huh? Is she excited about moving or having second thoughts?"

"She hasn't said anything to me about second thoughts. How's your place?"

"The same. But weirdly different. I liked having someone to cook for, and you're an easy roommate."

"With benefits, no less." I mock-leer at her, but we go silent rather than laughing. Her eyes flare with heat. I run my hand over my beard. "I haven't trimmed my beard recently. So if, say, you wanted to retest, I'm betting there wouldn't be any evidence."

"I shouldn't." She sips the last of her wine.

"That's not a no."

"No, it's not, is it?" she asks, raising a hand to get the server's attention. "Your place?"

I nod as I fiddle with my smartwatch and pay by flipping it over the little handheld device the server brings, adding a tip and signing.

As we walk out to my SUV, I lean toward her. "I was a good boy and stayed on my side of the table. Will you pet me now?"

She sinks against me, her spine a little more fluid from the drinks. Leaning up, she runs a gentle hand over my beard, one cheek after the other.

My body hums with recognition. Her skin, her dark liquid eyes, that mane of dark hair is like home to me. If only I could keep her.

* * * *

I plied Saylet with pills and water to minimize her hangover before we slept. Because my flight was early, it was still dark when I drove her to her car then followed her to her apartment to ensure she was safe before going to the airport. That one night, one taste was not enough, but it'll have to be. At least she's scent-marked my condo again.

The security system in Grams' new house was installed a couple days ago, and movers already packed her apartment and transferred everything. Grams has signed the release paperwork from the rehab center, and I'm taking her to her new home.

"How's Saylet?" They're not the first words out of Grams' mouth, but it's close.

"Still fine."

"Hmm. In more ways than one, don't you think?" Without waiting for an answer, she continues. "When did you see her last?"

I fight the urge to squirm and keep my eyes on the

drawers I'm checking in her room.

"Drew?" she queries.

Dammit, she's not going to let this drop. "Yesterday." Really, early hours of this morning, but let's not pick at nits.

"Excellent." Grams' voice drips with satisfaction. "So you're working on finding a way?"

"No. Look, I'm a doer, not a thinker. She's the smart one in our rela— She's smarter than me. And she hasn't found a way."

Grams rolls her eyes, thankfully not addressing my slip, although from the gleam in her eye she caught it. "Book smarts do not equal life intelligence. Clearly, you both need help. Have you spoken to her about children?"

"What? Of course not. She—we—went into this knowing it was short-term. Because of her *job*. So no, children weren't part of it. We'd have to get past the job thing first, and that would mean one of us leaves Austin."

"You like her a lot, though, right?"

"Yeah."

"More than the women you've slept with in the past?"

I flush. I hate discussing my sex life with Grams. "Yeah."

"So in a relationship," she tips her head and sends me a look telling me not to argue given that I nearly said it a minute ago, "you think of multiple aspects of the future. Whether you like her family, what holidays are most important to each family—by the way, I'm flexible, I'll come to you…"

I laugh, and she grins before continuing. "…your vacation styles, what sort of home you'll live in, where you'll live given your jobs, and children."

"Even on *your* list, they're last. So why are you bringing that up?"

"Because I want great-grandchildren while I'm young enough to enjoy them. But also because you have some things worked out already. For the aspects you don't, like the jobs, sometimes it's easier to have the long game clear to motivate you to work out the other stuff."

I shrug. "She was here when I reminded you I don't plan to have kids until I retire from hockey."

"I know. Did you ever think that's why she hasn't looked for a will or a way? She's a few years older than you, Drew, and she wants children."

I frown. "How do you know?"

"Girl chats when she was up here between your visits."

"Then that's that. Another way we don't work." I love kids, and I enjoy teaching hockey camps every chance I get. Rationally, I know I'll never do what my mother did. However, the amount of time I'd be absent for hockey season could feel the same to a child and that's not something I'm willing to risk.

"My word, you're a stupid man for such a smart boy."

"Hey, now." It was said with love, but still. Also, her saying that means that she's about to school me in one subject or another.

"You say you don't want children because hockey requires so much travel. But with the right partner, you wouldn't be abandoning them. That's the beautiful thing about having a partner. When one needs support, the other steps in."

Hockey has been my sole focus. Kids were always in the future. Grams has a point, but I'm struggling at the abrupt switch, trying to wrap my head around negotiating parenting. "That's a lot to ask of anyone, especially someone who is career-focused. Plus, she travels with the team sometimes."

"First, as evidenced a couple weeks ago, she can work from anywhere at least some of the time. Second, she made it sound like some of her travel is discretionary. Third, all I'm saying is that it's worth a conversation if you love her. Oh, excuse me, like her a lot." She rolls her eyes.

Love? No way. I'm not ready for that. Anyway, that doesn't happen without spending months with someone, knowing them inside and out.

But Grams is always right. And the two months Let and I spent sharing space round the clock is equivalent to five times as many dates. My head spins, unable to process the idea that I could be in love with Let. I clamp that down because I still don't see a way to make this work. "Just because my partner can take care of these hypothetical children doesn't mean I'm willing to miss their formative years."

"With today's technology, you wouldn't. You'd just experience them a little differently. And depending on how you timed them, you'd retire around when they start having school sports and performances and the like."

"What's your point?"

She heaves a dramatic sigh. "My point is you're not your mother. Out of sight won't equal out of mind. But if you don't consider different approaches to a problem, you can't solve it. And if you don't communicate, no relationship will survive."

"Well, this one is dead anyway, so let's leave it in peace." I grab the handles of her suitcases and gesture.

We're done with this place as well as the conversation.

Chapter Thirty-Two

Saylet

The acetaminophen and water Drew made me take before sleeping help. Coffee solves the rest of my drag from a hangover and fewer hours of sleep than normal.

The chafe of beard burn on my inner thighs brings a smile to my face every time I walk. This time it was deliberate. His beard was soft enough it took a bit of effort to get the effect he was looking for. But holy fuck, that man's tongue is worth any scratches.

He said he wanted me to have something to remember him, since he's traveling until training camp starts.

As if I'd forget any of our time together.

On Saturday, I decide to make enchiladas. Except my pan doesn't fit them as well as Drew's. I shop online for a few minutes, but I want them tonight and the pan won't come until at least tomorrow. Nor will I have the energy to make them if I went out and bought the baking dish at a brick and mortar store.

He's not using his. Hell, he's not home, and I doubt he changed the code on his lock. I contemplate for a minute. Fuck it. I text him.

Me

> I hope you don't mind—I'm going to run over and borrow your enchilada pan. I'll repay you by bringing back enchiladas with it to stock your freezer.

No answer after five minutes means he's probably helping Grams unpack, so I grab my keys and go. I've just finished locking my front door when I realize that driving back and forth twice makes much less sense than doing it once. I've cooked over there numerous times. What's one more?

Letting myself back in, I gather the ingredients into a reusable shopping bag and lock up again.

An hour and a half later, the enchiladas are finished and going in the oven—I've decided to eat here, too—when my phone chimes.

Drew

> Of course, you're welcome to my place any time for any reason. Bummed I'm missing them.

> And you.

He's killing me.

Ignoring that text, I give the first one a thumbs up and sit in my usual spot at the bar to eat.

After two bites, I'm fidgety. I enjoy music while I cook, but my music is not conducive to good digestion, more for dancing or raging. The silence is as deafening here as it was in my place, which forces me to admit that the missing piece is Drew. It's not the venue or kitchen layout, or simply getting used to a roommate. It's him—his deep voice, soft beard, and warm arm to cuddle under when watching TV. I grab my enchilada plate and settle on the couch, tugging down the fleece throw on the back as I don't have him to keep me warm.

But when I turn on the TV, it's set to some crazy hockey…channel? App? I don't know. Nor am I sure how to change the input. Drew always handled that.

Navigating the menu, I see their whole season of games stored.

So this is how he tortures himself after games and apparently all summer long. It appears that he's watched through February at this point, but that leaves a lot of games to go, even without the playoffs. He didn't watch these when I stayed here. Well, in the beginning he did while I worked or after I went to bed, but once we were sleeping together, I'm pretty sure he stopped.

Shit, he's probably stressing out about not finishing last season before this one starts. Grams would probably tell me to delete them all, if I even knew how, but I can't do that. Every player, besides being superstitious, has his own method of motivating himself, adjusting his practice, and improving his focus. If this is Drew's, I can't interfere.

And yet, I did just that by being here for those two months.

I'd love my presence to be a different motivation, but that can't happen. I worked too hard to get where I am.

Thinking about my job reminds me of all the emails waiting for me. But I didn't bring my laptop, and I'm too cozy to move right now. The remaining enchiladas are already in his freezer. In a few minutes, I'll get up and load the dishwasher. For now, I'll just snuggle here with the fleece that is a shitty substitute for Drew.

Hours later, I wake to a backlit blank TV screen and the kitchen lights still on. Turning the TV off from its sleep mode, I stagger up and glance in the kitchen. I'm not dealing with that right now. Instead, I grab my phone, flick the lights off, and strip as I walk to Drew's bedroom, bypassing the guest room he gave me at the start of my stay.

In my underwear, I dive under the covers and inhale his pillow. It smells like his lemon and cedarwood bodywash. I smile as I drift back to sleep.

* * * *

Drew

How were they?

Me

Way too spicy for you, LOL.

I hope you took those home then.

Don't worry, I made your gringo level of spice and then added for mine. You have six servings in your freezer.

I thought it made eight? Did you eat with a friend?

His question makes me wonder if he's jealous.

Let?

Okay, he's definitely jealous. Yet another thing that makes me wish I could reassure him as I would a boyfriend.

I'm not allowed to take one additional serving home for me?

Fuck. I just outted myself.

Oh, did you eat them at my place?

Yeah, it was easier to cook there. Not like I don't know where everything is. Is that ok?

Of course, I said that yesterday. Damn, gotta run, our coffees are ready.

Love to Grams, hope the move is going well.

I wander the condo, coffee cup in hand. Drew's coffeemaker makes better coffee than mine, although admittedly that's in part because I left some of my good stuff here. Walking down the hall past the bedrooms, I stare at the laundry closet's louvered doors. His machines are newer and fancier than mine. I would never dare put my silk work blouses and lacy underwear through my machines, even on the hand wash cycle, but I did here. The first time was because I'd neglected to take them to the dry cleaner, but it worked, and I've been saving money on dry cleaning ever since.

After showering in his fancy bathroom, I dress in yesterday's clothes, apply whatever little makeup I have in my purse, and run my errands.

Back at my apartment, I start to unload groceries. Putting the new bag of coffee into the cabinet, I eye the almost full bag already there.

Huh. I shopped as though I was replenishing Drew's kitchen. I stare at the half-unpacked grocery bag.

Fuck it. He said any time, any reason. Refusing to consider the fact that I'm undoing any progress I'd made in getting over him, I repack the bag and throw any perishables from the fridge into another bag. Hauling them downstairs, I return for my laundry basket then my roller bag with clothes for the week.

Two loads of laundry and another family-sized meal later, I section it out to package up Drew-sized servings for the freezer. I've already used the easy-to-reach plasticware from the pantry for the enchiladas, so I need to find what he did with the other ones I bought as he emptied them. I spy a box tucked in the back corner on the pantry floor and see he hasn't yet started placing things up high again.

Kneeling, I tug it forward and open it. Canned vegetables, boxed mashed potatoes, and macaroni and cheese fill the space. I gasp, sitting back on my heels. My heart breaks as I picture him fighting himself in the store as he loaded his cart, hiding these away out of…guilt? Embarrassment? I never want him to feel ashamed. With me or anyone.

I consider unpacking it, but this isn't my home, I'm just squatting. Even if we were together, my last misstep with the pantry reminds me that it's not my place to rearrange anything. But damn if it doesn't make me want to cook him enough that he'd need a second freezer, so he'd always have enough healthy food to eat.

I find the plasticware in a corner cabinet that had previously been empty, and finish cleaning the kitchen. Ignoring the emails still calling my name, I snuggle on the couch with his fleece throw and read a book—a luxury I haven't attempted since my last trip to see my family at the holidays. I manage not to fall asleep there this time, and shift to his bed for the night.

Waking rested and energized for the first time in weeks, I head into the office, where Kayla immediately gives me shit.

"Huh. You getting some again? The bags under your eyes are half as dark as they were. Ohh, if that's makeup, you must tell me the brand."

"It's not makeup."

"Sex then?"

"Nope. Just a good night's sleep." *In a bed not my*

own, but whatever.

"Huh. What changed?"

"I moved"—well, that part's true, anyway—"on."

She gives me some side-eye but says only, "If you say so. Where is the bearded beauty these days?"

I grimace at her ridiculous nickname for him. "Duluth. Then who-knows-where. Apparently there's a vacation rental somewhere some of the players have been invited to."

"Let me guess. Christina, Greg, and Amy are all out at least part of next week, so they're hosting."

"Really Christina and Cam."

"At least they kept you informed, especially if Landry is going. Do you have attorneys in every state on call?"

"Ha. Nope, just the ones with NHL teams." At her wide-eyed look, I add, "Kidding."

"Must be nice to have invitations to week-long parties. Like the nobs in Regency England."

"Maybe the wealthy passed their preferred privileges down? But, yeah. I guess. I might go stir-crazy with nothing to do for a week." I've never taken a beach vacation for that reason. On the cruise I tried, I did every activity I could get to, all day every day. The crew all knew me by name by the end of it.

I'd enjoy some downtime if I was with Drew.

But I'm not going to be. So my inner devil needs to shut the fuck up.

Chapter Thirty-Three

Drew

Opening the door of my condo, I sniff the air. It's almost like Let is here. The place smells like traces of cooking from the kitchen to my left, mixed with her unique spicy floral scent.

When she texted me that she cooked here, I almost asked her to curl up in the fleece throw again to reimprint it. Spying it on the couch, I rush over and stuff my face in it.

Ahh. The sweet smell of Let. I miss her all over again. Another sign I might be in love with her, an idea I've yet to come to terms with. Damn, I'm pitiful, but I can't seem to care. Even staying in the same hotel we used in Duluth was easier than being here without her. And of course, settling Grams in her new home was a good distraction. I swear she bought out Target, which I was happy to see. Same with high threadcount sheets and fluffy towels from a department store. She's finally embracing the idea that while I'm saving for our future, I want her to have all the nice things we couldn't afford.

I want my hypothetical, way into the future kids to have everything I didn't. Two loving parents, clothes that fit and are new, not just new to them, presents under the tree, and paraphernalia to support whatever extracurricular activity that captures their fancy.

But to be comfortable doing that, I need more in the bank. Okay, and a wife, of course, but there's time for that.

Not if I want Let. She wants kids sooner rather than later.

Either way, my focus must shift to what I can control. Earning my keep with the Tornadoes and grabbing one of those long-term contracts that alternate captains attract. Which means my game has to stay in top form. I've already lost a week to helping Grams move, and while I was able to skate with a few friends from my junior league days, now I'm headed to Arizona of all places for this crazy house party Christina and Cam are hosting. She's sworn that we'll have ice time with the trip so close to training camp, but I don't know how she'll find that in triple digit temperatures.

Sighing, I put the fleece down and drag my luggage into my room. There's no reason why I can't watch last season's mistakes while huffing the fleece. One of the benefits of living alone. Of course, if Let was here I wouldn't be reduced to snorting inanimate objects.

Shaking that thought off, I throw my roller bag on my bed to unpack. Tilting my head, I breathe in. Damn, this room smells like her too. Maybe it's in my beard from the fleece blanket. I walk into the bathroom. A towel is stretched out over the bar, just like she would do. She usually showered in the morning and hung her towel in a single layer to help it dry faster.

Glad there's no one to see me, I grab it and sniff. Yep. Let was here. Long enough to shower. Oh, hell yeah. That means she might have slept here. Racing back into my bedroom, I dive onto my bed and grab the pillow on "her" side. Sure enough, it smells like her again.

Me

Am I going to have to start calling you Goldilocks?

Saylet

Huh?

Someone's been sleeping in my bed. :) And I love it.

Three dots appear, then disappear a few times. Did she really think I wouldn't know?

It's cool. Like I said, whenever. Although of course I'm bummed I wasn't here to share the bed with you. <smiling devil emoji>

Sorry/not sorry

I wish you missed me as much as you missed my pans and bed.

Don't forget washer and dryer :)

I've dragged my suitcase to the bedroom, tossed my dirty clothes in my hamper, and am back in the kitchen. When I open the freezer my jaw drops.

> OMG you didn't have to make all this!

> Seemed the least I could do as a squatter.

> I'll take this in trade any day.

One of the plastic trays is marked "Let's ground turkey mac and cheese" so I take that down and toss it in the microwave. My fingers are crossed that she made the version with her mild taco seasoning. I go turn on the TV as her next text chimes.

> Your TV left a lot to be desired, though.

> LOL you should have learned to change the input, rather than relying on me all the time.

> Or let me know you were coming and I would have changed it for you.

So…when do you leave for Christina and Cam's thing?

Why? Want me to leave it on the cable feed for you?

Well, I mean, should a squatter come by to continue to cook for you, that would be the good host thing to do.

Let, you're killing me. I want you in my bed, sure, but with me in it.

Not once training camp starts.

Her last text was a good reminder. I nod and toss the phone on the bar, deliberately leaving it as I take my dinner—with spinach and black beans thrown in there because she knows I won't make a salad half the time—to study my old games and work on being indispensable to the Tornadoes.

* * * *

Christina of course arranged for some gear to be sent to the vacation rental for the group. Nicole, ever the planner, sent the list of attendees and bedroom assignments out while I was in Duluth, which I skimmed and promptly forgot.

As the rideshare pulls up in front of the house in a private gated golf community in Scottsdale, I stare. It's enormous. Possibly as big as Greg Donovan's house in Austin. Maybe Christina and Cam have claimed a pool house here like the one they live in back home on the Donovan estate.

When she said vacation rental, I'd pictured a regular house with a bunch of us sleeping on couches, pull-out beds, or air mattresses. Maybe a pool in the backyard. This is a whole other level. No matter what I make, I don't think I'll ever think or spend like a billionaire. Between this house and whatever she's arranged for ice time for us, this week probably cost her as much as my car when I bought it new. Only someone who knows the next three generations of their family are set for life for will do that.

As I walk up toting my roller bag and flowers for our hostess, the front door opens. Jack is in board shorts and flip flops, his long blond hair dark with water. He's carrying two beer cans and offers one to me.

"Sweet welcoming committee," I say with a smile.

"Yeah, well, we gave the butler the day off—I shit you not. Come on back. This place is the bomb." He leads me through a huge living room with multiple seating areas. To my left, a bar area with twelve barstools and pendant lighting above it is in front of a kitchen that runs the depth of the house. The entire back wall of the living room is glass that apparently folds out to the pool patio, which also has multiple seating areas, including a dining table that rivals Greg's in a covered area with a ceiling fan overhead.

Only one glass panel is accordioned because of the temperatures, but I suppose like the rent on this place, she's not worried about the utility bill.

Outside, Christina, Nicole, and Amy are on cushioned lounge chairs to the left. Cam, Mattie, and a few others are strewn between the right side of the pool and the shady area where Jack's dog, Tom, lies. He's wet but panting, apparently not a fan of the heat here, despite Jack having played in Vegas before getting picked up by the Tornadoes.

Everyone cheers when I step out. Jack points to a table where all the phones are kept in the shade away from the pool, and where YETI koozies are set out. We'll see if they can match 111 degree temperatures.

I head to the ladies. Leaning down, I buss Christina's cheek and hand her flowers. "Thank you for inviting me. This place is awesome."

Cam yells, "Hey, step away from my woman!"

I flap a dismissive hand at him and move on to kiss the other two, while Christina gives him a hard time about who belongs to whom.

My shoulders drop away from my ears and I grin. I hadn't realized how much I'd been worried about Grams, Let, and my future, until I got here and felt that vacation vibe. This week is a timeout. I've done what I can. I'll do more training this week then do the best I can at training camp and next season. For now, it's all on pause, and I'm ready to have some fun.

I wander over to the guys. As I pass Jack, he grabs my beer. I'm used to this—he likes to test how fast everyone else is drinking and if they're keeping up with him, child that he is.

What I don't expect is for him to then ram me like he's sending me into the boards.

"What the f—" My words are swallowed by pool

water closing over my head.

I come up, shaking my head like a dog, seeing grins on everyone's faces, no one's bigger than Jack's. "Oh man, you're going to regret that, Landry."

"Ha," he says through laughter. "Said everyone. No one's managed to get me in yet."

Cam, Jaden, and Remi walk up behind him in what appears to be a choreographed move. Cam comes around and grabs his beers, but he won't let go. Looking over his shoulder, he spies Remi, who is built long and lean. Jaden has stepped sideways to his other side to remain out of sight.

Jack laughs. "No way a forward is going to get a D-man in."

As he takes a step back, Jaden says in his ear. "How about two?"

Picking him up bodily, Jaden gestures to Cam and Remi. Cam wrests the beers away as Remi grabs his legs. Together, the two men swing Jack like he's a child before tossing him out into the middle of the pool. I'm waiting when he comes up to dunk him one more time for good measure.

"You were saying?" I ask. Everyone else is laughing too much to talk.

He laughs and bows for the crowd, then yells, "Beer me!"

Mattie comes over and sits on the pool's edge as I wade over to take my shirt and—gross—wet sneakers off. F-ing Landry.

"Is this everyone?" I ask.

"No. Lauren arrives tomorrow night—some big client deadline or something. And Greg will come out Tuesday if he can, Wednesday otherwise."

"Who's that?" I gesture with my beer that Cam returned to me. The only guy sitting upright rather than lounging is typing like a mad man on his phone screen. He looks familiar but I can't place him.

"Oh, that's Travis. Greg's best friend, Christina's ex-boyfriend, interestingly enough."

"Does Cam know?"

"Yeah. He doesn't care. There's some story there, and no love lost." He answers my next question before I can ask it. "Apparently, Greg wanted him here. Anyway, Christina brought a private chef in. Oh! And you gotta see downstairs."

"Okay."

"But not while you're wet."

"Okay." Now I'm curious, but not enough to get out of the pool quite yet.

* * * *

I've been here two days, and I might be over it. This house has an ice rink in the basement. Like, real ice. It blew my mind when they walked me down that first afternoon.

Given our size and the relative size of that ice, Christina knew we'd want more this close to the start of pre-season, so she also made arrangements with the arena used by Arizona State's hockey team during the school year. Must be nice, but I'm not one to complain when it was done for my benefit. Never mind that the amount she spent could probably provide gear for every underprivileged kid in Duluth for a year.

So mornings are spent on the ice running drills and half-rink scrimmages. We sort of made up rules similar to half-court basketball, since we only have the one goalie and no one else was willing to deal with hundred-mile-an-hour pucks coming at them, even in borrowed protective gear.

Afternoons are spent either checking out the greater Phoenix area or hanging at the house. There is of course a fully-equipped gym for those who want extra workouts. Christina and Cam are managing without a barre for stretching, thankfully in private. No one wants to see that. And then there's a pool table and the pool for chilling.

I've tried to relax and enjoy this downtime. Then I tried joining every activity proposed. No matter what I do, I find myself wishing Let was enjoying it with me. Or worse, picture her in my home, my bed, without me.

Greg arrived late last night. He has his own room, as do the couples. Amy and Lauren are the only two single women, so they each get a room. All us single guys have been relegated to a room that has eight bunk beds, as though it was for the grandchildren or something. It doesn't help that they're not extra-long twin mattresses, so we keep stubbing our toes on the ladders at the foot of the beds. And Jack's dog has gas. I haven't shared space with this many guys since junior league hockey, and it's far less pleasant than my most recent roommate experience.

Jack, Remi, and Jaden are aggressively single, as I've always been. Jack, as usual, is the purveyor of excess and frat boy competitions. Who can pocket the most balls in a row at billiards, who can hold their breath under water for the longest, you name it and he's thought of it. And as he has zero filter, he's also shouted it out and challenged someone to chug a beer if they lose. It's exhausting. He also sleeps at odd hours based on when he comes in and out of our shared bedroom.

Interestingly, Travis hasn't been here much either. He was in with us the first night, but I haven't seen him come and go since. His stuff is still here, though.

All of which makes me wonder if they're also coupling up, either with the two single ladies or each other. But I can't figure out the matches there. Either way, it makes me miss Let more. I share a bed with her happily, yet here I am being grumpy about sharing a *room* with these guys for a few days.

Grams wants me to find a solution. Hell, so do I, but my brain is going to break from how much thought I've given it, and I still don't know what to do. But Cam would.

I can't out Let, but the next morning I pull Cam outside to have coffee away from some of the other early risers.

"You ready for training camp, AC?" he asks.

"Pretty much. I need to catch up with Saint beforehand to talk about how to mentor some of the newbies, and Kyle to see how his summer has been, since he's been strangely absent. But that's not why I want to talk to you."

"Okay. What's up?"

"When you were dating Christina on the sly, how did you handle knowing it could be a career-limiting move?"

"What? Wait. I mean, I'm more than happy to answer your questions, but where is this coming from?" He cocks his head. "Who are you dating? I know it's not Amy."

Huh. So maybe Jack did hook up with the granola-girl owner. "No one at the moment. But if I was interested in someone within the org, they'd have more to lose than me. So I'm not naming names, but I'm trying to figure out how to…I dunno, support them."

"Hmm. Interesting. Okay, I'll put that aside to noodle on later. Chris might have some good guesses." At my eye roll, he drops his grin and thinks. "Without knowing her role, how much you interact, and for that matter, what you're looking for, it's hard to say. Is this for a one and done, à la Jack, or more?"

"More." I raise a hand when his mouth drops open. "I don't know how much more, but without understanding how to avoid risking her job, I can't really figure it out, can I?"

"Aww, Buzz-bee has found a flower he wants to do more than pollinate."

I grimace. A poet, the man is not. My phone rings before I can thank him. Charlie's name is on the screen. I suck in a sharp breath. "Excuse me. It's my agent."

He nods. "Good luck, man."

"No inside info?" I toss over my shoulder as I walk away, knowing he wouldn't have it. Christina isn't involved in that side of the organization, and if she was, Greg would keep her separated from contract conversations because of Cam.

He laughs behind me.

I tap the phone and bring it to my ear. "Hey, Charlie. What's up?"

"Buzz! How's Arizona?"

"Hot. You're such a damned tease. Why are you calling?" Am I vacationing with the wrong team? I gulp.

"Did you see the sports news this morning?"

"No." It's early here, and my focus had been on having a private conversation with Cam. We've all been watching the contracts roll out since July. Seeing who got picked up by which team and the resulting off-season trades are a rite of passage with hockey players, as we all try to manage our stress levels about being traded ourselves. Except Cam, of course.

"Chicago picked up Peter Lee from Philly in a trade announced this morning."

My knees go weak with relief. My desire to remain a Tornado has only grown since my last conversation with Charlie, but I hadn't realized quite how much. I glance around. I'm in a hallway to some of the bedrooms, with no idea how I got here. With no chairs in sight, I slide down the wall and plant my butt on the floor. "Thank you."

"Once we're through training camp, I'll put out some feelers with Link."

The GM won't give away anything until he's ready, but Charlie knows how to play it without making me seem too eager. It'd be good to see how that interaction goes.

"I wanted you to enjoy your vacation. Go find some bunnies in bikinis and relax. Just be ready for training camp."

"I stopped hanging with bunnies months ago."

"Huh. Any reason you care to share? Anything that changes your priorities for contracts?"

"No. Yes. I don't know."

"Alrighty then. We'll cross the contract bridge when we get to it. In the meantime, try to relax and have some fun. You're wound so freaking tight, Buzz."

"Thanks. You, too. Enjoy the last of your summer."

His question lit a fire in me to do whatever I can to figure things out with Let. Grams' words echo through me yet again. There's definitely a will, now I just have to find a way. But I can't do that from here. Besides, I could be alone and surrounded by couples here, or home where I'm almost positive Let is sleeping in my bed.

I pull up flights on my phone.

Chapter Thirty-Four

Saylet

I'm having the best dream ever.

As I have every night since Drew texted me "All yours" when he boarded his flight to Arizona, I'm sleeping in his bed. His smartass-ery didn't stop me from packing up some stuff and heading right back over here.

I'd love to say it's his pans, shower, or bed that I crave, but it's not. I miss him less when I'm here. His ghost helps me recall our fun evenings together, and I don't mean in bed. I also find I work less here. I still end up on my laptop more evenings than not, but not every one and not as late.

Once—only once—I found myself imagining that we were in a committed relationship, and he was traveling with the team. I shut that down so hard my brain hurt and haven't let myself consider it again since.

But I can't control my dreams, and this one is a doozy. I'm on my stomach as usual, and dream Drew slips in behind me on his side of the bed. He's naked, having ditched his sleep t-shirt and cotton pants, which is how I know this isn't real. He skims a big hand down my back, petting me as I did his beard the last time I saw him. Cupping my ass, he leans over and sniffs my hair.

I moan and push my butt back into his hand, tilting my hip up. His dream hand slides around and up my belly to cup a boob. Fuck, yes. I scoot back farther to press my back to his front, his heat and touch lighting a fire in me, fueled by the sensation of his cock catching in the lace of my panties.

I reach back to hold his thigh and rub against him.

"Let," he moans in my ear. "I missed you."

"Mmm, ditto." I confess what I'd be loathe to say to real Drew, given our circumstances.

"Let. Are you awake?"

"Do I have to be? This is an amazing dream."

"Hmm." I can feel that from his chest as much as hear it. "I guess not."

He plays with my nipple, sending sparks through me. Then he lifts my leg over his so his fingers can dabble between my thighs, slipping inside my underwear. Rubbing, petting, even gentle pinching get the blood flowing more than the nipple play did, until I'm undulating against his cock. Dream Drew shoves my panties down. Licking his finger, he slips it between my pussy lips to circle my clit. With a shift of his hips, his cock is there, rubbing along my seam to bat against his hand.

Usually, I'm fighting for my time to pet him, but if I move, the dream bubble may burst, so I remain languid. Maybe I can orgasm in a dream.

He coats his finger with precum leaking from his cock and uses that to relubricate my clit, and the sparks of heat become fireworks. I gasp.

"There, eh?" His rough whisper sends shivers through me as much as his touch, and I arch my back another inch.

He grunts and his hand disappears, foil crinkles— dream Drew is as considerate as the real guy—then his cock is notched at my opening, thrusting inside in short bursts, sinking a fraction deeper each time. After a minute, this too is taken away, and I moan in disappointment.

"Shh. Come here." He rolls me to my back, and his cock surges into me in one long smooth press of his hips. "Ahh, Let."

My eyes flutter open. "Holy fuck."

His teeth gleam in the darkness. "Hi. I take it you're awake now?"

"You're real. I thought I was dreaming."

"Yeah, I got that." He draws back and plunges into me once more. "Is this okay? I felt a little weird, taking advantage of you sleeping like that. But damn, I missed you. I'm so happy you're here."

He came back for me. That sounds strange at first, until I remember I'm in his bed. Apparently, as pleasurable as this is, sex is not as good at waking my brain up as coffee. I shift under him, frustrated at him holding still, as I process the rest of what he said.

He leans on one arm as though to disengage, and I rush out, "Totally okay. Great, in fact. Just move, please."

Another flash of his smile and he complies.

As we fall asleep after, I realize I still don't know if I can orgasm in my sleep. But if anyone could get me there, Drew could.

* * * *

I wake to the faint smell of coffee over Drew's lemon and cedarwood scent. I never noticed those before, but after a spell here without Drew, I take note of the subtle differences.

He's here! My first inclination is to jump out of bed, probably for the first time in my life. But I take a minute to regroup.

My thumping heart with a Drew magnet in it aside, this changes nothing. And in fact means I need to get my ass back to my own apartment and my own world ASAP. On top of all that, I have work today, so I should get a move on.

Throwing on my favorite robe, I head to the kitchen, where I'm greeted by Drew in low-slung athletic shorts and t-shirt, holding out a cup of coffee.

"Thank you." I slurp an appreciative glug. "Not that I'm complaining, but what brings you home early?"

"You. Knowing you were likely here and in my bed, it was hard to enjoy a bunk bed in a room I shared with a bunch of guys."

"The paradox being that if you were here—now you are here—I won't be."

"Come on, Let. Don't be like that. Look, is there any chance you can go in an hour late to work? I'd really like to talk to you. You know I wouldn't ask if it wasn't important. And if you can't then I totally understand and we can talk tonight?" he asks, expression somewhere between hopeful and worried.

The sweet man is trying to respect my career. I grab my phone and check my calendar. "Hmm. I'm good. I'll tell people I'll be offline for an hour or so then work from home the rest of the morning. But I do have to be in the office for an afternoon meeting."

"Great." He sighs with relief. "Thank you."

I slide onto a stool and type out an email, then close the laptop so I don't get sucked in. For Drew to ask something like that, it must be major. "Can I get dressed for this? Seems like a serious topic requires clothes, maybe even a bra."

"Sure. Although nothing requires a bra if you ask me." He grins as he shoos me toward the bedroom. At the last minute, he strides forward and grabs my coffee cup to top me off while I change. Fucking annoyingly thoughtful as always.

When I return, he's in the living room sitting on the chair facing the couch at an angle, so I sit on that end of the couch.

He leans forward, elbows on his thighs and hands clasped between them. "Let, where do you see yourself in five years? Professionally?"

I frown. Does he think I'm going to say home taking care of kids for some man? Even when I have kids, I plan to work. I've put my blood, sweat, and tears—well okay, not blood—into this career, and I love what I do.

Hold on. That doesn't sound like Drew. Why don't I just ask him for his reason?

Nevertheless, I condition my response. "I'm not sure why you're asking. Our jobs are very different in a myriad of ways. But I see myself doing what I do now, hopefully balancing my career with a husband and children."

"So no aspirations to travel the world, climb further up the corporate ladder? Move closer to your family?" His hands twitch as though maybe he's going to reach for me or stroke his beard, but he doesn't.

"I love Austin and this organization. This type of job presents new challenges all the time, particularly as the team matures. So I don't need to change roles to be fulfilled. I like traveling with the team, and having the choice not to. I'll continue to do that until I have children. Then, if I have to switch"—I cut myself off. "Wait, why are you asking about this? It's not like your career gives you choices."

He takes a deep breath, his eyes steady on me. This time he does reach for my hand. "I had a trade scare the past couple weeks, and it helped me realize how important this—you and me—is. Let, I'm in love with you."

I suck in a breath; my hand spasms in his. He's in love with me? My heart goes all gooey at that, ready to leap into his lap. I'm frozen, though. His questions feel more ominous now.

He swallows at my silence, but continues, "I want to respect your priorities, but I'm dying to see where this could go. I've racked my brain for ideas, but you're the smart one between us. What can I do to get you to stay with me?"

My head puts my heart in a chokehold. I've been trying to figure this out, too, with no clear answer. A huge part of me wants to throw caution to the wind, scream out my love, and jump his bones. But my family's history and the repeated double standards I've seen in the workplace—although not the Tornadoes'— keep my fears too strong. My career is my jewelry.

So I ignore his declaration of love for the time being to say, "I don't know. It would be so much easier if we didn't work for the same organization. But there's no other comparable job in Austin for me, and there sure as fuck isn't for you." I haven't explained why I've been focused on hockey PR, so I add, "Did I tell you that when we moved to Denver, my brother started playing hockey. He was really good. Enough to play in college, although not at a division one school. So my whole family loves hockey. Even though I decided to make my own way and didn't like the idea or expense of grad school, I wanted to do something they could relate to. None of them really understand the world of public relations, but they watch the Tornadoes every chance they get."

My heart is still doing cartwheels and singing "he's in love with me" over and over, so I'm not sure I was coherent or addressed his concerns, but I shut up, not knowing where to go from there.

He closes his eyes for a long moment. "I was hoping you'd thought of a way for this to work."

"Don't you think I've tried?"

He blinks. "You have?"

"Remember? Smarter one." I jerk my thumb at myself, and we smile. "Of course I have. I love…being here with you, being roommates in all the best ways."

He lit up when I said the word "love" but I'm not giving him that ammunition. It's all I can do to stick to my guns. I never want to be the little woman following her man around, taking whatever time she can get from him, to say nothing of taking whatever job she can get where he's traded. My parents' stories of starting over from nothing stuck with all of us, and that's where I'd end up if the Tornadoes don't like exes working together.

"Did you come up with anything?"

"No. Anyway, I heard you tell Grams you don't want kids for years."

"Yeah, she told me off about that. Reminded me that lots of people travel for work and technology has made it easier to be part of their children's lives. And that by the time they're ready to play hockey, I might be ready to retire."

I snort. Sounds like Grams. But also, my heart beats

double time as one hurdle to us being together falls. Regardless, I don't see a way around the rest.

"That's great. I'm glad you can be flexible. I can't, not when it would jeopardize everything I've worked for. If we date then break up, no other professional sports organization would have me. And it's not like we can be together on the down low. You're too high profile."

"I'd never do anything to hurt you."

"I understand you wouldn't mean to. But so much of it is public perception when it comes to NHL players. As a PR Director, I've seen the shitstorms. I want nothing to do with that. I'm serious, Drew. I've thought about it and thought about it. I'm thirty. Do you know how many men have said they love me and want to be with me, yet here I am, still single? It's too risky."

Those men weren't half as mature as Drew, but it doesn't matter.

His shoulders droop, and his hands come to cover his face.

Fuck. If he cries, I might give in. My heart is already in shreds. Knowing I'm hurting him as well is killing me.

He swallows audibly and drops his hands. The look on his face is as devastated as when he came to find me after Grams' fall. Double fuck.

"Okay. I'm not done trying, but I'll keep all attempts quiet." Then he twists the knife that I've driven into my own heart. "Just remember I love you."

Chapter Thirty-Five

Drew

I stay in the living room while Let packs her stuff. When she wheels her suitcase out, I walk over and surround her in a hug.

She's stiff, but her arms creep around me. She sniffs.

"Shh. It'll be okay. I love you. I want what's best for you, even if it isn't me."

She tears out of my arms. "Don't say shit like that. It makes it worse when you're nice."

I gulp, torn between my own tears caught in my throat and a smile at her statement. "Maybe that's my tactic. I'll wear you down with niceness."

"I have to go."

I nod. We both need time to regroup, and I want to talk to Cam again. Unable to move to even hold the door for her, I watch as she walks out, my hands fisted at my side as I swallow back the lump of tears. The door clicking shut makes me flinch and bursts me into action.

Arizona is an hour behind Austin, so I text Cam.

Me

> You up?

Cam

> Sort of. Give me 5 to get out to the kitchen and brew coffee and I'll call you.

> Thanks.

An hour or maybe six minutes later, my phone rings as I pace the hall. "Hey, thanks."

"What's up? You had me worried between your crazy question and your agent's call. You and Saint are supposed to be the calm and steady ones on the team. I was scared enough to check the trade news and text Coach."

"There'd been rumors with Chicago, but my agent called to tell me they'd gone in a different direction."

"Oh yeah, I saw that. By the way, since you're apparently safe, I'll tell you that Coach was very close-mouthed."

"He has to be, I'm sure."

"I think they're working on something, but at least we can be pretty sure it's not you or me."

My brain can't process that right now.

He continues, "As for the other, ya gotta give me more to work with for me to help you."

"I'm asking for your perspective as the one with more at risk."

"Okay, we can start there." He sighs and ponders. "First, top level NHL goalies don't grow on trees. So worst case, I was going to work somewhere else, where I could get over her—as if such a thing was possible.

Second, I made enough that I wasn't going to starve even if I got booted midseason. That's really different than, say, Becky in Accounting."

I hoot a laugh. Becky is a lovely woman who is almost my grams' age. "Nice pick."

"No judgment here," he says through snickers. "Okay, I'm sorry. I was trying to cheer you up. You get the idea. There's a huge difference in what we risk versus what back office people risk. Yes, we have more money on the table, but in a way, that mitigates the risk."

"Dammit."

"Here's the flip side. If it was someone in a role like Becky's, then you'd rarely if ever have to interact with her at work, so there's not a ton of risk. But if it's someone like oh, Saylet maybe,"—he draws out her name—"then there's more."

I throw myself onto the couch, groaning. "Please tell me Chris didn't come up with that guess."

"I wouldn't have, but it makes sense. Don't worry, Chris is a vault. She's not going to mention anything to anyone, even Amy. I promise. Amy didn't know we were seeing each other until well into the season. So Saylet, huh? She's such a firecracker, I'm surprised."

"What are you, a hundred and hanging with Becky? A firecracker?" I spy the throw out of the corner of my eye and hug it to me.

He laughs. "I'm just saying, your energies don't match."

"We meet in the middle. She helps me be less intense about my play while I help her take a break from her endless emails and planning."

"I heard she cooks like a pro, too."

"Jack has a big mouth, but yeah, that doesn't suck.

However, she's worked really hard to get where she is. She's one of the youngest PR Directors in any industry. And she comes from an overachieving family." I'm beaming with pride even if he can't see me.

"And she interacts with the team a bunch, especially the captains."

"Yeah." Big sniff of the blanket. Memories of that purple dress.

"Have you thought about what it would mean for you if it didn't work out?"

That one I have thought about, unlike Grams' pressure for grandchildren. After all, we both went into this with an end date. "It would be awkward, but we were friends before this. And if it was too weird, I could step back from AC, or ask to work with someone else on her team."

"Would you really step back?" Cam doesn't see half of my obsessive behavior around my performance, but he apparently noticed enough.

I put the blanket down and pace the hallway again, picturing seeing Let at every game as well as working out PR appearance assignments with her. Then I consider trying to do that if she were with someone else. "I'd like to think that we'd be friends, or at least professional. But yeah, if I had to, I would."

He pushes. "What if you didn't believe it was necessary, but she needed you to step back?"

Sheesh. This is starting to feel like an inquisition, but it's what I need, and it's easier to field from him than Grams, whom I never want to disappoint. "We'd find a way. Without hurting the team."

"Look," Cam's voice is serious. "You're asking me as a friend, rather than my AC, so I'm going to answer you in that vein. Don't kick my ass for this."

"Okay…"

"That's easy to say, but harder to do. Emotions don't belong on the ice. You have to be able to shut that shit off, and if you're seeing her in the tunnel as you head out to the ice, I have my doubts that you can be professional. And that affects us all. What happens when she shows up with a big rock on her ring finger?"

I grit my teeth. I can't fathom such a thing. My lizard brain is shouting, "*Mine!*" Out loud, I reply. "Maybe I haven't been clear. I'm in love with her. If I'm in agony, I'll remove myself. If she's hurting, I'll remove myself even faster because I can't handle seeing that. If she's happy, then I'll be happy for her."

"Wow." Cam blows out a breath. "Have you told her that?"

"Most of it. She doesn't trust it. Especially as a woman in a man's world, and a non-hockey role in a hockey organization. All of which I understand and respect. So how do I make it safer for her?"

"I don't know," Cam says flatly.

"What the hell? You ask me all these damned questions then your answer is 'I don't know?' You're killing me here. What about Chris? There must be some—what did Mattie call it?—grand gesture I can make."

"She said the only way is to show Saylet. But short of quitting the team, which I don't think either of you want, I don't know how you do that."

Well, to quote Let, *fuck*. Sorry, Grams.

* * * *

Let is at training camp almost every day with Sara

and LaRhonda. They interview us about our off season, what we're looking for out of training camp, how ready we feel, any other players we are watching, you name it. They roll out the edited footage throughout the pre-season, re-introducing Austin and Tornadoes fans to the team on a personal level.

She studiously avoids my interview about the off season, but my answer to LaRhonda is meant for her. "It was surprisingly relaxing. I golfed a little, coached hockey camps here, spent time with my grandmother and a good friend, and ate some amazing food. I really expanded my palate and improved my nutrition, and I'm hoping that will help my play."

The box of canned and dry goods in my pantry had been moved, so I know Let saw it. When I started compulsory buying that stuff again, I filled the box then forced myself to stop. Enough is enough. She was right, nutrition is important to an athlete, so I'll force myself to either cook more, buy more salad, or fork over my hard-earned dollars for a meal service. Regardless, I hope she'll focus on the fact that I valued my time with her for more than her cooking.

The rest of training camp is spent evaluating the guys up from the AHL, and checking my teammates' readiness for play. Saint and Kyle are moving a little slow. The guys who were in Arizona are in decent shape. Most of us have been training for a month or more now, but even that can't fully prepare a player for the competitive skating for hours in training camp. Bergstrom looks amazing, as fast as ever after spending the summer in Sweden, where he must have been on skates more than off them. The second line is solid, and there's a D-man from our AHL affiliate who looks promising.

Saint is leaning against the boards by the bench talking to Coach Steele during a break, and I glide over.

Saint gives me a chin jut.

Coach asks, "Thoughts?"

"Offense or defense?"

"We were talking about the defense," Coach says. At my continued silence—I'm wary of jumping in with an opinion without getting the lay of the land—he adds, "Scott looks slow."

"Yeah, but we all know he had a rough summer," I say watching him carefully. I'm still dying of curiosity about why he bailed Kyle Scott out. He holds my stare. Which is why he's Coach and I'm AC. I nod toward the AHL D-man, Kenji Yamaguchi. "What about Kooch?"

Coach tilts his head side-to-side. He's on the fence.

Saint looks thoughtful. "You think? He's definitely keeping up speed wise and in drills. I'll watch him more in scrimmages. Is he ready for the rougher teams, though?"

I smile. "Only one way to find out."

"Jack," we all say in unison, and laugh.

Unable to stop myself, I add, "He also fits the bill with L-uh, Saylet's PR campaign for us to be the face of the new NHL."

Coach blinks then nods. "True. Okay, let's keep evaluating, and we'll talk closer to the end of camp. Thanks, gentlemen, now get back out there and train."

Saint pats me on the back as we head back into the fray. "Good eyes, Buzz."

As soon as my phone is in reach, I text Saylet.

Me

Watch Yamaguchi. He looks good and I mentioned to Coach that all things being equal, he'd be a great addition to your PR campaign on diversity.

Saylet

Thanks.

I wasn't expecting a blow job out of appreciation, but a little enthusiasm would have been nice. There's no reason for her to doubt my professionalism, but I guess re-establishing trust after our affair will take a while. I'm sure Grams'll remind me if I forget.

Chapter Thirty-Six

Saylet

Training camp is torture. Hockey players look hot in the suits they wear to game days, their sweaty workout apparel, and pretty much everything, but never hotter than in uniform and skates making hockey look like a choreographed dance. These guys come from all sorts of backgrounds and have worked their butts off to be the best at this sport. To see someone excel at something they love is the sexiest thing I can think of. And also, aforementioned torture.

I sigh. And Drew. He's just so fucking *nice* as always. Not only does he look for opportunities to improve the team, but he also helps me pursue my goal of being one of the most diverse organizations in the league. Fucking asshole. I'm trying to be indifferent here. I'm sure he found my "thanks" curt, but anything more would have given away how much I miss him.

I stayed away from the tunnel for the pre-season games that are part of training, taking the opportunity to start new traditions and save myself the agony of seeing Drew. The organization finally hired a dedicated media liaison, so Greg now expects me to spend more time in the owner's box to shmooze with sponsors.

Less interactions mean there's less risk in you dating Drew.

The following week, the team leaves for three pre-season road games. The day they fly out, I come home to his enchilada pan sitting on my doormat. I grab it, stab my key in the lock through tears, and barely get the door closed before I'm sobbing. Sliding down the door, I clutch the pan to my chest and rain tears and snot on the stupid fucking pan.

Finally, I get my act together and text him. I avoided looking at their flight schedule so I don't know if he's landed in St. Louis yet.

Me

You're willing to sacrifice a pan to keep the squatters out, eh?

Drew

I thought you might not be comfortable using my place right now. But I meant what I said. You're ALWAYS welcome there.

Thanks. I was kidding. You're right, I'm not. But I will accept the pan on loan and return it to you with 'interest' in the form of enchiladas if you're cool with that.

> Keep it. I never used it anyway. I'll get another to Grams' specifications when she visits.

I have nothing else I can say. "Do you miss me as much as I miss you" is not going to help either of us move forward. And he clearly doesn't listen to "Stop being so fucking nice." And now he's taken away an excuse to see him by not accepting the offer of enchiladas. I noticed he had LaRhonda interview him for the pre-season introductions we ran. Maybe he wants nothing to do with me now. No. He said I was always welcome. There's no sense in arguing with myself because I have no business thinking about excuses to see him. I need to move on.

* * * *

The team has been back a day, and there's a home game tonight. It'll be the second to last pre-season game, not that I'm counting.

Kayla has already commented on my lack of vivaciousness again, hoping to get a laugh out of me at her repeated use of the old-fashioned word. Now I'm faced with having to attend a game and watch Drew be excellent at his profession while I maintain a professional façade with Greg's clients and associates.

I grab her and go for coffee in the break room. Once we have caffeine in hand, I ask, "Any chance you want to switch jobs today?"

She tilts her head. "Are you sure this is the better path? Sure there's no risk, but there's no reward either.

What if being together worked out?"

I grimace. "We've had this conversation several times. The risk is too high."

She nods. "I'm still going to keep asking here and there. One of these days your answer might surprise you. I'm hoping you realize being miserable alone without even trying is worse than that risk you're so afraid of."

I make a noncommittal noise and sip my coffee.

"Here's the thing," she continues. "You broke up because you're worried about your career being at risk. He's showing respect for your job and staying out of your way. So sure, you could end up back in this state"—she gestures—"but you might not. You might find he's the love of your life and it all works out. But you should at least try."

A sliver of hope shoots through me, but I scoff. "I never knew you were a romantic, Kayla."

"Just like you, I know better than to show my weak underbelly around here. The testosterone poisoning would kill me."

I snort a laugh, but I'm stuck on her reasoning. Finally I admit, "I'm afraid."

Her reply is softer. "I get it. Okay. I'll leave it for now."

I hadn't realized how little contact I'd had with Drew. Probably because I could be standing next to him and still miss him like crazy because we're not together. But Kayla's right. The risk at least within the organization is lower than I imagined. The idea of there being a long game to get back together gives me more hope than I deserve. With it comes pressure to think harder, to find a path. Since I was the one who broke us up, I'm probably the one who has to put us back together.

Chapter Thirty-Seven

Drew

Management chose to keep Yamaguchi here, as he played well in the pre-season games. Tonight is our home opener, and he looks a little green at morning skate.

Saint gestures me over to the edge of the ice by the tunnel.

Saylet is there with him, along with Mattie, Cam, and Jack. She asks, "Y'all going to have Kooch do a solo lap?"

Saint adds, "I called her down to talk about getting him introduced to the home crowd. Last year was different as an expansion team, but I'd like to start the solo lap tradition here. You guys good with that?"

The league has an unofficial tradition of sending a rookie out for a solo lap before warmups for the first NHL game he plays. Some teams warn them, some don't.

We all reply in the affirmative.

"Fuck yeah," Jack says, "Let's not tell him."

I reply, "Have you seen how off he looks? The guy's freaking out. We'll tell him but only a few minutes before he goes on or he might lose his lunch, and he's going to need his energy to beat the Vortex."

Saint adds, "I agree. Jack, you can play whatever

pranks you want, but as a team, we should be supportive."

Saylet nods in agreement.

I'm using my peripheral vision so hard to watch her, my eyes hurt.

"Do you already have material on him, for snippets up on the jumbotron?" I ask her now. As I finish, I look her dead on. If I'd turned earlier, I would have garbled the question.

She meets my eyes, then flicks hers down to her tablet. "Yes. We interviewed him for social media, and there's film from training camp and the pre-season games. We already have short clips for all the players for this season."

"Cool." Of course she does, because her brain is as sexy as her body. I suspected as much, or I wouldn't have asked in front of others.

Saint nods. "Do you need anything else from us then?"

She nods and taps a finger on her screen. "We're set, thanks. Good luck out there, boys. Take 'em by storm!"

Each player bumps fists with her and pushes back onto the ice. With me conveniently directly across from her in the huddle, I'm last, and I bump knuckles then skim my fingers over her fist, closing my eyes for a minute. I'm dying to tell her I love her and I miss her, but that's not fair. So I lean in and take an exaggerated sniff of her hair. "There, got my fix. You look good, Let."

Her eyes are dark chocolate pools of liquid, unblinking, as she stands frozen. She swallows and as I push off, whispers, "You too."

I'll take it as a win.

* * * *

For now, though, my focus has to be on tonight's game and kicking Nashville's ass. Our starting lineup is the same as most of our games last year. No reason to fix it if it's not broken. Saint, Mattie, and I are front line, Cam's in net with Jack and Scottie on defense, ready to help all of us.

Coach switched Kyle out with Kooch for a couple of the pre-season games, but for the start of the regular season, the top six spot is Kyle's to lose.

It's a sellout crowd, and half the seats are already filled when we head out for warmups. Saint grabs Kooch and walks him forward in the tunnel. "Take a celebration lap. Deep breath. You're in the big leagues now—" he turns the young player to face him "—because you deserve it. So go enjoy. You'll remember this for the rest of your life."

His press picture comes up overhead, and the announcer's deep voice calls, "Please welcome," he draws out each of his next words, "Kenji Yamaguchi…to the Texas Tornadoes!"

Saint calls, "Take your bucket off so they can get to know your face."

And Kooch steps onto the ice as we all roar for him, in sync with the fans. Candids of him in practices and pre-season games flash on the jumbotron. When he's about three quarters of the way around, they announce the starting lineup, and we all join him on the ice to circle and take shots on goal.

I'm buzzing. Itching to play. This is what I'm born to do. The ice feels different tonight, and the arena is warmer with every seat filled. Saint has already given us our pep talk after Coach's pre-game speech in the dressing room. Now it's time to internalize it. We made it to the Conference Finals last year as we learned to work together. Our team is stronger, more cohesive, and we can make it even further. It comes down to doing it one game at a time, pacing ourselves.

My thoughts stutter to a halt. *One step at a time.* The idea is just out of reach, though, and I have a face-off, then a game, to win.

I win the face-off, batting it to Jack, and we're flying. Our blades scrape across the ice as the crowd roars. Out here, the world makes sense. Get the puck, keep the puck, pass the puck, take the shot. Lead the team alongside Saint. I'm stronger than ever before in a season opener, ready to take on the world. One game at a time.

When Kooch is on the ice, all of us give him encouraging words. When Scottie is, we urge him to be faster, more aggressive in his defense. We all want to win for the home crowd.

Cam is a wall in the net. Nothing gets by him in the first period. However, we didn't get anything by the Vortex's goalie either.

In the second period, Nashville presses us hard, spending way too much time down our end. Jack and Scottie swap out for Kucera and Kooch while Mattie takes the puck, Saint and I one stride behind him. Mattie drops the puck back to Lukas, who sets up the play trading it with Kooch. I duck between two Vortex players, and Kooch sees an opening, winging it to me.

Taking it in at an angle, I can't get a shot off with two defensemen on me, but as I approach the left goalpost, I see a small opening. It's a tight angle. They expect me to send it over to Mattie since I'm righthanded. Instead, I backhand it over the goalie's shoulder into the far corner of the goal.

First blood! I beeline for Kooch, grabbing him in a bear hug and twirling him on the ice on our razor sharp blades. Patting him on the helmet, I thank him for the assist, and I swear he's more excited than I am about the point.

The Vortex tie it in the third period, but a quick slapshot goal from near the boards by Bergstrom gets us back to a one-goal lead, and our home opener goes down as a W in the books.

When the media asks me about my game, I focus on bringing Kooch to the forefront. "Kenji Yamaguchi came up ready to play from the first day of training camp. He saw an opening and got the puck to me. I made use of it. I'm happy to be a part of his first point of his NHL career, and I look forward to seeing what he'll do with us this season."

When my inquisition is over, I step out of the press room. Let greets me with a warm smile and a nod. "Great game. And thanks for your comments about Kooch."

"I said that because it's true, and because I agree with you."

"Well, thanks anyway. At least with a win, I can hope you'll get some sleep tonight."

I shrug, unwilling to admit to my continued obsessive watching of game tape. Tonight, though, I need to figure out how I can convince Let to give me a chance, one step at a time.

Chapter Thirty-Eight

Saylet

It's early November, and the team is at the top of its division. There have been more than the usual number of meetings in the conference room, and Greg seems to be around quite a bit. Even Christina has been pulled in, with a spreadsheet up on the wall-mounted flat screen monitor.

The font is small enough that I can't read it through the glass walls, and I can't very well stop and stare.

But Coach Steele is in there as well as Stephen and once when I was passing, Stephen, who was sitting with his back to me, was holding a list of players' names. So it's either trade negotiations or, more likely given the team's performance, contemplating who they'll lock in first.

The list was five names long, but even strolling at a snail's pace, I didn't see any beyond the first one. Drew Busbee. This is his last year under his current contract, so the other guys on the list probably are as well.

I have no idea how they finagle numbers for the salary cap. And what about someone like Saint whose contract is up in two years, and who would command a larger contract? Presumably, they'll hold a lot of room for their captain, unless they're planning to offer an extension right now to lock him in.

My head hurts. This is why I prefer jobs that don't involve numbers much. Christina or someone will always support me on presenting the financial pros and cons of sponsorship options. I'd rather focus on the relationships.

I may or may not make extra trips for coffee or water these days while those closed-door meetings are in progress. And therefore extra trips to the ladies' room. Finally, they're taking a break as I walk by, and the door is open while the spreadsheet remains on the monitor. Only Chris and Stephen remain in the room, and they're deep in conversation, gesturing to the numbers.

I swivel my head. No one is in the hall. Taking a quiet step backward, I hover, peering in. Yep. Salary cap stuff. They have names slotted in with number of years and salary projections, with a total at the bottom that is red. A line below it is labeled "room under cap" and is smaller than the red number. Shit.

I turn back to my office. I want so badly to text Drew and tell him they're working on a deal for him. This is yet another reason dating a player would be a bad idea. How would I go home every night and keep a secret like this?

Of course, if I stopped spying on stuff that's none of my business then this wouldn't be a problem.

Two hours later I'm wrapping up for the day when my cell phone rings. "Meak" flashes on the screen. I snatch it up and swipe. Meak and Ba were on night shifts at the hospital for the past month so it's been longer than we usually go between catchups.

"Hi, Meak. Are y'all back to days yet?" I get up and close my door and grab my ear buds as I greet her.

"Mhm." She continues in Khmer as always, even

when I speak in English. "Damn, I hate those months. Hey, I'm switching to video." Then she's onscreen, her smile so like mine, her grey-and-black streaked hair pulled back from her face. "Kaun, it's so good to see you. But you look tired."

Her use of kaun, a Khmer endearment meaning child, reflects her concern, and my heart warms. "I'm fine, Meak."

"You're back in your apartment, no more electricity issues?" I nod, so she continues down her checklist. "You still close with the player who let you stay with him?"

My eyes pinch, just for a second, but she sees it. "What's going on, Neang Let?"

I wave a hand, hoping to avoid tearing up. "Nothing. He and I are friends. But it can't be anything more."

"Why not?"

"I'm trying to protect my professional reputation. My career is my safety net, right? If I date a player, then we break up, they're going to keep him, not me. Worse, no other team would have me."

"I get it. But you look really sad. You never seemed bothered when relationships ended before."

"No one else I've known is like him."

"In what way?"

"Oh, Meak. He's young, but so mature. He's such a gentleman, such a caretaker. I told you how close he is with his grandma. It's like our relationship. I don't really have a word for it, it's so beyond courteous. Even when we broke up, he said he understood because he wanted what was best for me and wanted to respect my career."

I'm definitely tearing up by now, but interestingly so is my mother. "Oh kaun, he sounds wonderful."

"He is."

"You know, I met your ba at work. You can imagine that as a man and the doctor in the mix, he had less to risk than I did."

I nod.

"I had to decide whether he was worth the risk. Turns out, he was." She grins, still so in love with my ba that it shines out of her. "Some risks are worth it, but it's hard to tell which ones. Remember Walt?"

"Ugh." I roll my eyes at the mention of the first guy I fell in love with. I was nineteen, in college, and thought I knew everything. But the minute he graduated and moved away for work, it fell apart. We didn't communicate that well when there were different demands on our time and spending time together took more effort.

"That time, the risk wasn't worth it. But that was more than a decade ago. Your judgment has improved. Trust yourself."

"Meak, if you could have only had Ba or your bracelets which allowed you to get out of Cambodia, which would you pick?"

"You know the answer to that. We've told that story too many times. We'd have found a way to get your sister and brothers out, with or without the money the bracelets brought. But I hear what you're saying. This is a bracelet-level decision. I can't wait to meet him." She is smiling, her eyes shiny with maternal happiness.

But after we say our goodbyes, I still can't let go of the fear of losing my independence.

Chapter Thirty-Nine

Drew

Once I figured out what resonated with me about one step at a time, I knew what I had to do. As much as Charlie is my supporter, he still has a vested interest in the outcome. So I talked through the idea with Cam first.

Still crickets from the organization, but I want to be prepared, as I know Charlie's setting expectations with them.

Two games after our home opener, we traveled to Denver for an out-and-back road trip. I snagged the seat next to Cam on the return flight, ignoring Jack's protests.

Cam grinned. "More questions, huh?"

"Yep. I think I have a plan."

He winced when I outlined it. His verbal response was, "As a teammate, I hate it. As someone who would have done anything to stay with Christina, I respect it and think it's smart. Risky, but smart."

I get it. Accepting a one-year contract—and only a one-year contract, not open to negotiation—goes against everything I've been striving for to date. But people's goals and dreams change, and both of mine are now Let. Worst case, like the "i" word none of us say or even think, I'm young enough I can recover, or else I'll coach or something. Whatever. But I'll be with Let.

Grams' and my homes are paid for, the rest I can

manage. What I can't manage is being without Let. And she can become comfortable with us dating, one step at a time. If need be, one year at a time. I'll take short-term contracts until she's ready for me to do otherwise. If that means a ring on her finger, I'm ready. But I won't use a ring to try to pressure her.

Now, I have to tell Charlie.

"Hey Buzz! You know I'd call the minute I had any news." His voice reflects his surprise. I've never been a nervous ninny, checking in with him on negotiations, and after an initial conversation about what I wanted and what I didn't, I trusted him to pursue sponsorships and bring them to me.

"I know. This is news on my end."

I can hear his mind racing, trying to figure out what I'd know before him that impacted my hockey career. It clicks. "Is this about the non-bunny?"

"Yeah. Look, she works for the org."

"The Tornadoes? Ah, man, what have I always told you? Don't shit where—"

"Don't finish that sentence," I cut him off. "She's the real deal; she's *it* for me, man. But she's not as confident as I am, so she's understandably nervous about the impact on her career if it doesn't work out."

"Yeah, there's no dating a hockey player privately." He thinks. "I thought you'd ask for a NTC, but that doesn't fit with what you're saying about her."

"You're right. A no-trade clause would hurt rather than help. I need a one-year contract for the time being."

"What?!"

"Charlie."

"Dude, I hear you. She's the one, and all that. But this is a huge risk. Saint's contract comes up that next year, as do some others. You've got the salary cap, making the post season, and staying healthy, to be where we are now in negotiating power."

I smile. "Yeah, but I'll be in a way better negotiating place with her."

"Oh, shit. You're a goner. I expected more rational thinking from you of all people, Buzz."

"Love isn't rational. Or at least, this is as rational as it gets. Even Grams is on board." I discussed it with her after my conversation with Cam and she was a thousand percent for this approach. "Look, this way she can try me on for size, knowing that if it goes horribly wrong—which it won't—she won't have to deal with me for longer than this season, because I can go to another team."

He groans, long and low.

"Then, hopefully next year, I get that fat seven-year contract. And that's when I'll want the NTC."

"Huh, I figured you'd ask for a NMC then."

"I might."

"Fuck. Let's deal with this year's contract first. We'll worry about that stuff later. Here's what I'm going to do." I hear a rhythmic swish of clothing from him pacing as he thinks through his strategy. "I'm not going to call them. If they come up with the deal we asked for, we'll know what we're looking at next year. It'll be our little sneak peek. Then I'll wallop them with how much can they do for us in a one-year deal, and hopefully keep it close to what you'd have made in a longer one. Yeah, I think that'll work."

He's mostly talking to himself, but I answer anyway. "Whatever you think best, Charlie. You know I trust you."

"What happens otherwise?"

Basically, I'll do whatever it takes to show Let that I won't impinge on her career. So it'd likely be a year without hockey. But I'm not ready to think about that too much yet, and I know it would give Charlie heart palpitations, so I just say, "Let's worry about that if we have to."

Saylet

The following week, I'm wrapping up my review of LaRhonda's social media plan for the next month when my phone buzzes. Finishing my email signing off on the project, I grab the phone.

Drew

> Hi. Do you have time for a late lunch today? We have morning skate until 1:00 then I'll need a shower, but I'd really like to run something by you.

Me

> Maybe come to my office?

> It's not something I can discuss in the office.

> Grams ok?

Yeah. Coming for Thanksgiving weekend as a matter of fact. I'm bringing her to Greg's shindig.

Yay! I can't wait to see her.

Gee, I wish you were that enthusiastic about meeting me for lunch. :/

My relationship with Grams is much less complicated, you big baby.

<winking face with tongue>
We'll see. Meet me at my car at 1:30.

Fuck. I just flirted with him. As though I want to be in a relationship. Which, of course, I do, but complicated is a gross understatement, despite my meak's encouragement.

So what does he want to talk to me about that can't be discussed in the office? It has to be something personal, but unless he's magically found a way around the risk to my career, I can't think what it would be.

By 1:20, I'm agitated and have lost the ability to get any work done. I might as well take my laptop because I have no idea if I'll be in a headspace to return to work after this lunch. After sending a "WFH" email to those who might look for me, I pack my computer in its sleeve, sling my purse over my shoulder, and head out.

Drew is already there, hair wet. Apparently, we're both eager to see where this conversation goes.

"I was thinking maybe if you're okay with this, we could get takeout and go to my place? Only because I don't want anyone interrupting a private conversation."

This is getting stranger and stranger. I shrug. "In for a penny, in for a pound. Sure."

After navigating food, which I go in to pick up, we are sitting at his kitchen bar unwrapping tacos. He passes his little containers of hot sauce over to me. An unsettling combination of déjà vu and awkwardness churns in my gut. Maybe the hot sauce will solve it.

He eats a few bites, then puts his taco down. For Drew not to scarf everything on his plate is not a good sign.

"My agent called me."

Fuck. My stomach drops. They traded him for someone cheaper. Stupid management and their stupid salary cap. I've lost my appetite now, too, and the knot in my stomach is worse. How could I have not wanted to spend every minute with him that I had? Now I don't have a choice or a chance. I'll always wonder what might have been.

In the next instant, I'm worrying for him. The risks to my career are minor compared to the risks involved in his. He could have to pick up and move his whole life every year, reproving himself to a new team. I can picture what that would do to his stress level about his performance.

No, wait. If he'd been traded he'd probably have to

be on a plane already, as it's mid-season. And I likely would have heard about it in the office. Then, what?

Drew only hears the silence, not my extended internal freaking out, so he continues. "The Tornadoes offered a multi-year contract extension with a significant salary increase."

Oh! I clutch his hand, ostensibly in celebration of his news, but really as an anchor while relief makes me dizzy. He'll still be here. Suddenly, all my wishes become confused, and my own risks get bigger again. "Congratulations, Drew. I know you were hoping for a multi-year contract. Hopefully the money is what you want, too."

"It's close, and we could probably negotiate more. But I declined it."

"What!" I'm aghast.

He nods. "Here's the thing. Recently, my priorities have changed. A long-term contract would be comfortable, sure. But it wouldn't make me happy."

"What?" I'm confused. It's only been a couple short months since he craved that with every fiber of his being. "What changed? Grams having a home that's bought and paid for? Or is it her health?"

"Stop worrying about Grams. It's hurting my ego. And she's fine. We'd both tell you if she wasn't. I respect that friendship…" he trails off on a mumbled, "if it doesn't supercede ours."

"Then what?"

He shakes his head at me, his eyes soft, and one side of his mouth curling in a lopsided smile. "You really can't guess? When I told Grams why we broke up, she said that where there's a will, there's a way, and that I had to figure out the way if I wanted you badly enough."

I swallow. He better not have turned down a multi-million dollar contract for me. And he can't quit the team, or I'll be run out for scaring off our star alternate captain.

He takes my hand, my sweaty palm as the freaking out recommences, and says, "Let, I'll recap. I am in love with you. I crave you in my life more than hockey. Which—" he gulps "—is hard for me to say and please don't tell the guys that."

We both chuckle.

Sobering again, he finishes. "Therefore, however uncomfortable I might be on a year-to-year contract, I'll be less uncomfortable knowing I'm minimizing the risk to your career the only way I know how. Please. Give me the rest of this year. By the end of the regular season, if you want me to leave, I will. And even then, I'll sign a one-year extension, so every year until you feel safe, you'll have the option to send me packing. We can't keep things entirely quiet, but I'm pretty sure we can keep them off social media for the most part, because the Tornadoes have a kickass PR Director."

I can barely smile at his last comment. My mind is reeling. He turned down a multi-year, multi-million contract. For me.

He should be freaking out, nevermind me. Where is the guy who obsesses over every imagined misstep he's made? The one who worried about buying a house, despite his seven figure salary. The one who dropped everything when he heard his grams got hurt.

He doesn't look stressed, though. In fact, his face is remarkably calm; he's not stroking his beard or anything as he watches me, waiting for an answer.

I can't breathe, much less think. "Oh my fucking god,

Drew. I can't believe you did that. I mean, most romantic thing ever, but that's bonkers! I'm losing my mind over here trying to wrap my brain around it. Give me a minute, all right?"

I gently extract my hand from his grip and stand to circle the living room. "Why wouldn't you talk to me before doing something this drastic?"

"What would you have said?" He props his head on his hand to watch me from his barstool, elbow on the bar.

"To not fucking do something so stupid. You've worked your whole life for this, and I know how important stability is for you. Call your agent and ask for it to be back on the table."

"No. Now, tell me why you would have told me that." His voice is calm. I guess I can at least be confident he's thought this through, as he seems prepared for my answers.

"Because I want what's best for you."

He nods. "Exactly. And I love you, and I want to be with you. That's what's best for me. Likewise, I want what's best for you. For you to be happy with us being together, you have to feel your job is safe. This does that. We both get what we want."

"Drew. Oh my god." I have no words—me! The PR Director. This would be funny if there wasn't fifty million or some crazy amount of money on the line.

"What would happen if I called them back?" he continues. "Would you be willing to take a risk on us? Or would you secretly worry that this was all a ploy on my part, and I don't value your career enough? Either way, my bet is you'd still have some fear about your job. So no. I'm not signing a new contract until the end of the season and only then if we're still together and you give the okay."

I'm still overwhelmed at his gesture. Fuck, it's more than a gesture, it's a whole rework of how he's structured his life. I want this so bad I can taste it. I'd never have come up with something this crazy, but it does indeed go a long way to addressing my fears. However, I'm not ready to commit to a timetable, even with the crazy amount of money probably at stake.

"What happens if I'm still afraid to try?" I say in a small voice.

"Then I keep trying. Although at some point, I'll need to figure out if I can handle staying here while you move on and potentially date other people, or if I have to look for another team."

"Drew! Fuck." Too. Damned. Nice.

"We've established that you remember my name. This is a good start." He chuckles.

"This is not funny." I stamp a foot.

He presses his lips together to try to stop his laughter. After a moment of fighting for control, he says, "I talked to Cam about this. And by extension, Christina." At my wide-eyed stare, he adds, "I didn't give them your name. Their point was that given how much players make, there are much bigger numbers at risk, sure, but there is also less risk in a way. I could take a season off and not be homeless. Or at the very least, take a much less lucrative deal and still ensure Grams and I have security. I knew your risks are higher, but they put it in terms I could understand."

"I doubt either of them recommended you do something so reckless. I should call Grams and tell her you're putting both your futures at risk with crazy ideas."

"You're welcome to call her, but I already told her

what I was doing. She's in full support. She said, and I quote, 'Go get the girl. She's worth it.'"

My eyes well and my throat closes. He'll probably get mad that I respond to Grams' words more than his, but really they were the last straw to the pyre burning down my walls. We're really doing this. He found a way. Ohmigod.

I'm so glad I thought to bring my laptop. There's no way I could return to the office sans makeup with swollen eyes.

Drew is in front of me in a heartbeat, gathering me into his arms. "Please don't cry, Let. I wanted to do this. I want to do this. Even if you don't say yes immediately, I want to give us every chance. I love you so much."

I bat at his chest with a fist. "I love you too, you stupid man. How could you do that? You're just so. Fucking. Nice."

His chest rumbles a laugh under my cheek, the wet patch on his athletic shirt moving against my skin. "Sorry not sorry."

It feels so good to be in his arms again, crazy multi-million dollar contract be damned.

Chapter Forty-One

Drew

Holding Let in my arms, the smell of her hair wafting to me, is heaven.

This was a lot for her to take in. I'm trying to give her a minute, but I'm on tenterhooks waiting to see if she's ready to try being together. I have a Plan B, complete with a Grams visit, more gifts, and showing up wherever I can. She's my drug of choice, and this addict craves a fix.

Unable to resist and maybe hoping to convince her, I palm her head and tilt her face up to capture her lips with mine.

She moans into my mouth and returns the kiss for a few moments before breaking it off. "We have to talk about this more."

"After." My tone is firm, and in a surprising reaction, my strong PR Director melts. I sweep her up in my arms and head to the bedroom.

Stripping her down, I gently shove her backward onto the bed and kneel. "I need sustenance. I've been starving for this."

Hooking my hands behind her knees, I tug her closer then prop her legs on my shoulders. I nuzzle her folds with an appreciative hum.

"Drew." She pets my close cropped hair, but her

voice is still distracted.

"Shh. No thinking. Just enjoy. Unless it's to tell me to do something different," I say, looking up her body with a wink. After all, I've gotten this down to a science after two months of exploring her body.

I mouth her pussy lips, tugging them open, and nibble on them with my teeth. Recalling our conversation about beards, I brush my chin along her inner thighs, making us giggle for a second, before getting serious. I start with a slow rhythm and pattern of lips and tongue, encouraging her clit out of its hood, coaxing it to grow and expand. When my tongue delves into her, I press my nose against her burgeoning flesh.

She moans, signaling me to speed up a notch. I slide two fingers into her pussy, waiting to curl them until I've sucked her clit into my mouth again, tonguing it in time with internal taps.

"Ahh." She arches off the bed and clutches my hair. "Please. It's been too long. Come here."

I pause sucking long enough to say, "First one is this way. Hope you don't have any afternoon meetings." Then my mouth is back on her, my other hand climbing her body to grab a breast and flick her nipple with a thumb in time with my mouth and fingers against her G-spot.

She detonates, writhing on the bed. I hold on as she quakes, gentling my lips and slowing my tongue and fingers after her keening moan trails off.

Rising, I whip my shirt off, wiping my beard with it before tossing it aside. Then sneakers, socks, pants, and underwear fly before I climb up the bed. Grabbing under her arms, I tug her toward the pillows, wanting more contact right now. My emotions are at a boil, and I crave the intimacy of making love, not standing at the end of the bed and fucking her brains out. That can come later, hopefully tonight.

As soon as the condom is on, she wraps her limbs around me and clings, which soothes my soul.

I plant one hand on the bed and align my cock with my other hand, spearing through her swollen folds to slide home. Hovering over her on my knees, arms straight so I can take her in, I sigh in happiness.

In typical Let fashion, she pinches my side. "Move already."

"Don't rush me. I've missed you. I'm savoring."

Her eyes get glassy again, and she mutters, "Shut it. No being nice right now. Fuck me."

Damn, I love this woman. I tell her, and she slams her eyes shut. Another pinch to my side spurs me to obey her demand.

Gliding backward, I thrust forward. And repeat slowly. I grin. She didn't tell me how fast to move.

She opens her eyes and sees my grin. Frowning, she pinches me again. "Faster."

I raise my brows. "I like a little pain with my pleasure. Or should I say, I've learned to since being with this feisty little demanding PR Director."

She rolls her eyes, which is not going to earn her any speed.

I keep sliding in and out, enjoying the slow glide, though it'll get too much for me in a minute too.

"Please?" she asks, all sweetness and innocence suddenly.

"Oh, well, since you asked so nicely. Okay." I scoot my weight back so I can use my leg strength for speed and impact, and piston my hips. Dammit, I'm not going to last.

"Good, neither am I," she pants, and I realize I said that out loud.

"Please," I gasp, "tell me again."

"I love you, Drew," she wails as her pussy clamps down on my cock. That's all I need to let go, my hips quaking in double time against her in micro-thrusts as ecstasy and love shoot through me, and I explode into the condom.

I collapse next to her, getting rid of the condom in a tissue for the moment. After I catch my breath, I say, "Now we can talk."

She laughs. "Oh sure, after you've made me incoherent from two orgasms."

"I just need one word from you right now. Then we can figure the rest out later. Please, give me a chance?"

"Yes."

Now my eyes are glassy, so I duck my head and sniff her hair before going to the bathroom, ostensibly to get a warm cloth to clean her with.

After splashing my face with cold water, I stare at myself in the mirror and take stock. How do I feel knowing my future with this team is up in the air for months? Calm. Surprisingly calm. No freak out in sight. Sure, I'll have to prove myself in every damned game, but that pressure is familiar. My personal standards will never accept less than being the best. And it'll likely get exponentially worse when we have kids. Which is why I need Let's calm, sane influence in my life. Well, that and because I'm totally in love with her.

Now, we have to work out the details, but that's her area of expertise. I could barely figure out how to get us this far.

Chapter Forty-Two

Saylet

I clutch Drew's hand as we walk from my office to the conference room. It's the one where management spent hours finding a way to offer Drew his dream package.

Now we're going to use it to disclose our relationship to Stephen, since we both report to him.

Drew and I brainstormed how to frame this and what questions might be asked. We're as ready for this conversation as we can be, but I still worry it will reflect poorly on my professionalism. Of course, if his contract decision is linked to this, I'll be labeled a demanding, controlling bitch by some men, although those same people would see it as natural if a woman deferred to a man's job. There's no winning as a woman sometimes.

We drop hands as we enter the conference room. Might as well start as we mean to go on, which includes minimizing PDAs. I blink twice. Christina is sitting toward one end of the table, chatting with Greg. Greg is always welcome to attend these, and when I scheduled the meeting in Stephen's calendar, I invited him. But Christina?

My brain fires off potential reasons for her presence before figuring it out. She's not there as an owner. She's been clear that she doesn't want to be part of the day-today operations of the hockey enterprise. So she is there in solidarity for me, as a woman, and as a member of management involved with a player. I grin and sigh in relief, feeling less pressure already.

Stephen rushes in, obviously direct from another meeting, drops his laptop and a notepad, and asks for two more minutes.

Drew offers to get me coffee, but I'm nearly shaking already, so that's a bad idea.

Stephen returns with a glass of water and throws himself into his seat. "All right, what's this about that needed two owners and a GM? That sounds like the start of a bad joke."

Drew speaks for us, as we'd agreed. "L—Saylet and I established a friendship last season that became something more in the off season. We're in a relationship now, but wanted to assure you in person that it will not affect either of our jobs. If it does, we'll address it immediately and will work with you to resolve it."

Stephen's brows quirk up at the first sentence, and he slides a glance to Christina, but other than that his face remains impassive. "You couldn't have put that in an email?"

I step in. "We could have. But tone is important here, and we wanted to be able to address any questions or concerns."

"No questions. No concerns. You both, along with Saint, are the most professional members of the organization. Unlike someone who snuck around for half a season." He flashes a grin at Christina as he says this.

"I'm not in this organization," she says mildly.

"I was referring to Cam." He laughs at her fierce frown. Another reason why I love working here.

Everyone is comfortable and friendly.

Greg leans in. "I have a question. Does this have to do with you refusing our very generous offer?"

Drew and I trade glances. We'd hoped to avoid this.

Drew turns to Greg and Stephen. "First, can we agree to keep anything discussed in this room quiet?"

I tap his arm and add, "Second, we plan to keep a low profile. That's my request because blowback would be directed at me."

Christina nods and murmurs to Greg, "True."

"Neither of us is online much personally, and I conveniently have control over the team's social media, so assuming you're okay with this approach, we can avoid a lot of hoopla. We're not going to hide, but we don't want to flaunt it either."

Stephen nods.

Drew continues, "Now, to answer Greg's question, for some of the same reasons, yes. Although it was the other way around. I refused your moderately generous offer—" Stephen and Greg chuckle and roll their eyes and Christina covers her mouth to hide a smile "—in order to ensure Saylet was comfortable dating me. I refuse to jeopardize her job or her future."

Stephen frowns. "Why would her job be in jeopardy? She doesn't interact with you that much."

It's my turn. But before I can say anything, Christina replies, "This is a hockey organization. If they had a nasty breakup and it affected the team, who would you trade?" She took the words right out of my mouth.

I sit back, because otherwise I'd round the table and hug her with all my might.

She continues, "This puts the power in their hands, however they want to balance that between them."

Drew pipes up. "I have every intention of staying with this team as long as you'll have me and continue to offer reasonably generous contracts," he adds with a wink and a grin. "Nor do I plan to give Saylet up. But she needs time, and I can give her that."

I have a lump in my throat again at the magnitude of his gesture. I really hope no one asks me a question.

Christina slants me a fierce look and a tight nod to say, "You deserve this."

Stephen laces his fingers and taps his pointer fingers against his lips. "Sadly, it makes sense. He's a caretaker. Always looking out for teammates. It's why we made him AC. I wouldn't expect him to do any less for a romantic partner. It tracks."

Greg throws himself back in his chair. "Ugh. I had no idea that the new face of the NHL would be this riddled with relationships and hockey players walking away from contracts as romantic gestures."

Christina presses her lips together. "Ignore him. He's the only single person in the room, after all."

Stephen has been happily married for a decade with two lovely children we've met at family and friends events.

Drew cuts to the chase. "Any other questions? Otherwise, I should get to the gym."

"By all means, go to the gym. But we're regrouping at the end of this season." Stephen glares, but ruins it with a small smile.

I like the sound of that threat. Drew shouldn't subvert his goals for mine. This is the one and only year I'll let him do this. We have to hope they'll offer this or a comparable deal for him at the end of this season.

* * * *

"Grams!" I shout, jumping and waving at the bottom of the escalator as she descends to the baggage claim and arrivals level in the Austin airport. Sometimes I really hate being so short.

"Saylet girl!" Her shout annoys the person in front of her on the escalator but she doesn't care.

We embrace for a long moment before I take her bag. She told us ahead of time she wasn't going to check anything, so I texted Drew as soon as I caught sight of her. We told her to look for me, as Drew would be recognized by fans, making it harder to get out of here.

"How's the hip? How was the flight? I'm so happy you're here." I am beyond excited. Thanksgiving is going to be amazing. I'm with my new family for this holiday, then Drew and Grams are coming to Denver for Christmas. It's a nice short flight for Grams, and we booked the tickets so we'll get there first to meet her.

My family is excited to hear I'm dating, especially Meak. Ba was less than thrilled it was a hockey player, as he'd prefer a doctor or lawyer, just like they wanted me to be. On the other hand, they were impressed when we described how we were addressing my professional reputation. Drew laughed at their mild response, but I was incensed they weren't raving about him effectively considering me more valuable than his dream contract. Which still freaks me out when I think about it, but right now I'm focused on the pleasure of Grams' company.

"Hip is like new, stairs are no trouble at all. I've been to visit my friends in the apartment complex a few times, although they like to come to my house," she says with a grin as she passes me the handle to her roller bag. She's in love with her little house. Size doesn't matter, it's all about location for her.

"That's awesome. So, is there anything specific you want to do while you're here, other than see Drew play?"

"Nope. I'll be visiting regularly, so it'll happen naturally. I'm here to spend time with you two, and meet Drew's teammates who I've heard so much about. Plus, why would I want to go out when Drew raves about your cooking so much?"

I laugh and climb into the back seat of Drew's SUV so they can hug and catch up.

Back at Drew's condo, I pull out stuff for dinner. Grams and Drew sit at the bar so I can participate, and she regales us with stories of her friends' oohing and ahhing over her beautiful home. I slide a glass of champagne in front of her and slide Drew a glance to say, "I told you so."

He smirks back as he accepts the beer.

Grams pokes him. "Why don't you help her? I know you know how to chop vegetables—and cook for that matter."

I jump in to defend him. "This is my happy place, I promise. I prefer to rule the kitchen alone, especially from helpers who consider salt a spice."

Grams cackles.

Drew's phone buzzes. Looking down, he says, "It's Saint. Give me a few minutes." He accepts the call on the way to our bedroom.

Okay, it's officially his until I finish moving in. I haven't given notice because I haven't decided what of my stuff to bring over. He's offered to replace everything here with my furniture but I don't want that. I've loved being here as it is, but I love my apartment, too.

I'm usually not indecisive, so Drew thinks it's one last risk to my independence that I need to get over, and has told me to keep it as long as I need in order to be comfortable.

Right now, with him out of the room, is the opportunity I've been hoping for to have a heart-to-heart with Grams. Putting my knife down, I come to stand across the bar from her. "I've been wanting to ask you this for weeks, but I wanted to do it in person. I feel terrible about Drew declining the long-term contract."

"Hmm," Grams hums through a sip of champagne, her eyes dancing. "That's not a question."

Rolling my eyes, I try again. "Okay, I guess I wanted to apologize. I hate that this interfered in his career."

"Did it, though?"

"Maybe. What if he gets inj—the 'i' word?" While I don't share his superstitions around certain words like injury and retirement, I don't know how Grams feels about them. "Or they decide they want to use that salary cap room to bring someone else in who'll commit to the team for more than a year?"

She puts her glass down and leans forward to hold my gaze. "The bottom line is that he is happy. You are happy. I am happy. Doing that got us here. As for the long term, consider this. His goal is to be with you for the rest of his life."

My eyes flare.

She adds, "No, he didn't tell me that in so many words, but the one rule I taught him is that actions speak louder than words."

We snicker at that, as Drew has warned me that she has a fuckton of "one rules."

Sobering, she finishes with, "You need this time. You haven't even moved in here yet. Take the time this gives you. You're worth it. Now, welcome to the family."

We clink glasses and toast.

The bedroom door clicks. Drew rounds the corner, and they ask in unison, "What's for dinner?"

Drew

I exit the elevator on the executive level in athletic shorts and a tee from my biggest clothing sponsor with a big swoosh across my chest. I figured the "just do it" attitude felt right for today.

Charlie is waiting for me, an enormous iced latte in hand as always. We head to the conference room. Let must sense my presence because she flies out of her office to hug me.

She doesn't look nervous, but I ask her again, "Are you sure?"

She laughs up at me. "Remember me? I'm the one who's been begging you to get Charlie on this for months."

It's true. After we went to her family's for Christmas, and rang in the new year, she got out of the lease on her apartment and started pushing me to re-open negotiations on my contract. On my side, that box in the corner of the pantry floor was downsized twice, and last week I noticed the last items in it had expired and tossed it. I had one or two restless nights, but every time I open the freezer I'm amazed at the many healthy, fresher food options, thanks to Let.

We've had a few disagreements. More than one about the hours she works and how hard she pushes herself, and probably the same number on how much I beat myself up over past mistakes with game tape. But overall, we're the happiest we've been in our lives, and our families are in full support. However, I was determined to give her as much time as possible. So here we are in early August, another fantastic year under our belts with me at the top of my game, ready to sign a seven-year contract worth over fifty million with a no-move clause.

Charlie turns from two steps inside the conference room and glares. "She did? You giant pain in my ass. You made me sweat this."

I shrug. "All those calls where you'd make small talk and keep me waiting for the reason you called me? Payback's a bitch, man."

He laughs. "You're lucky you'll be done with me for seven years after this."

All the details have been ironed out, so this will be short. Frankly, I think it's a formality or Stephen likes to see the whites of our eyes as we commit or something. I mean, I closed on my condo and Grams' house without leaving my computer thanks to all the e-signature software. But doing this in person works because I can walk down the hall and celebrate with Lel afterward.

We lift the pens, we shake the hands, and I'm a Tornado for the next seven years—really eight as that one year contract will cover this season—unless something goes terribly awry. My salary will also more than double.

In an out-of-character move, I've already bought something significant in anticipation of this. Let's not ready for a ring, and while she could use a newer car, she's probably not ready for that either quite yet. Maybe in a few months.

For now, I have a surprise for her being delivered this afternoon while she's at work. I walk down the hall to her office and get my celebratory kiss.

She asks, "How do you feel now that you have everything you want?"

I give it some thought. "No different today than I did a month ago when we began these negotiations. I had everything I wanted when you agreed to try this."

Her eyes glisten and she thumps my chest with a fist. "Fuck. What have I told you about being nice? And especially making me cry in the office."

I snort, but manage to avoid outright laughter. "Sorry? We're celebrating at dinner tonight, right? The guys demanded lunch with my shiny new salary, then I have to run a couple errands. You sure you want to cook *again*?"

"I don't feel like it would be a proper observance of this momentous occasion without macaroni and cheese."

"Okay, then. I'll see you at home. Love you."

"Love you, too, hockey boy."

She's better about coming home at a reasonable hour these days, so Let walks in the door at 6:05. Mid-reach to place her laptop case on the bar, she freezes, her gaze caught on me in the living room, standing next to her gift. Well, part of her gift, anyway.

"Drew! Oh my god, what did you do?" There's a four-foot high Khmer Apsara statue next to me, flanking the built-ins that line one wall of the room. Let has a pair of tabletop sized ones that are on a shelf, but I'd seen standing ones at her parents' house. She said she was waiting until she owned a place to get larger ones.

Our home is a pretty good blend of both our

belongings, but with her apartment being smaller, her attitude about accumulating things as a renter, and my furniture better suited to my hockey-sized body, I haven't been entirely happy with the balance. I want her to feel like this is truly her place, not just mine. A few throw pillows and books (her stereo system and TV were seriously inferior and didn't make the cut) won't do.

She races past me to admire the statue up close, peering at the detail and the red and gold accent colors. Then she glances around the living room, her brow furrowed.

"Is it okay?" I ask.

"It is…it's beautiful," she answers slowly. "They usually come in pairs, that's all."

"I put the other one in our bedroom."

"Oh." She blinks and turns to hug me. "First, thank you so much. This is wonderful and thoughtful, although you didn't have to."

"I wanted our home to reflect both of us more equally. I know you're happy with it as is, but I wasn't."

"Fucking *nice*," she sniffs.

That sentiment is my favorite way to be thanked. It's like a game with us now.

She tilts her head. "In that case, how would you feel about bringing the other one out here? They're actually supposed to be displayed as a pair."

"Damn. Sorry. In that case, I'd say I'm glad they only weigh about thirty pounds each, rather than the stone ones I saw."

She giggles. "I think the stone ones are more for outside. You're good."

"You tell me where to put them and I'll move them."

Once they're in place, she throws herself into my

arms. "This was supposed to be your big day, your celebration. Instead, here you are, you nice fucking man, buying me more gifts. What am I going to do with you?"

"You could feed me?" I ask innocently.

"I could, and I will. But first—" she starts to sink to her knees, then casts a look back at the statues. "Hmm, those might take some getting used to. Follow me."

By the time I make it into the bedroom, she's down to another pair of skimpy lace panties, the lime green bright against her warm skin, and her floral tease of a robe, open over her bare breasts.

My cock leads the way over to her, but I miss my opportunity for a kiss as she's already sunk to her knees, onto a pillow that we've found improves the angle. I don't give her the chance to do this much, as I like giving oral as much or more than receiving it. But she's right. Today I deserve to celebrate, and I'll take it.

Whipping my shirt over my head, I shove my shorts and underwear to my ankles. I tangle a hand in her thick dark mane and bend to huff it, making her grin.

Then her hand wraps around my cock and my fingers tighten convulsively. She moans at the tug on her hair.

I guide her to me, wanting to feel that moan around my cock. She levers it down and licks my length in long wet laps before sliding me all the way in. Her throat bulges. Fuck me. Then she's retreating to slurp me in again.

"Damn, Let. Not too fast. I'll come."

She withdraws and reminds me, "Your party. Your day for multiple orgasms." Her cheeks hollow as she sucks me in once more. And a moment later when she releases me to take a breath she says, "You can recover over dinner."

The woman is going to kill me.

It's hard for me to relax and enjoy without knowing I've satisfied her, but her mouth forces the issue. There's no relaxing. Instead, everything in me winds tighter. My teeth clench, my quads go taut, my pecs twitch as I fight not to shove her head against my pelvis.

Her tongue undulates along the bottom of my cock, especially under the head as she withdraws, and I'm done for.

My fingers clench, and my balls draw up.

She moans around me at the tug on her scalp, and I can't even warn her.

"Let—" I'm already coming, spurting into her throat as she swallows around me and hums in satisfaction.

Finally, she slides off me with gentle suction to clean me. My shorts are still around my ankles, but I'm an empty husk of a man. Without attempting to dress, I stumble one step and collapse on the bed.

She stands and leans over me, brushing her nipples across the dusting of hair on my chest. "Hmm. Dinner will be fast. I'm so wound up. I'll cook like this for you, to help your recovery period."

"Recovery period?" I grab her and flip her under me. "What, do you think I'm thirty or something?"

"Hey!" she kicks out at me half-heartedly.

Just then, my stomach rumbles. "Ignore it, it'll go away. Let me give you a quickie now then we can both enjoy later."

"No way. Youngsters need their sustenance, too. Let me up, or I'll put my ugliest sweats on to cook."

I release my hold on her wrists, but remain over her for another moment. "I love you so damned much, Let. Thank you for taking a chance on me."

She blinks hard. "Get off me, and stop being fucking nice." Bouncing up, she gets the last word. "Thank you for being patient with me. I love you too."

Sneak Peek at Book 4

Kyle

I slump on my stool, propped on one hand with my elbow on the bar, staring into my fifth or is it my sixth beer of the night.

Renee, Chasers' manager/bartender, comes by. It's the team's unofficial hangout bar, and it's quiet on a Tuesday night now that the Tornadoes' season is done. Unfortunately that means she has more time to check on me. "Y'all made it to the Conference Finals, Scottie. You should be celebrating, not to mention enjoying your off season."

"This is me celebrating." I'm not in the mood for chatting, and definitely not for being cheered up.

"By drinking alone? There's a group of women over there"—she tilts her head—"who have been eyeing you for the past half hour. Why don't you let them help you with your celebration, hmm?"

I bark a bitter laugh. "If only."

She blinks and wipes the bar in front of me. "Ah, okay. Well, if you need to talk to someone about whatever's stopping you, I'm a vault. Part of the bartender code."

I stare at her for a long moment. Fuck, her offer is tempting. As a defenseman for the Texas Tornadoes in the NHL, it's hard to know who to trust. My childhood friends fell by the wayside when I moved to play juniors. After the NHL draft two years ago, I was with an AHL team in yet another city before being acquired by the Tornadoes in the expansion draft last summer. My two closest friends tried to stay in touch, but their lives were so different, they couldn't understand why I felt overwhelmed by the travel, the pressure, and the PR demands of the League. I am making close to a million a year on an ELC, an entry-level contract that's standard for players under twenty-four, and they see my life as one long party with an even longer line of pussy. Which, to some extent it was.

Until it all came crashing to a halt three months ago.

No one I've played with in the hockey world is safe to talk to about what changed, for sure none of my teammates.

Maybe, just maybe, I could talk to Renee…

Another customer leans on the bar next to me to ask for drinks for their table, and I twitch at the sudden intrusion. Nope, this is way too public a place to share my struggles, even with the bartender. Who knows who might overhear. Until I decide what to do about it, I have to keep quiet. Some guys on the team might be cool, but it's too risky. Because if they're not, it affects the whole team and my entire life.

I've always assumed I was bisexual because I'm attracted to guys and girls. But with the NHL being the only Big 4 league with no openly gay active players, women have always been the safe bet, so I've never even kissed a man.

Hence why I attached myself to Jack Landry, biggest player of them all, as soon as I arrived. That, and he's so damned pretty the girls flock to him, so I could get sloppy seconds without having to work too hard. Or as has happened a couple times, share and get the added bonus of watching him in action.

So, yeah, pussy has never been a problem. The problem arose when I met up with a friend from the AHL on a road trip earlier this season, and we walked into a club he liked on the wrong night. It was men's night. As professional hockey players, we were torn about not wanting to be seen there, but didn't want to turn tail and walk out and be labeled as homophobic if someone caught us on camera. So we stayed for one beer.

Closing my eyes, I'm back in that place.

After our drink, I excuse myself to the bathroom before we leave. As I exit the men's room into the dark corridor leading back to the club, a guy approaching slows then stops in front of me. He's small and lithe, his movements dainty. "Looking for a dance, big guy?" That throaty, come hither voice pulls at something low in my belly.

"Uh, no thanks." I shove my hands in my pants pockets to hide my nerves.

He tilts his head up. "Ah. You one of those curious types?"

"What do you mean?"

"You're sure you're straight, but you're with a friend and you're"—he raises his hands to do air quotes—"'just curious.'"

"Uh, no. I'm not." My dick might be, though. I've been half hard since I saw what some of the guys dancing were wearing. Skintight pants, mesh tops with nipples poking through, and tank tops. I swallow the saliva pooling in my mouth.

He steps closer, and I turn and lean against the wall

to create space. He closes the space by stepping closer. "You're not which? Cuz, honey, that bulge in your pants tells me you're very curious, and you shouldn't be sure you're straight."

Then, bold as can be, he plants a hand on my bicep and squeezes, his eyes closing as he hums in pleasure. My hand grabs his wrist in a firm grip as I bleat, "Ahh!"

He blinks his eyes open and sees my expression. I must look like a frightened deer in headlights or something, because he opens the hand still in my grip, and says, "I beg your pardon. That was assault and is not okay. You have my deepest apologies."

I stand there like the dumb deer, gaping at him.

He tilts his head and licks his lips, glancing down to where I'm still holding him—against my arm. I never pulled his hand away. Then lower to where my cock strains through my pants. "Unless…I surprised you, but not in a terrible way?"

I finally close my mouth, still helplessly ensnared by his knowing gaze.

"So, here's the deal. You say no and I stop. You move my hand"—he wiggles it in my grip—"and I stop. I'll go really slow."

His hand creeps back to my bicep, both of us watching it. He squeezes it. Fire licks through my veins, and my cock is about to punch him in the belly, it's so hard. I'm completely lost to this interaction. There could be paparazzi at the end of the hall recording all this, and I wouldn't be able to move. I swallow again.

He flutters his lashes, and I realize I've slouched down a couple inches. His exhale over my throat nearly does me in. What the fuck is happening to me? I've been having sex—and orgasms—with women since my teens.

I mean, blow jobs are my favorite part, but I attributed that to being lazy.

My brain short-circuits when he brushes his stomach gently against the bulge in my jeans. I gasp another, "Ahh."

"Oh you poor misguided man. God, I love being the lumberjack type's first." He leans in. "Okay, we're going for the holy trinity. A kiss. Then I'm going to go in the bathroom, and you can either follow me in, or I'll finish alone."

I lick my lips, and he grins. My eyes flutter as I realize that had always been my sign of consent from a woman. Holy fuck, this is really happening.

His lips find mine, and my world implodes. Fireworks. Gunfire. I don't know the hell what. But the firmness of the body against mine, the abrasion of his stubble around my mouth, and his assertive-but-not-aggressive tongue, all combine to make my dick throb. No sexual interaction has felt anything like this. It was like the world was in black and white, but this is technicolor. I'm on the edge just from the brush of his hips and cock through our clothes.

Too soon, he leans back a few inches to check in.

I stare at him in shock, my mouth still wet and open. My brain is trying to come to grips with what this means, but instead just keeps shouting, *I can't be gay!*

He arches a brow and releases me, stepping back too late to undo the damage he's caused. No, it's not his fault. He had my consent, and frankly, given our relative sizes, I was in control the whole time.

"I—I—" I stammer, still looking for my brain to connect to my mouth.

"I know. You're not gay. This never happened." His

mouth twists.

"It's not that. I mean, I thought I was bi-, but *this*—" I stop before trying to describe how overwhelmingly better this feels. I'm not getting into my inability to be gay with a stranger. "Just please, please don't say anything to anyone. You could ruin my life." Now I'm begging.

"Honey," he says through a laugh, patting me. "Relax. I don't even know your name."

I blush. I. Blush. What would my teammates think of that? I'm spiraling. Needing to get gone, I try to extract myself. What had women said to me if I got my signals crossed? "I, uh, apologize if I gave you the wrong impression."

"You didn't. Pretty sure 'curious' covers it. I hope you figure it out, hon." He adjusts his cock in his tighter-than-ever pants, making me fucking salivate. He snorts when I swallow visibly and gives me a short nod before continuing his path to the bathroom.

Returning to the bar, I find my friend and tell him I don't feel well. I sure as fuck don't feel alright, so it's mostly true.

After that night, I tried watching hetero porn in an effort to distract myself from the fact that a single kiss from a guy was hotter than anything I'd ever done with a woman, and the fact that I *can never have that while I play hockey*. The Tornadoes may be super progressive and open to diversity, but I've only got one year left on my ELC with them. Then I could end up anywhere.

But of course, my self-control was absent when I watched, and I clicked into MM porn. In doing that, I've realized that the guy from the bar wasn't my type. I prefer someone closer to my size, and more masculine.

I'd be afraid that I'd break someone smaller, as I was always careful with the women I was with. But also, I want sex to be more equal in give and take, sizewise and otherwise.

I kept clicking on videos with more mature guys who know what they want and are willing to manhandle their partners to get it.

Then, a new worst thing possible happened.

I got my first man crush. I'm not sure the summer will be long enough to get over it.

Renee comes back over. "Hey, I texted a few folks to see who is in town, so you don't have to drink alone."

Fuck me. First, back in January, Coach caught me leaving after a few too many and took me to his place for the night to sleep it off. Then in the spring Drew had to take me home from an owner's party. They probably all assume it's another youngster struggling to adjust to the NHL. "No, no. I'm going. Let me pay my tab and I'll get a rideshare home. Please tell them not to come."

"Too late," a voice says beside me and a heavy hand lands on my back in a hard pat. "Remember? I live close."

I squeeze my eyes closed. *No, no, no, no, no. This can't be happening.* But it is. I can smell his Speed Stick deodorant from here. Because I've been obsessing over this man for months.

Opening my eyes, I swallow, and aim for normal as I say, "Hey Coach."

* * *

Preorder **Intentional Offside** now for $0.99
Want more hockey romance?

Get Emil Bergstrom's second chance love story when you sign up for my newsletter at
https://bookhip.com/TFJRZCH
Future Texas Tornado books will feature (in no particular order):
Jack
Saint
Greg
and others
(tell me which you want next when you sign up for my newsletter!)

Also by Debbie Charles

Written as Maggie Sims

Acknowledgements

First, a reiterated heartfelt thanks to my two most valuable resources, Milly Bellegris and Stephen Meserve.

Milly, you wear so many hats—or as you might say, toques. Editor extraordinaire, multi-lingual phrase checker, immigrant accuracy checker (it's a new title, work with me here), and all around cheerleader. You're amazing.

Stephen, your patient responses to my questions—even the ones I should have websearched for myself—and encouragement ("*shows how much you understand the backend of the business side*") and tips and hints ("*If you need a crowd moment here, you can also note that some of the folks who made the trip in the crowd are waving brooms, which is a real thing people do when their team sweeps someone*") go above and beyond. I'm so glad your friends are getting in on the act now too, with Book 4's title.

As you did with Books 1 and 2, you both made this far better than I could have.

Last, the person who this book is dedicated to—the very real and very lovely Saylet. For the hours of videos, emails, texts, and now the narration of this book, done out of the goodness of your heart. I hope this honors you and a few Cambodian-American traditions the way I intended. All mistakes are my own.

About the Author

A lifelong romance reader, I cut my teeth on Johanna Lindsey, Jude Deveraux, and Kathleen Woodiwiss, along with Silhouette and Harlequin for palate cleansers.

Opting for a career that provided both a food and travel budget, I earned a BA, CPA, and MBA, and spent far too long being a corporate drone, then consulting other corporate drones.

Along the way, I was one of the few 1990s NBA season ticket holders never to see Michael Jordan play ('93-'94). I also attended a few NFL games, the Belmont Stakes, the NHL playoffs, the World Series, and managed to see more than twenty MLB parks, several of which have since been demolished. More recently, I've enjoyed the Texas Stars, the AHL affiliate of the Dallas Stars.

I have published a number of spicy Regency romances under the pen name Maggie Sims (www.maggiesims.com), along with hot hockey romances set in Austin as Debbie Charles, where I now live with my husband and a varying number of furbabies.